GHOSTS OF
TRUMBALL MANSION

A Contemporary Novel

WHAT READERS ARE SAYING ABOUT LINDA WOOD RONDEAU'S BOOKS

... magical gift of words.

... not your usual romance writer.

... wise and gentle way of explaining how God moves in people's lives

... makes the reader part of the story

... using metaphor, description, and humor, this author is wonderful at setting a scene.

... characters that come to life

... creates quirky characters with finesse

... grabs and keeps your attention right from the beginning

... strong vibrant characters and great storylines

... doesn't fit neatly into any niche but one: Inspiring Christian Fiction!

... great mix of love, relationships, suspense & mystery.

... perfect in writing style, story theme, and characters

... not your typical cookie-cutter romances

... themes of mystery, romance and restoration, sprinkled with humor

... one of my favorite writers of Christian fiction

... liked the Upstate NY setting, especially in the Adirondacks, one of my favorite places.

... surprising twists and turns in her storylines

... satisfying endings are worth every tear

... be prepared to have your attention riveted

... draws you into the story early on and keeps you there

GHOSTS OF
TRUMBALL MANSION

A Contemporary Novel

Linda Wood Rondeau

ELK LAKE PUBLISHING INC

PUBLISHING THE POSITIVE
Plymouth, Massachusetts

COPYRIGHT NOTICE

Cover and Interior Design: Derinda Babcock
Editor(s): Kim Autrey, Cristel Phelps, Deb Haggerty
PUBLISHED BY: Elk Lake Publishing, Inc., 35 Dogwood Drive, Plymouth, MA 02360, 2022

———————————————————————————————————

Library Cataloging Data
Names: Rondeau, Linda Wood (Linda Wood Rondeau)
Ghosts of Trumball Mansion / Linda Wood Rondeau
306 p. 23cm × 15cm (9in × 6 in.)
Identifiers: ISBN-13: 978-1-64949-503-7 (paperback) | 978-1-64949-504-4 (trade paperback) | 978-1-64949-505-1 (e-book)
Key Words: Mystery, Romance, Ghosts, Separation, Family, Contemporary, Redemption

Then they cried out to the LORD in their trouble,
And He saved them out of their distresses.
He brought them out of darkness and the shadow of
death,
And broke their chains in pieces.
(Psalm 107:13 – 14 NJKV)

PROLOGUE

FIFTEEN YEARS EARLIER

Sylvia Moore Fitzgibbons steadied herself against the balustrade surrounding the upstairs promenade. Henry stood at the door, much like Scarlett O'Hara's Rhett. In her mind, Sylvia could hear Scarlett say the words, "Oh, Rhett, whatever will I do without you?"

She expected the same final condemnation to pass from Henry's lips. "Frankly, my dear, I don't give a ..."

Sylvia screamed her petition. "Henry, don't go."

He paused—his gaze sorrowful as he opened the double-paneled door. "I'm sorry, Sylvia. I told you last night. I can't live here."

She pushed away from the rail, her knees wobbling, wanting the floor to swallow her whole. Should she pray? She hadn't needed or thought about God since childhood.

Instead, she summoned the author within, the strength she'd always leaned on. If she were to survive, Lana Longstreet must take over. "Then go."

He glanced toward the marble-floored ballroom. "I tried, Sylvia. For a brief while, I thought I might eventually learn to manage the commute." He pointed toward the infamous ballroom. "But whatever's in there hates me."

Of all the excuses she'd ever written, Henry's fiction surpassed Lana Longstreet's most creative pages. "Will I still see you Wednesday?"

"As agreed—a weekly business meeting at Chez Phillipe."

With that, Henry was gone, leaving Sylvia to mourn the life she'd lost. Only Lana could help her make a new one. What now? She surveyed the staircase and the portraits of the ancestors. Lana Longstreet would not let sentiment stand in the way of enjoying this mansion, a piece of New Haven history. She shook her head at Henry's idiocy.

Sylvia surveyed the lower rooms, the lure to the old Trumball Mansion that was now hers. Every room, even the servants' quarters on the left wing beyond the ballroom, remained as the edifice was when Trumball built the place. Of course, she'd modernize the kitchen for Rosalie. She couldn't expect her cook to manage with a wood stove.

Anger heated her cheeks as she surveyed the perfect symmetry and Georgian architecture. How could Henry have resisted the breathy charm filling each room, the engraved woodwork, and plaster of paris etched ceilings?

Last night's sharp criticism still stung. "Of all your impetuous schemes, this is the craziest thing you have ever done," Henry had said. Lana Longstreet thought her decision to buy Trumball Mansion the smartest move she'd ever made.

She walked through the living room to the kitchen, then looked out the window at the rose gardens—the only feature Henry found alluring, though he couldn't name a single species. She'd laughed while Henry referenced each bed by its color and location rather than use their common name.

Apparently, not even the roses were enough to keep him here. He'd rejected her gift and thrown their marriage to the wind. He made his choice—now Lana Longstreet would make hers. The once bustling Trumball Mansion would live again through twenty-first century galas, and Lana Longstreet would emerge as New Haven's sauciest socialite.

A last tear trickled down Sylvia's chin. She pulled out a hankie from the sleeve of her knitted long-sleeved tee and wiped her eyes. No more regret, no more conniving. She'd salvage what she could from her broken marriage and find contentment within Lana Longstreet's independence. Though Henry refused to call the mansion his home, he would not divorce her. Her books brought in the bulk of the profits for Fitzgibbons & Associate Publishing. If love didn't motivate Henry's faithfulness, the fear of poverty would. And, they would have Wednesdays at Chez Phillipe's. A small part of him better than none.

She gazed at the beveled archways gracing the entrance to both the ballroom and sitting room. She'd fashion a life for herself and the children here. Let Henry keep his predictable Manhattan existence. Lana Longstreet's genius needed surroundings that juiced the creative spirit, one richly fed in this historic home.

She scanned the open ballroom, the cornerstone of Trumball's influence on a nation in the making—the place where Henry claimed ghosts danced.

Ridiculous.

She joined Julie in the ballroom. A residual pungency coated Sylvia's throat. "Let's get out of here. Smells like rotten eggs. Tomorrow, I'll hire a cleaning service to purge these odors."

Julie stood with cocked head, her gaze fixed on the angel-engraved marble fireplace. "They're gone, Mother. They jumped back into the walls when Daddy left."

CHAPTER 1

THE PRESENT

Wednesdays were as predictable as the whole of his life—and for Henry Fitzgibbons, predictable was good enough.

She had slid into their private booth at Chez Phillipe's, all Saks Fifth Avenue and Max Factor perfect. For one ecstatic moment, he thought he still loved her.

Until she spoke.

He had come steeled against the inevitable arguments doomed to follow their business luncheons, the prelude to their Wednesday afternoons at their old apartment. Why bother? These last few years were more torture than comfort. He tried to stay interested, but she just wasn't Sylvia anymore. He mourned the gulf between them.

The conversation always ended with the infernal question, "Why haven't you been to Connecticut lately?" Since Sylvia refused to believe the very house itself hated his presence, he'd quoted enough excuses to write his own book. Sylvia's latest ploy, however, had thrown him off guard.

"For the last time, Henry, you have to do something about the mess in the backyard."

She hurled her spears with deadly precision and leaned forward in the replicated Louis XVI chair, her tantalizing no-use-arguing-about-it stare, a weapon for which Henry had no defense, a deliberate Lana Longstreet cool, a frostiness, though delectable, not the least bit desirable.

"Very well, Sylvia. You win." Perhaps to wallow in victory, she rested her back against her throne and nibbled the remainder of her salad. She dabbed her red lips with the corner of her starched linen napkin, then twanged her sentiment like a broken guitar string. "The rose bushes, Henry. We can't let them die."

Yes, the rose bushes. His enjoyment of them ... the closest to a religious experience he'd known since—when? He'd grown up in church but could never bring himself to believe his father's God was as loving as his father preached. Where Pop saw only love, Henry saw only wrath.

"Why do you have to drive the nail beneath the wood? I already promised I'd come."

"I know how much you love the roses." She pinned her shoulders against her regal seat, a queen at court. "I'm only thinking of you, Henry."

He doubted Sylvia comprehended why he doted on the roses and not her. As a writer, shouldn't she grasp their symbolic importance? For Sylvia, the centuries-old gardens serviced as conversation fodder or fanciful bouquets in her porcelain vases.

"Henry, is it such a chore to stay one summer with me? You haven't spent more than a day or two in Connecticut since the kids graduated from college and started their own lives. If it weren't for Wednesdays, we'd never see one another."

Slam—like a hard-lined tennis serve—her unstated accusation would squelch any hopes of a pleasant Wednesday. Sylvia no doubt conjured up all manner of false explanations for his absences. Always the dramatist, she preferred to view him as emotionally disturbed rather than admit the house might be inhabited by something not human. Then again, her assessment of a deranged husband might not be too far afield. What other answers could explain his visions?

"Not true, Sylvia. You are still my wife. I come to all your dinner parties like a good husband should. What more do you want from me? I don't come to Connecticut more often because nothing much interests me there. All I need or want is right here in Manhattan."

Sylvia grimaced.

Maybe he'd been too harsh, but she'd recover ... Lana Longstreet would rebound with even more caustic remarks and jibes.

"Except the roses, Henry, and they will die if something isn't done soon. The vines are strangling them."

"I can't afford to be away for the whole summer. I have a business to run, you know."

"I thought you liked the roses."

Like hardly scratched the surface of his attachment to them. The roses intrigued him. And as far as Connecticut was concerned, they were his only comfort during his infrequent visits to Sylvia's house, especially after the children grew up and started life on their own. That something so delicate endured the cold winters, and against all odds, bloomed with indescribable beauty in the spring, gave him hope somehow he and Sylvia might reclaim something of their lives together. He owed the roses whatever hapless attention he could muster.

Sylvia cupped her head into her palms, her eyes widening, her frenzied façade the prelude to the rest of this Wednesday. She must know he had no resistance to her damsel in distress routine. "I know how much of a sacrifice coming to Connecticut is for you. Remember, I'm starting the *Johnny Gallant* series, and I have an August deadline. I need you, Henry."

"That's right. I'd forgotten."

Careless words.

Sylvia slammed her barely used napkin onto the table. Lana Longstreet surfaced yet again as she persistently had since Sylvia had bought Trumball Mansion. "How could you forget? You know how rich my books have made us."

Of all Sylvia's barbs, the truth of his uselessness hurt the most. Anger washed away desire. "My dear, you always have a deadline, and you've always done a superlative job maintaining your house without me. Why now?"

He regretted the words. Even he tasted their acidity.

"Henry, Trumball Mansion is your house too, whether or not you choose to live there. I'm only thinking of you. I'd take care of the garden casualties myself, but I—"

"I know ... *Johnny Gallant* is of more importance to you."

Like a Victorian mistress, Sylvia took the porcelain cup in hand, inserting two dainty fingers through the tiny handle and artistically caressing the opposite side. He imagined the coffee dribbling down her chin, a river of sensuality. He used to wipe her lips after sharing a slice of blueberry pie. How sad that he'd lost interest in sharing pie of any kind. She set her cup back down. Not a drop escaped.

"So why can't your gardener ... what's his name? Ah, yes, Fernando. Why can't he take care of things?"

"He quit last year, and you didn't care enough to notice?"

True ... Henry distanced himself from the affairs in Connecticut and possessed no defense against his wife's indictment. He knew little of what transpired there because little interested him—including her hired help and, least of all, Sylvia's lavish parties. He loathed them, forced to don the costume of a dutiful husband, only attending as business required. "You should have told me Fernando quit. I'm not a mind reader."

Sylvia played her eyes into a droop while her lips merged into a pout. "Now, Henry. Don't get upset. I didn't think the matter worth mentioning. David has been coming over every weekend, but his wife's expecting. She needs him more than I do."

"Bonnie's expecting? When?"

"Christmas. I thought David told you the last time you golfed together."

"The subject never came up."

Should he admit the shallowness of this relationship too? Still, a wife should let a husband know when he's about to become a grandfather. Sylvia crooked her head to one side and her hair fell over her shoulder, a maneuver meant to subdue more than seduce.

He smiled at the thought—a grandchild to bounce on his knee, compensation for a hard life's journey. Hopefully, he'd be a better grandfather than he'd been a dad, the greatest regret of this crazy arrangement—married but not married—his part-time fatherhood.

"Why do you keep things from me, Sylvia? You could've left a voice mail or sent me a text."

Sylvia placed her forefinger over his lips. "Shush. Let's not argue, darling. It's Wednesday."

Yes … Wednesday. Once a week, the Fitzgibbons sealed both their business and marital contract in a meaningless afternoon of pointless chatter while Sylvia countersigned paperwork.

A willowy blonde sauntered toward the table and dropped a black leather wallet onto the laced tablecloth. Henry slid his credit card inside and offered a smile when she returned for his payment. He disliked the secrecy, but Lana Longstreet would not have approved of the hundred-dollar bill he'd slipped inside. The waitress turned on her heels like a well-trained soldier and headed toward the cash register.

Henry forced his attention back toward Sylvia. "Will Donald drive you over to the apartment, or do you want to walk with me?"

"Let's walk. By the way, Donald quit last week. Erik—with a *k*—is my new chauffeur." Sylvia flung her shawl over her shoulders. She grabbed her purse, retrieved her cell, then texted a message, mouthing words as she thumbed the letters. Henry had few skills, although he had learned to read lips while in the army. *Erik, pick me up at Mr. Fitzgibbons's apartment in two hours.*

The waitress returned with Henry's receipts, her eyes a fountain of gratitude. Sylvia glared. Perhaps she had noticed the generous tip. If only she were jealous instead of displeased. Then again, how was she to know this waitress had a huge car repair bill and needed the money. Sylvia never bothered to get to know the men and women who served her, while Henry found great pleasure in idle chit-chat with the less advantaged.

"Well, dear, my attention is yours for the rest of the afternoon."

Her face softened. In the dim restaurant light, she seemed more like the Sylvia he married, the Sylvia he still loved. If only she would surface more often, command Lana Longstreet to disappear, there might be hope for this marriage. He heaved a silent sigh. Little hope Lana Longstreet would ever disappear. The marriage and his misery needed to end.

Sylvia's stiletto heels clicked against the sidewalk three times for every one of Henry's long strides. "Slow down. I'd like to look at some of these window displays."

At least twenty storefronts lined the sidewalk on the four-block stretch from Chez Phillipe's to Henry's apartment, and Sylvia enjoyed admiring the displays, especially Nanette's Boutique.

"Oh, look, Henry. Isn't this sundress simply darling? I can picture Julie wearing it for her art exhibit next month."

Henry waited, as rigid as a statue, as she admired Nanette's display. His brooding, always troublesome, seemed far more intense of late, turning once enjoyable Wednesdays to a test of endurance. Perhaps the time had come to end this horrendous masquerade.

They passed Antonio's Delicatessen, opened a month ago, replacing the old donut shop. "I'm curious about this place. How's the food?"

Henry squinted as he read the sign. "Haven't been here since the Coffee Clatch moved out. Miss it. Pity. The whole neighborhood is changing, especially the tenants in my building. More riff-raff moving in every day."

Henry's weekly complaint.

"You don't have to put up with a decaying neighborhood, Henry. You can easily afford a place on the East side. Why not move?"

"Don't go there again, Sylvia. I like *this* apartment. Our children were born here, and you know how much I despise change. Besides, I can walk to work from my place."

In the early years, Henry's rigidity brought a measure of comfort, pulling her from the precipice of her impetuosity, his steadfastness the rock she could lean on when afraid. Now, in middle age, his stodgy bearing and idiotic claustrophobia dulled him.

She'd offer to discuss a movie, but Henry never went to the cinema and rarely watched television except for sports. Since he disliked talking about Connecticut, their only common ground remained the children and the business. She pried open a conversational door with her detective series. "You'll like my new hero, Johnny Gallant. He's handsome but aloof ... friendly but private. I modeled him after you, you know."

"I'm hardly the poster kid for a detective series, Sylvia."

Another decapitated conversation. What did she expect? Henry hadn't read a single one of her books. Why frustrate herself with his feigned interest in anything she wrote. No use talking.

Once in the apartment, Henry, always the gentleman, removed her shawl, placing it on the back of the winged armchair, the first piece of furniture they'd bought together when they took occupancy of the Manhattan apartment right after their wedding. Not even a honeymoon. She had a deadline on her first book.

His hands, as cold as his heart, brushed against her bared shoulder. She'd give away her entire fortune if only Henry would cover her with smoldering kisses. If she thought God cared, she'd pray, though unlikely even the Almighty could bridge the chasm between them.

She filled the room with more chit-chat, trying in vain to interest Henry in Johnny Gallant's manly virtues.

"I know you love your characters, Sylvia, but you seem to live inside your books. Why can't you stay in the real world for one afternoon a week?"

For a publisher, Henry had no clue how a writer's mind operated. She could no more manipulate the muse than the weather. Then again, perhaps she preferred Lana Longstreet's worlds because so little good happened in her own.

Henry assumed a sentinel posture by the unopened window, his eyes glued on the street below. "Looks like a drug deal going down across the way."

"Never mind the street, Henry. Talk to me."

He stepped aside from the window, allowing the fading sun to cast its last beams of the day. In the brighter light, Sylvia noticed Henry's black suit, nicely accentuated by a gray shirt and a striped tie, the ensemble setting off his blue eyes. Maybe today he'd notice her *L'amoureux* perfume, his birthday gift to her, the scent she wore only for him. She inched next to him, removed his tie, and threw it to the floor. "Isn't that better?"

"I suppose so." He smiled—maybe embers did lie beneath his frozen veneer.

"I've never seen this suit before. Is it new?"

"Monique picked it out."

Lana Longstreet begged to be loosed. "Where, a secondhand store?"

His face reddened as he moved to the other side of the room. "That's a low blow, even for you." An emotion expressed, even if not the one she'd hoped for.

Sylvia thought herself a rational person, incapable of pettiness, yet thoughts of Monique birthed a typhoon of resentment. For a twenty-something, wanna-be-royal-princess, Monique performed far too many favors for her middle-aged employer. Ridiculous to be so jealous. Despite their futile marriage, Henry would die a faithful husband. For one reason—he lacked the courage. Infidelity required too much deception and was not in Henry's wheelhouse.

Henry returned to his spot by the window, pulled aside the sheer white curtains, and resumed his watch. She'd let him have his space for the moment. If this Wednesday were to be rescued, she had to forget Monique's intrusions. She sat on the brown leather couch she'd gladly left behind when she moved to Connecticut and imagined the walls a vivid gold rather than their off-white hue, unchanged since she left.

"You should get a D'Roma, Henry. The brown and gold silk stripes will give the room a manly aura, and this place screams for renewal."

Henry ignored her suggestion like he did her perfume.

"Where's the Monet print I bought you for our anniversary last year, *Poplars in the Sun*?" She searched across the barren living room walls. "I thought a landscape would look nice over the fireplace."

Henry went to his kitchen counter, retrieved a file of paperwork, then set the file on the coffee table in front of her, apparently more interested in business than her perfume. "Monique brought the painting into the office. She said the bright colors got lost without morning sun, and this apartment's on the west ... the office is on the east. You don't mind, do you? If you want, I'll take it down and bring it back here. Makes no difference to me."

"It's a gift. Yours to do with as you wish."

"Do you want coffee?"

Coffee—Henry's panacea for every bad moment.

"No, thank you."

Sylvia shifted her weight to free her stuck legs. She should have worn the longer black skirt rather than this short, strapless shift dress. She patted the couch. "Come here, Henry—sit with me. Tell me what's new at the office. I should stop by more often."

Henry obeyed, still rigid but less pensive. "Bridget Sperling is expecting her second soon."

"Book or baby?"

"Baby. Another boy."

"Really? I hope she gives this one a better name than Elmer. If she's going to name her children after her characters, she should stop writing westerns."

At last, the start of a real conversation and a lead into the workings of Henry's everyday life. On most Wednesdays, Henry shoved documents in front of her to sign, yet rarely told her anything about the day-to-day life of Fitzgibbons & Associate. She knew little about the other writers Henry published and even less about Henry's employees. "Tell me more, Henry. I love it when you share office gossip with me."

"We hired a Pakistani boy, Asaim I think he's called, through a work exchange program. He doesn't speak much

English, and Higgy thought he'd do the least damage in distribution."

"Paul Higgins is a smart man. And how is our dear Paul?"

"He misses his wife. Other than that, he seems fine."

She should have sent him a card after Anita died. She had often accompanied Paul to book launch parties in Connecticut. They seemed devoted to one another. The two would hold hands while strolling through the rose gardens. Sylvia wondered if she and Henry ever loved one another that way. Perhaps ... in the early years. Their marriage died when Henry refused to live with her in Connecticut, though he would argue Sylvia abandoned him first. Regardless of who left whom, the truth remained—their marriage was now beyond resuscitation. Only a miracle could save it, and Lana Longstreet would not allow Sylvia to believe in miracles.

Did Henry want a divorce? If he did, he'd never make the first move. Their arrangement did have advantages —a peaceful existence if not very fulfilling. And, though inevitable, a divorce right now might be majorly inconvenient. She needed Henry's help this summer. Besides, the children were planning a party for their anniversary in August.

Henry had moved to the window again.

"What time do you want Erik to pick you up Saturday?"

"Saturday?"

"Henry, have you forgotten already?"

"Sorry. Momentary lapse. Have Erik with a *k* pick me up around one o'clock." Lana Longstreet wanted to leave— to end Wednesdays forever. She began signing Henry's documents. How she hated this tediousness. Perhaps she should just sign over her shares to Henry ... no more Wednesdays and no more paperwork.Once Henry moved in for the summer, Wednesdays would be like any other day.

CHAPTER 2

Henry checked off the last item on his list and placed his cell into his shirt pocket. No need to reiterate office matters with Higgy, the well that watered Fitzgibbons & Associate. Henry Fitzgibbons, the company's president and founder, proved to be the most useless rich man in the world.

"I think we've covered everything. Thanks, Higgy."

"You're welcome, Fitz. Give my regards to Sylvia."

"I will. She asked about you too. Just Wednesday." Higgy needn't know how much Sylvia remained out of touch. She liked the man. No surprise. Higgy understood women, especially women writers. No wonder all their women authors adored him.

"Don't worry about a thing. Besides, you're only an hour away. Not like you're off to China." Higgy laughed. One never tired of a contagious laugh like his.

Henry smiled despite his determination to find no amusement in the summer's prospects. "You know how I dislike the commute."

"I understand."

"Wish Sylvia did. She likes long car rides. She takes the train every so often just to study people."

"That's what writers do, Fitz."

Higgy must have a psychology degree tucked away in his long list of credentials. The man knew people, got inside their skin, including his partner's phobias.

"You never told Sylvia about your service in the Gulf War? Why you dislike closed places?"

"Sylvia hates war talk, won't watch the news either. Besides, Higgy, it's not just my claustrophobia and the commute. The house doesn't like me."

"Nonsense, Henry. Houses neither like nor dislike."

Of course, Higgy probably wouldn't believe a house was haunted. Ghosts did not fit into his religious beliefs. Besides, a brilliant man, Higgy could explain everything from what made Brazil nuts hard to the cheapest way to produce a book.

"Higgy, the house *is* haunted."

"I don't believe in ghosts. But if you say there's something unnatural there, who am I to argue? Not everything in this world can be explained away by scientific rationale."

"Sylvia doesn't believe me. She knows the rumors. She tells the stories as conversation starters—especially when a stray wind blows through and conveniently knocks over a vase."

Higgy laughed. "True. I've heard her tell a few. Very entertaining, but that doesn't mean—"

"Either there're ghosts in the house, or I'm delusional. At any rate, whatever spirits reside there seem content to remain in the ballroom. So, if I let them have their space, I might survive the summer."

"What will you do in a sprawling house with just the two of you?"

What *would* he do? The very question made him shiver. Before he could answer himself or Higgy, the security buzzer chimed. "That's my ride, I believe. Erik with a *k*."

"Sylvia's new chauffeur?"

"Yes. I'm not surprised Donald quit. Sylvia's tongue cuts worse than a razor. A category five hurricane is a mere blustery wind compared to Sylvia's temper tantrums."

"Come on now, Henry. You don't appreciate Sylvia's passion for her work."

Higgy's words always welled with truth. Her passion held Henry at bay, an elusive trait, beyond his experience or comprehension. Why some consumed their life on a single pursuit was a mystery. Dreamers were a sorry lot—self-absorbed, pushing aside those who loved them. Like Pop. More passionate about God than his family.

"Higgy, sometimes I think you understand Sylvia more than I ever will. Well, I suppose I shouldn't keep Erik with a *k* waiting." Henry tilted from sudden disorientation. Could he manage without Higgy's daily counsel? "I'll miss you, my friend."

"I'm only a phone call away, Fitz. Don't worry so much."

"No. I won't. I trust you."

Henry could almost hear Higgy blush, the man far too modest.

"I'll pray for you."

Offer of prayer was Higgy's signature goodbye. He believed prayer solved everything—his infantile dependency on prayer was the solitary fault Henry could find in his friend. Only the desperate prayed. Higgy claimed prayer made him a stronger person. Prayer hadn't helped that dead girl in Iraq.

The buzzer chimed again. Henry peered at the security camera. A tall, blondish man dressed in a black uniform rocked on his shiny black shoes.

Henry pushed the intercom button. "I assume you're Erik with a *k*."

Hesitation followed by a response coated with a thick Swedish accent. "*Ja.*"

"I'll let you in on the condition you address me as Henry, with a *y*."

"Ja, I vill, Mr. Henry."

Not the slightest chuckle. Maybe Swedes were humorless. No. Not true. Bubben Larrson was voted the most popular female Swedish comedian in 2006. Henry heard her perform once, and she was hilarious. Too bad. Henry's best joke of the day had been wasted on a witless chauffeur. "Apartment 1C—at the end of the hall."

Henry stifled the urge to whistle when Erik entered his apartment.The overhead view had not done justice to the man's warrior build. Mid-thirties and with his Fabio face and Schwarzenegger physique, he looked more like an action movie hero than a chauffeur. At least the man's mystique might provide entertainment for the long ride to New Haven.

"I'm almost ready. I suppose I should pack a few things. What do you suggest I bring for clothes?"

"Excuse, please, Mr. Henry. I know little of fashion."

"I see. Doesn't matter. I've got a full wardrobe at the house, complete with a tuxedo. My wife is up on all the latest male fashions. Oh, well. Let's go. If I need anything, they have stores in New Haven, don't they?"

Erik the Deadpan remained silent.

Henry grabbed his computer, carrying it more for show than need. Then again, he never knew when it might come in handy. He pointed toward the door. "Lead the way."

They walked in silence to Sylvia's new car, the sporty look so unlike her previous black sedan. He shouldn't be surprised. Sylvia varied every aspect of her life except her writing routine. She must think her husband the dullest man on earth. For Henry, the slightest variance brought on a panic attack—the reason he walked the same route to work everyday. Still, Sylvia's penchant for spontaneity mesmerized him like a firefly in the dead of night.

Sylvia thrived on spontaneity, something Henry could not give her. If he could do one thing differently, maybe she'd move back to Manhattan. Once, he took the subway to work and traveled an extra four blocks. He ended up in the hospital with near respiratory failure. Sadly, he must choose the predictable, solitary life.

Erik opened the passager door, and Henry stared from the curb as he sucked in a deep breath, then another and another until he conjured enough courage to slide in. With a half bow, Erik closed Henry's door. Like a solitary guard at post, Erik marched to the driver's side and positioned himself behind the wheel, every limb jerking in robotic efficiency. He started the engine and eased into traffic with expertise worthy of a NASCAR racer. Once they reached I-95, Henry finally breathed but refused to release his grip on the door handle.

He trained his thoughts on his driver. "So, I'm guessing you are from Sweden?"

"Ja."

"How long have you lived in the United States?"

"Five years I am in dis country, Mr. Henry."

Cagey. Give just enough to answer but don't offer more than what's asked. "What did you do before Mrs. Fitzgibbons hired you?"

Erik broke his cardboard posture to tilt his head to one side. "Mrs. Fitzgibbons?"

"Oh. Sorry. I meant Miss Longstreet." Henry's cheeks heated. True, the name Lana Longstreet tripped off the tongue with more glamour than Sylvia Fitzgibbons. That his wife wrote under a pen name gave him no concern at first. That she now lived exclusively by this name enraged him—her final rejection.

"I forgot. My wife prefers her pen name."

"Lana Longstreet ist gud name for writer."

Erik's too-agreeable persona pegged him as a spy. "Have you always worked as a chauffeur?"

"Ja."

"Who else have you driven for?"

"I drive for Dr. Gordon before Miss Longstreet."

"The plastic surgeon?"

Most humans, Henry observed, leaned either forward or backward while they sat or drove. Not this Nordic Adonis with a spine made of unbendable steel.

"What kind of work did you do in Sweden?"

"I vaz chauffeur for dignitary to US of A. Miss Longstreet have my history."

For the next hour, Henry machine gunned questions while Erik with a *k*, as evasive as a jihadist operative, answered with as few words as possible. Henry's dossier on *The Incredible Swede* remained pitifully opaque. The little he gleaned was more like an unimpressive biography than a blockbuster thriller.

Born outside of Stockholm, Erik had a wife named Martina and two children, twin three-year-old boys, Svenbjorn, Sven for short, and Gunnar. In Swedish, Sven meant young bear. Gunnar meant bold warrior. Both names seemed prophetic. Perhaps Erik primped them for a career in soccer.

Henry could easily glean the information from Sylvia, but putting Erik to the test was a lot more fun. He probed for one small nugget Sylvia might have overlooked.

"My Swedish is a little rusty. But doesn't Erik mean eternal ruler?"

"Ja. Very good, Mr. Henry. But I do not wish to be a ruler. I am just a chauffeur."

"And you don't aspire to anything else?"

"Vhat means aspire?"

"You know. Dream of being anything other than a chauffeur."

"Ja. I am student at Yale. I take night course."

Now we're getting somewhere. "And what are you studying?"

"I study law."

Sylvia paid her employees well. But how could Erik afford to study law on a chauffeur's salary? "Does your wife work?"

"She does housework for elderly peoples."

"Forgive the intrusion, Erik, but being an immigrant, how do you finance a law degree at Yale?"

"I have what you call scholarship?"

Erik Hagstadt might be an opportunist, after all—his story too squeaky clean for believability. Every Adonis had an Achilles heel, and Henry felt energized from the challenge before him. He'd have his private investigator do some digging as well. An immigrant left his native country for one of two reasons: either to better one's lot or to escape a past. Which brought the Swedish Hulk Hogan to the hallowed halls of Yale and to Sylvia's front seat?

FROM JOHNNY GALLANT

C1

Johnny Gallant tipped his Fedora at the pretty waitress. Some men might not appreciate her less than slender form, but Johnny found all women attractive—the tall and short as well as the hefty and slim. Heaven designed each woman as he did each man—for a singular purpose. When a woman stumbled upon her divine destiny, she wore an expression borne from her inner beauty, an aura of confidence and charm. For some women, pregnancy brought a visible joy. For others, particularly younger women, first love showed through their innocent blushes. Given the girl's ruddy complexion, she had recently won the attention of a young man. Another clue. Her voice, soft and hushed, gurgled through throaty giggles.

What face would he wear if he discovered a great love? Would he ever find such wonder? Not likely. He expected to go to his grave with the question unanswered. Only the righteous deserved the bliss of reciprocated adoration.

Johnny possessed intimate knowledge of many women. His sexual conquests, though numerous, failed to satisfy. A part of him yearned to experience that purest conjugality—when a man and woman's hearts beat as one.

Johnny placed his order. As the waitress retreated, he pulled out the rose-bordered letter. Another job in another city. Another victim who begged for his help, the best of the best. Another wealthy woman whose fame and fortune brought fear and oppression. The rich failed to realize their prisons were as unsavory as the masses.

Kings could not dictate the tenor of their days. Protocols and expectations mired the soul as much as destitution. Every benefit of privilege came with a price, if not gold, then from the sacrifice of peons.

Johnny Gallant was neither prince nor pauper. He owned his time, and no one forced their will upon him. He could accept or refuse this entreaty he held in his hands. In some ways, that made him god-like, didn't it?

He sniffed the jasmine-scented letter the courier had brought him and rescanned the appeal so delicately penned. She cited two attempts upon her life. The first came by way of an attempted hit-and-run. She described the green SUV that nearly ran her down. If she hadn't stopped to give the custodian a tip, the car would have found its mark.

If her account were true, she was a kind woman. A guardian from some realm protected her. Why did she want to hire a hellion like Johnny Gallant?

Maybe the first incident was a mere close call. But the second incident in the sanctuary of her own home left no doubt someone wanted to harm her. Her maid noticed the masked intruder lurking in the bushes. Unfortunately, the man escaped before the police arrived.

Johnny read the next paragraph aloud but in soft enough tones to be heard by only him. "The police think I'm making the whole matter up as a publicity stunt to promote my next movie. I assure you, Mr. Gallant, I've never stooped to such levels. I implore you to consider my predicament, and I will spare no expense to bring you into my employ."

Should he accept? Money ceased to be an enticement. Johnny's bank accounts already bulged with more wealth than he could possibly use, though his assets were hidden, stuffed away in foreign accounts under presumed names, waiting for his elusive retirement.

An intelligent man would hand the plea back to the waiting courier and say, "Tell your client to find someone else. Johnny Gallant is no longer for sale."

Was he allured by the perfume or by curiosity? Which prompted his response as the waitress returned with a Texas T-bone steak? She set it before him, blushed, and spun on her heels. Johnny motioned the courier over. "Tell your client, I'll be in touch."

CHAPTER 3

Sylvia stretched her arms toward the ceiling. She stood and arched her back. A start, at least. She could tweak what she'd written later. Henry should be here soon. She ran through her mental checklist. She'd spent the better part of yesterday getting his room ready. Henry probably thought she sloughed the task off to Rosalie.

He never shopped for his clothes. Not once, as far as she knew. When he visited, he brought nothing with him except his cell phone and laptop, which he probably never took out of its case. She spent tedious hours arranging his wardrobe, making sure to buy the latest and best. He never took any of the clothes she bought back to Manhattan. If he did, Monique wouldn't need to shop for him. Maybe he treated Monique's efforts with the same ungratefulness.

Sylvia sighed. Henry seemed to drift through his existence with no inkling how much she enjoyed doing these things for him, no acknowledgement or half-grunted thank you, treating her hired help with more regard than his wife. Well, Henry could go to blazes. She'd endured his passivity long enough. Years of tepid waters had congealed her heart.

Maybe she could find love elsewhere. An affair, however, out of the question. Whatever sins Heaven held against her, she'd not add adultery to the list. She'd ask Henry for a divorce after the anniversary party. After all, she couldn't disappoint the children. In the meantime, she'd have to endure his callous complaints.

She picked up their wedding portrait from her worktable. Henry's hair had frosted with age, and his waist had expanded a few inches. He looked much the same, however, from his grin to his short hair cut, a style he'd worn even in high school, according to his yearbooks.

She remembered when laughter rang from the Manhattan apartment. The newly married Fitzgibbons were poor in possessions but rich with hope. She thought then happiness stretched before them like an endless river. Her first three books sold modestly. Then success exploded with more wealth than either could imagine. No amount of money, though, could buy back Henry's love.

The soft purr of her Porsche reverberated through the loft. A desk drawer eased open. Odd. Rumbles rarely made the furniture shake like this. Should she at least greet Henry? Lana Longstreet wanted to stay put, get back to her writing—to let him settle himself. Sylvia won the emotional coin toss. If hope sprang eternal, then perhaps she'd find some glimmer in Henry's face, some reason to stay a divorce for a year or two more.

She took hesitant steps from her writing loft through the upstairs string of closets and chambers, and down the grand staircase. A hazy glow coming from the ballroom caught her eye just as she reached the bottom step. Probably dusty. She'd ask Rosalie to give the room a thorough cleaning on Monday.

She blew out resolve and joined Henry at the circular drive. Insisting he spend the summer topped the list of her twenty worst mistakes. She could have found some other solution among countless alternatives than setting herself up for yet another heart-wrenching disappointment. Too late now. Whatever symphony summer played would be orchestrated one day at a time.

Henry took three deep breaths before getting out of the car. He scanned the front hedges, a geometric mix of squares and ovals.

Sylvia stood with hands on her hips, like a mother ready to send a child to his room. "It's a good thing I stocked your dresser. I suspected you'd traipse over here with nothing but the clothes on your back."

She wasted no time launching her attack, pecking his nerves. "Not so, Sylvia." He held up his computer valise. "I came prepared."

"If you need anything else, Erik will run into town for you."

He-man nodded like a bobble doll, too eager to please.

"I think Erik could use the rest of the night off." Jealousy reared, but Henry refused to let Sylvia get a whiff of his envy. A man on the upper end of middle age should not have to compete with perfection. He was forced to play Euripides to Erik's Hercules.

Sylvia took charge, the manor's mistress to the nth degree. "The weather report indicates we're in for a warmer season than usual. I hadn't bought your shorts yet. Erik can go into town Monday. I give all the staff Sundays off."

Erik couldn't be human—probably a highly-developed marionette, like a Disney prototype. "Ja, I vill, Miss Longstreet. Vat size, Mr. Henry?"

"Honestly, Erik. I don't know. I haven't shopped for clothes in more years than I can count. Miss Longstreet buys clothes for me here, and my secretary runs my personal errands in the city."

Sylvia cocked her head and scrunched her eyebrows, her Peppermint Patty stance a signal he was about to receive a verbal dousing. "And what other favors does Monique do for you?"

"Sylvia, that was completely uncalled for and totally beneath you. Monique's a nice girl. Besides, she's more like a daughter to me. Good grief, she's a year younger than Julie."

He should tell Erik to bring him back to the city right now while he retained a modicum of dignity. After one whole summer of Sylvia's persistent hammering, he'd be reduced to a stump.

But ...

He'd promised.

Henry Fitzgibbons never broke a promise.

Erik rocked on his feet and gazed in all directions except toward his argumentative employers. Henry oozed a sigh of resignation. "I'm going to my room to freshen up. What time is dinner?"

Sylvia flicked her hair to one side. "Rosalie brings me a plate at six o'clock sharp. I eat in my loft when writing. You may eat wherever you choose." She turned on her heels and disappeared behind the house, leaving him with the unsavory choice of entering by the main foyer.

The rambling estate had thirty rooms. With any luck, Henry might not see Sylvia all summer. For the best. The less contact, the fewer arguments.

"I take your things for you, Mr. Henry?"

Why not let him feel useful. "Sure."

Henry took hesitant steps, stopping at the top of the front stoop. He stared at the massive portico. Why hadn't he swallowed his pride and followed Sylvia to the rear entrance?

He opened the door, stepped into the foyer, and stared at the ballroom. The only access from here to the old servants' quarters where he slept when in Connecticut was through the ballroom.They waited in there for him, and he sensed their hateful mockery. Every creak made him shudder. He complained to Sylvia more than once, but she maintained rigid disbelief. Why did these beings torment only him?

If Erik hadn't been standing right behind him, he'd run back down the steps, go behind the house, and follow the cobblestone path to his room. Hindsight always precedes regret. Now, he must either withstand the horrific or admit his fear of brick and mortar to a younger, more robust man. "My room's through the ballroom at the end of the west wing, the old servant quarters."

Confusion reigned on Erik's face. Henry supposed all of Sylvia's help gossiped about the owners' sleeping arrangements. Erik asked no questions, and Henry offered no explanations.

Why had he listened to his arrogance and chosen a room as far away from Sylvia as possible? His anger equaled the same hostility he felt when he discovered she'd bought the house without his input. Why? Didn't she think him smart enough to give advice? Or maybe she knew he'd never agree. She'd forced his hand and moved without him. Now, his foolish ego kept him downstairs. He'd rather face a thousand ghosts than an hour of Sylvia's ridicule.

He stood in rigid protest against the derision awaiting him. When he reached the grand staircase, the sulfurous odor assaulted him on all sides. He fought his discomfort, hiding his unmanly dread from the Viking. Henry sucked up all the courage the putrid air allowed and faced Erik with theatrical calm. "I need nothing further today. Go home to your pretty wife and kids."

Erik handed over Henry's valise then executed a one-eighty sans salute and retreated to a kingdom of his own. Henry inched under the archway to face the horror alone where vapors in human form danced a minuet. If he could see them, why couldn't Erik? With the first step into the room, they ceased their revelry, turned, and taunted him with hysterical laughter. Henry's frantic exhales joined the mist by the fireplace.

He picked up his pace, thankful for the shaft of late afternoon light—a beacon guiding him through a contemptuous sea.

"Let me through, I say." The mist parted—not in obedience to his command for he held no power over them. They merely abided until the time of their choosing to devour him.

Once through the ballroom, he dared to breathe and hastened his steps down the hallway leading to the old servants' quarters. He rested a moment outside Sylvia's library, a museum to her highly successful career. The guilt pricked him each time he peeked in. Her books had made them wealthy beyond his wildest dreams, yet he'd never read a single title. Sylvia rambled for hours about her plots, describing her characters' conflicts like episodic soap operas. He gleaned enough from her reports to bluff his way through committee meetings. To read them meant rehashing her drivel.

He employed editors to manage her manuscripts, and they said her work needed minor if any changes. In truth, though, Sylvia's capability provided an excuse, a convenient out to cover up his inadequacy. Could a former sportswriter judge the work of a literary genius like Lana Longstreet? Ten million fans sang her praises. What more could he add?

Though he'd read the classics for his English degree, in the last twenty years, he'd read fewer than a dozen literary works. His current reading material was mostly comprised of sports books. He was the worst kind of fraud—a parasite who fed off the talents of others.

Tossing his briefcase onto a chair, he refamiliarized himself with the room. He opened the glass doors on the far end of the room, recalling how Sylvia installed them soon after his first visit. He had slammed a coffee cup on the counter and swore enough to make Satan himself blush. "I'm never coming here again, Sylvia. Not if I have to keep going through the ballroom just to get a cup of coffee." He waited a whole year before he came again. Fighting drained him. He couldn't remember a single visit that didn't end up with him storming out and vowing never to return. Somehow Sylvia always coaxed him back with some excuse or another.

Although he'd never tell her, he enjoyed the interlocking cobbled path where he could stroll through the gardens on his way to the kitchen. There, Rosalie kept a ready supply of her coffee. Except for Sylvia's soirees, he could avoid the ballroom altogether. For the most part, the ghosts behaved during her parties. They might tip over a glass or two as a reminder—sufficient unexplained happenings to keep the rumors alive.

With the exception of a few wall hangings and decorations, not much had changed since he slept here last. Henry walked over to the antique dresser, reportedly an 18th century hutch belonging to Trumball. Henry picked up a newly framed photograph, a five-by-seven of him and Sylvia in front of the retaining wall. Icicles crept along the stone ledge and glistened in the afternoon sun. They wore parkas and big smiles. Henry opened the frame and read the inscription on the back of the photo: *Henry and Sylvia at launch party honoring* Gordon's Promise, *Lana Longstreet's sixtieth release. Photo by Paul Higgins.*

He remembered the February party. He had brooded the whole time. Sylvia insisted he come when Higgy could have represented the company. Henry had been there for Christmas and stayed an extra two days. Since Sylvia barely spoke to him at either visit, he wondered why he'd even made the effort.

Maybe the time had come to be rid of all Connecticut entanglements. He could plant a few rose bushes around his patio off the back of his apartment. A poor substitute to be sure, but Sylvia could no longer use the roses as a ploy to drag him here. He should turn over his shares to Higgy, divorce Sylvia, and retire hassle free.

There.

Settled.

Somehow, he'd get through the summer.

Henry rummaged through the assortment of toiletries— not the brands he preferred. He'd make do. Next, he rifled through drawers stuffed with underwear, argyle socks, swim trunks, Ralph Lauren golf shirts, and an assortment of Levi casuals. He found two sets of pajamas. He preferred to sleep in his boxers, but Sylvia insisted he wear pajamas while in Connecticut, especially when she entertained overnight guests. Could he stand them for a whole summer?

He opened the closet doors: a robe, slippers, pillows, blankets, oxford shirts, dress trousers, his summer tuxedo, and several lightweight suits. He should thank Sylvia for the new set of golf clubs. He pulled out the putter and made a couple of phantom putts. For a non-golfer, she had chosen well.

Raindrops pinged against the window. Henry fumbled through his room in vain for an umbrella. He'd have to ask Erik to get him one as soon as possible. In the meantime, he would either drown or have to go through the ballroom. He grabbed one of the lightweight jackets in the closet, threw it over his head, and made the dash to the kitchen where Rosalie stacked pots into the dishwasher.

"Any coffee, Rosalie?" He hung his soaked jacket on the coat rack next to the door.

Rosalie winked. "Yep. 'Bout done brewin'. You'll have to fetch it yourself, though. I'm a mite busy here."

"You sure you don't want to come back to Manhattan? I'd stake you for a coffee shop if you'd make some just for me once in a while."

If not for the ballroom, Rosalie's banter might entice more frequent visits. Henry loved her like his Aunt Doris, the two women equally matched in sass and flesh. He cried when Rosalie and her husband decided to move to Connecticut. Sylvia took the best of everything when she left him.

Rosalie wiped her hands and faced him. "Hope you still like my pot roast. Miss Longstreet never tells me what to make except when there's a big party goin' on. I remembered how you like my pot roast."

Henry sniffed the air with exaggerated snorts. "So that's what I smelled." He opened cupboards in search of his Bubba Watson cup, a personalized autographed photo of the legend, embossed over white enamel. Sylvia surprised him with the gift last Christmas. He'd expected the usual heavy knit sweater and kissed her on an impulse when he opened the package.

Rosalie's coffee deserved a man's mug, not one of Sylvia's too-delicate teacups.

As if reading his mind, Rosalie pointed to Henry's right. "Top shelf."

He nodded as he reached with his full height, jumping when the intercom buzzed, making a Johnny Bench maneuver just before his mug hit the counter. "Whew! Too close. Miss Longstreet sure keeps you hopping. I don't know how you tolerate the noise."

Sylvia's voice boomed. "Rosalie, is my tea ready yet?"

"Comin' right up, Miss Longstreet."

"I'm sorry. I distracted you."

"I don't mind, none, Henry. Miss Longstreet has a schedule she likes to stick by when she's writin'—breakfast at nine, dinner at noon, tea at four, supper at six. When her schedule's off, she gets a little perturbed."

"Give me the tray. I'll bring it up to her. I don't have anything better to do at the moment. No interesting golf tournament this weekend and the baseball game isn't on until later."

Rosalie clicked excitement. "Henry Fitzgibbons, you're a kind man. Those steps get harder to climb every year. Well, only a few months more."

"What are you talking about? You're not quitting, are you?" He'd miss Rosalie's coffee as much as the woman herself.

"Housekeepers get to retire, too, you know. I turn seventy in September. It's high time for Mister and me to start enjoyin' ourselves. We bought a little trailer in Florida, and we're movin' the first part of October. Thought ya knew."

Henry's jaws clenched. "No, Miss Longstreet and I don't talk much since Julie and David left home. When we do, our conversation is usually about business. Sylvia ... er ... Miss Longstreet ... doesn't need me for much. I'm only here now because of the garden problem."

"You sure do like those roses, don't you, Henry? I catch you staring at 'em every once in a while as if you're praying." She retrieved a wooden tray from a narrow cupboard. On it, she placed a glass of iced tea garnished with a lemon slice and a plate of Lorna Doones, adorning the setting with a short-stemmed rosebud perpendicular to the glass. She stepped back, readjusted the items to line up perfectly, whistled approval, and covered the tray with a linen napkin.

"There. All set." She chuckled. "If you dare."

"Should I be afraid?"

"Miss Longstreet gets into an awful snit when she's creatin'. Yesterday, she threw a print cartridge toward the landing just as I popped my head up on the last step. Near gave me a black eye. Oh, I know 'twas an accident. But I'm still none too careful when she's at the computer." Rosalie's laugh belied her gruff tone. Sylvia's worst days could do little to intimidate Rosalie Grady. Gaelic through and through, she gave back as good as she got.

"I'll take my chances. Go home if you want. I'll see to Miss Longstreet's dinner."

"I'm always glad when you come home, Henry. Almost always get me a few hours off. Pot roast's done at quarter to six. Let it set ten minutes before servin'." Rosalie yanked off her apron, picked up her purse, and scooted toward the back door. "Thanks a heap, Henry."

Balancing the tray with one hand, he carried his coffee in the other. He took the spiral staircase with slow, deliberate steps. Remembering Rosalie's account, he whistled as he climbed in the event Sylvia readied to launch another missile.

When he reached the loft, he found her staring at her computer. After a few seconds, she typed a sentence or two, then stared at her computer again while chewing on her bottom lip. Did he dare break her concentration? He boomed out a quick, "Here's your tea, Sylvia. I sent Rosalie home. I'll bring up your dinner at six."

Her eyes never left the computer screen. "Put the tray on the table."

Dismissed like a servant.

He hesitated with the realization he'd never been in Sylvia's loft before. He stole a quick glance around the room—shelving along every wall, a bookcase at his right. *Moby Dick* was positioned next to Sylvia's first nonfiction published work, *The Life and Times of Gloria Steinham,* each row of books a hodge podge of mysteries, romance, and biographies.

"Anything else you need?"

She grunted, "No, thank you," and resumed her typing.

Well, he tried to be civil, and she ignored his overtures.

Since Sylvia said nothing more, he returned to face the long night alone.

JOHNNY GALLANT

C3

Johnny Gallant studied the woman as her sombrero-like headpiece wobbled in the breeze. To Johnny, women lost themselves beneath their hats. Like the prophet of old, he believed a woman's hair was her crowning glory. Why cover the divine gift in the name of fashion? Yes, certain weather conditions required protection from the sun. True enough. Many women, he observed, used hats to hide a deep insecurity. Johnny forced himself not to look at hats. He focused on a woman's eyes. Did they droop, laugh, sigh, or sparkle?

This woman, however, seemed made to wear a hat ... its tilt enhanced her brown eyes, and ebony hair fell softly over her shoulders. Johnny avoided tracing the length of her curls with his glances, too much temptation in those tresses.

"So, Mr. Gallant. You will take my case? I can't tell you how grateful I am. My father recommended you."

"Your father? How do I know your father?"

"You saved his life in the Amazon. A hungry croc wanted him for his supper. Daddy said you jumped in, hit the croc's snout, and the beast dropped him. The bites healed nicely thanks to your medicinal advice. Daddy relishes in the story."

"Your father is Colonel Lester?"

Her eyes sparkled like the crystal fountains in Rome. "The one and only."

She laughed. Johnny imagined her laugh recorded and played back when dark moods descended. What a shame she danced in the shadows, too afraid to bask beneath the sun.

CHAPTER 4

Sylvia stared at the page. What should she call a woman who'd end up transforming the hard-hearted detective? The character hadn't whispered her name yet. Tough, macho Johnny Gallant could never fall in love with an Emily or an Emma. What about a symbolic name like Cherise or Chenelle? No, not Chenelle. Sounds like a perfume or one of those tacky bedspreads she had growing up.

Sometimes, a stroll into the village stirred the imagination. She looked at her watch, the only sense of time she allowed in her loft. Ten o'clock on a Sunday morning. She'd been up since six. Henry had brought her a muffin and coffee at nine. He didn't stay, nor did she risk asking him to. If he'd made one of his halting excuses, she would have sunk into a fit of depression. She thought she would relish having him so near, yet he distanced himself even more than ever before.

Maybe he hadn't left yet for his golf date with David. She should make some attempt at conversation. Feverishly trying to get a head start on word count, she hadn't spoken more than a dozen words to him since he arrived. She arched her back, picked up the plates, and set them on the tray. She took the grand staircase leading to the main foyer. Although less convenient than the back spiral steps, Sylvia treasured the feel of the cherry banister on her palm.

She stopped at the last step and squinted as she peered into the ballroom. Where were Henry's ghosts? Nothing. All she could see was the sparkling jade on the fireplace mantel. The pieces were said to be from Eleonor Trumball's collection. The realtor told her the fireplace was one of the few colonial constructions left in New Haven. History abounded in this room. Not just the artifacts, but what transpired ... a meeting ground for the American Revolutionary War generals. What better way to plan strategies than undercover at a ball? Yet, Henry avoided the whole house like spoiled lunchmeat. She hitched her ear to listen ... for what? A whistle, a moan—anything—if only a falling candlestick or an eerie creak, a hint of plausibility in Henry's excuses. She'd rather be stampeded by ghosts than accept the fact Henry no longer loved her.

Of course, she had heard the rumors but saw no mists or glows worth mentioning, no evidence of the supernatural afoot. True, the air temperature seemed ten degrees cooler in the ballroom than anywhere else in the house ... no central heating here. She reasoned the cooler temperatures were due to the lack of windows, no means of natural lighting except when the heavy mahogany veranda doors were opened. The drafts provided her guests with ample conjectures laced with jealousy. Lana Longstreet thrived on the envy of others.

Sylvia stood by the entrance, waiting, anticipating. Nothing. Not a peep or a breeze. Not that she expected to see or feel anything. Henry insisted the spirits danced while they taunted him. If they existed, they performed only for him.

On one occasion, a guest's glass tipped over as if disrupted by a surly child. She dismissed the spill as a quirky accident, but Lana Longstreet milked the well-timed disposition and regaled her guests with a fabricated story about an ill-mannered wraith who frequented the very room in which they dined. Her guests were enthralled. Her publicist suggested she include the rapscallion's antics in the next press release. Henry made no comment. He threw his napkin on the table, walked out, and didn't return for six months.

She thought back to other unexplained events like Julie's graduation party. The poor girl screamed, claiming a dark form flitted along the walls. But Julie saw shadows in the blazing sun. No one believed her, least of all her own mother. Henry believed Julie, of course. Finally, someone on his side. To placate him, Sylvia hired a ridiculous ghost hunter, Madam Eggleston. The woman was so eccentric, she passed for a character in a Noel Coward play, right down to her phony French accent. Evan North had recommended her. He'd met her researching his newest book, *Willows at Wingate*, a thriller about a ghost hunter.

Madam Eggleston proved as big a disappointment as Evan's book. Too embarrassed to tell Henry of the debacle, Sylvia passed the whole thing off as one of Evan's failed publicity stunts.

Henry's sightings remained a mystery. The logical conclusion? He manipulated the rumors to avoid coming to Connecticut.

Sylvia heard clapping as an announcer recapitulated Rickie Fowler's birdie shot. She walked through the ballroom, down the short hall to Henry's room, then knocked. No answer. She peeked in. Empty.

She turned the television off, then retreated through the ballroom, opening the doors onto the veranda. Henry sat on a wicker chair, lost in the vista, rocking away like an oldtimer. His gaze seemed fixed on the early blooms nestled against the retaining wall, his poise like one in prayer—only, to her knowledge, Henry never prayed. "There you are."

He roused from his trance. "Good morning, Sylvia. How late did you work last night? I thought I heard computer noises once or twice. Amazing how every sound echoes through this old house."

"I went to bed at one, got back up at six, worked on the book for a few hours, then took a shower before I went back to try to write a bit more. I'm stuck at the moment." Sylvia drew up a wicker chair next to Henry. The soft light cast a halo affect around his thick, multi-shaded gray hair. At least, he'd never go bald. She drank in his musk cologne, content he was near her, even if they didn't touch. Nor did he look at her now, his gaze resting on the array of rose beds. Didn't he care his wife had been violated by an empty page?

"I've never known you to get stuck for long, Sylvia. Your stories always fall together."

"Not true. I get stuck a lot. You might think I don't because I've never missed a deadline."

Henry took a sip of coffee as if she hadn't said a word. "You know, I've been looking at the yard for about half an hour. I can't see what the problem is."

No, Henry. I suspect you wouldn't.

"For a man who claims to have perfect vision, you see as much as a bridled horse." She cupped his chin in her palm then turned his head toward the other side of the yard. "Over there by the shed. Tell me you at least see the vines on the shed."

"Of course. They've gotten pretty thick over the years, I guess."

"More than that, Henry. Now follow those rows across the yard. See how they've spread along the back wall and around the rose stems?"

"I guess I see what you mean. I'll get on it tomorrow. I'm meeting David for brunch, then we have a one o'clock tee time. Sorry to desert you. Will you be okay by yourself?"

"I'm used to being alone on Sundays. At least, since Julie went off to college. Go. This will give you and David a chance to catch up."

Henry turned away from her again. She'd worn her red blouse, the one he said brought out her dark features, and doubted he'd noticed. "Just so you know, David and Julie have planned an anniversary party for us. They want to have a gala on the last Saturday in August. You do remember our anniversary, don't you?"

Henry nodded—a polite, short curtsy of the head, the way he avoided telling a bold-faced lie.

"Will I still be in Connecticut?" He asked the question like a convicted felon wants to know when he can be paroled.

"Hard to say."

"Well, I don't want to disappoint the kids. I suppose I could come back for the party if I'm gone."

I'd be disappointed, Henry. Does that matter?

Sylvia stood. For all the conversation Henry gave her, she should've moved Mother in for the summer. "I thought I'd take a walk. I'll get a sandwich at the coffee shop in town. I like to observe folks now and again."

Henry returned to his rose-crazed stupor. Why couldn't he look at her with the same admiration? He used to—years ago. What changed? What drove Henry into himself and away from her?

She turned to retrace her journey through the ballroom. The veranda doors were closed, yet a misty breeze like a small water eddy encircled her, then dissipated. Funny. She hadn't remembered closing the doors behind her. Then again, she was known to be absent-minded while in the throes of creating.

She took the cobbled path to the kitchen, grabbed a sweater off the coat rack, and took the winding trail through the western unmanicured back acreage—a flow of weedy brushes and poplars shrouding the estate's south boundaries, sometimes a photo op for her publicist. Once a buck scooted across the trail and turned his head. She snapped a quick picture … the perfect background for her novel, *The Deer Lover*. On days like today, when life drained her spirit, the walk into town bolstered Lana Longstreet's creative juices.

On any given day, Sylvia would have enjoyed the walk along the old street, now a touristy market place. While she appreciated the estate's isolation within a bustling city like New Haven, she sometimes yearned for the aroma of freshly baked bread and the drumming sounds of chattering shoppers instead of the persistent *tap-tap* of the resident woodpeckers.

The chimes from the old Methodist Church played *A Mighty Fortress Is Our God*. She stopped, surprising herself as she suddenly sang along, albeit in low tones in case someone might recognize her. Lana Longstreet was well known for her ridicule of religious people, claiming only the weak minded depended on an unseen God. For a few moments, she was taken back to her youth and the hymns of old that once gave her comfort. She must have walked this street a hundred times and had given little thought to the chimes before this. Why did they catch her attention now? She shook her head, willing Lana Longstreet to take control again, then continued her walk.

The height of tourist season didn't begin until after Memorial Day. With the early warming, the streets teemed with enthusiastic explorers. Three years ago, the city council voted to rope off the section from traffic. The town refurbished the cobblestone to give the block an eighteenth-century flavor. Some of the shop owners even dressed in period costumes.

She hungered for an éclair. No place but Gig's would do, her favorite café. She caught up to an elderly couple, in no apparent hurry, certainly not on a quest for a specialty dessert as she was.

She resisted the urge to pass them. Instead, she slowed her pace in order to observe them more closely. The woman wore a moth-eaten overcoat, and her pencil-box hat seemed a throwback from pre-hippy days. The man tugged at his cabled gray cardigan, then held the woman's hand as they continued their stroll like young lovers. Sylvia thought eavesdropping to be impolite, but Lana Longstreet seized the opportunity to study love in the twilight years.

The woman unloosed her hand and slapped the man across the arm. "Now, Ozzie, don't go so fast. You know I can't keep up with you when you walk so fast."

The old man stopped. "Sorry, dear." They walked along for a few minutes more, impossibly slower than before. "Is that better?"

In spite of their awkward shuffles, they walked side by side as if they'd journeyed together for decades. She envied the couple ahead of her—even their tiff seemed laced with love. Given their white hair and stooped backs, they probably had been together at least five decades. Maybe more. Wasn't that eternity? Even if by some miracle she and Henry revived their dead marriage, could they possibly achieve this kind of harmony?

She grieved for what might have been. Maybe if she had stayed in Manhattan, the closing chapters of Henry and Sylvia might have had a much happier ending. Remorse stabbed her as never before. Normally, Lana Longstreet shielded Sylvia from unwanted feelings; but the sight of these oldsters released knee-knocking sorrow not even she could barricade against.

When the couple turned into a coffee shop, Sylvia permitted the tears to flow, the first since Henry walked out of the portico of her dreams.

CHAPTER 5

The thumps woke Henry from a deep sleep, his limbs a trembling mass of fright. Apparently, these spirits never slept. Monday. Not his favorite day of the week. Had he been in Connecticut for a day and a half already?

He swung his feet to the floor and listened with a wakeful ear. The pings and bangs of rattling pots and pans brought relief. Not spirits but rather a very spirited housekeeper. He sniffed the air like a bloodhound. Coffee, bacon, eggs—pleasant aromas filled his nostrils—much more pleasant than the nauseating gas drifting into his room from the ballroom. He slipped on the first arrangement of clothing his hands grabbed and stuffed his feet into cardboard slippers. He should have brought his leather moccasins. He added *soft slippers* to Erik's shopping list.

Henry peeked outside, pleased to see the morning mist already dissipating. He pulled out a sweatshirt from the closet, opened the glass doors with gusto, and sprinted to the kitchen. No one made him breakfast in Manhattan. Coffee either. If he must abide the summer in this mausoleum, Rosalie's coffee might make his sentence bearable.

She whisked open a drawer and retrieved a potholder and tongs. "What are you doing today, Henry?" She turned the bacon, the sizzling pops as melodious as breaking waves to a surfer's ear. She removed Henry's cup from the dishwasher and handed it to him.

"Never saw a man so deprived in all my born days, Henry. Have a seat while I fix you a plate." She shook her head with motherly humor.

Henry filled his cup and whiffed the aroma as he sat at the end of the counter. Rosalie's coffee deserved slow sips but not before inhaling the hot steam for several minutes. "I suppose I should find a gardener. Suggestions?"

"Sorry, Henry. I clean, cook, and keep the books. I don't do gardens, and I don't know anybody who does."

His hopes for an early release dimmed.

"There's a nursery in town, though. I think it's called The Flower Store."

Henry laughed. "Not a very clever name."

Rosalie echoed his snorts with oinks of her own. "Might not be the cleverest name, I'll give ya. But with several stores along the east coast, I'd say the odds are these folks know a mite about gardens of the flowery kind. The one here in New Haven is the anchor store."

Henry brought the cup to his lips, imagining his first sip. Not quite time yet to reward his want, anticipation the best part of a morning cup of coffee. "Won't hurt to give them a call. See if they know anybody." A few phone calls, a couple of handshakes, and he could shake off Connecticut like a dog's bathwater.

He ate his breakfast at the kitchen nook while Rosalie busied herself in the laundry room. After two cups of coffee, a half pound of bacon, three scrambled eggs, and toast, he rubbed his stomach until he released a hardy burp. Rosalie never minded his gaseous pleasure. Too stuffed to think about the gardens, he contemplated a long morning nap. No. Better get right to work. The sooner he made the arrangements, the sooner life, for him, could return to normal.

He took out his cell, searched for the store's website, and laughed again at the lackluster name as he punched in the number.

"The Flower Store," an older voice answered. "How may I help you?"

"Henry Fitzgibbons, calling. Do you hire out any gardening services?" An exasperating silence followed. "Hello? You still there?"

"Sorry, Mr. Fitzgibbons. Your question kind of threw me off guard. No, we don't do landscaping as a rule. Our business is strictly cash and carry. I do a little work on the side from time to time. What do you need?"

"I need to hire a gardener for the summer. According to my wife, the rose bushes are a mess." Henry gulped. Might as well wear a dunce cap and sit on a stool.

"Nobody here's a gardener, Mr. Fitzgibbons. We're landscape architects."

Henry swallowed his amusement. *A rose by any other name*—had the whole world gone politically correct? "Whatever it's called, I need help. Money's no object."

That should get his attention.

"Well, I can't promise anything, Mr. Fitzgibbons, but I'll stop by tomorrow about six and see if there's anything I can do to help."

"In the morning?" To set an alarm for an eight o'clock tee time was one thing—getting up with the sun merely to discuss land issues was far too agrarian a concept for a city boy to grasp.

"Morning's the best time to examine your yard."

Henry pictured a naturalist Sherlock Holmes with magnifying glass in one hand and a shovel in the other adrift through the acres of foliage in Sylvia's estate. "Very well. See you tomorrow at six. Anything you need?"

The man's voice caught as if hiding a chuckle. "No. I'll bring what I need."

Rosalie shot him a smile. "Better get a reference, Henry. You know how particular Miss Longstreet is."

Henry nodded.

"Not to sound rude, but what's your name?"

"Not at all rude. Name's Charlie. Charlie Michaels."

Rosalie slid a pad over to Henry, and he wrote down the name. "Like the folk singer?"

"Some people say I look a lot like him. What's the address?"

Henry put his hand over the mouthpiece and leaned toward Rosalie. "He wants to know the address." She shook her head as she scratched numbers and a street name on the notepad.Henry brought the pad close to his face, wishing he'd put his reading glasses in his pocket. "5955 State Route 40."

Rosalie's stomach bounced. She grabbed the pad and wrote in a large scrawl.

"I'm sorry, Charlie. That's 5935 State Route 40."

"I thought a famous writer lived there by the name of Lana Longstreet." The man's tone bordered on accusatory.

"My wife … goes by her pen name."

"I see. I know the house. Used to work for the former owner, old man Donner,before he passed on."

"Then you're familiar with the lay of the land. That's good." Should be reference enough. "See you tomorrow."

"Tomorrow, it is, Mr. Fitzgibbons."

Friendly enough as landscape artists go. Then again, Henry had never talked to one before. Not a good measuring stick. Still, a friendly gardener ought to be a plus.

"Please, call me Henry."

"See you tomorrow, Henry."

He hung up the phone to Rosalie's snickers "Want I should tape your address to your shirt, Henry, before you go to town? In case you get yourself lost?"

"Not funny, Rosalie."

Addresses were inconsequential pieces of information stuffed into the hinder portions of his brain. He never sent mail to Connecticut, all communication with Sylvia was handled by text or phone call. Her chauffeurs always picked him up whenever he came to Connecticut ... as infrequently as possible. At any rate, Charlie Michaels would arrive in the morning. Henry smiled with assurance his stay could be a short one. Give the man a pat on the shoulder, a basketful of praise, keep him on his toes, and he could be home in time to watch the PGA Memorial Tournament in the comfort of his Manhattan apartment. He'd suffer through the next few days and prove to Sylvia she had not married the most inflexible man on the planet.

CHAPTER 6

Henry had spent the remainder of the morning and afternoon watching the sports channel on television and napping here and there. He looked for something to fill the evening and told Rosalie to go home early.

She tilted her head and put her hands on her hips at his suggestion.

"You sure you can manage, Henry?"

"What's to manage? Supper's in the oven, and you've already delivered her afternoon snack. You've even set our supper trays, right down to the cream and sugar for the coffee. Just have to put food on the plates, fill Sylvia's cups and my mug, then carry the trays upstairs."

"It's not the carrying part I'm worried about. You eating supper alone with Miss Longstreet is the thing that's bothersome. Seems anytime you two occupy the same room for more than five minutes, World War II starts up all over again."

Henry scowled, a pretense, but Rosalie's sarcasm called for rebuttal. "This time, we're eating in her loft, not the ballroom. And she doesn't have a passel of socialite geese to flock around her. I'm certain we can keep the conversation to a neutral subject."

Rosalie took off her apron, picked up her purse, and headed toward the kitchen door. "There's extry in the refrigerator if you need more. Better get up there afore the chicken veal gets too cold. Miss Longstreet likes her food piping hot, exceptin' her salad. Cold things cold, hot things hot."

"Good night, Rosalie."

"I'll pray for you, Henry. You're going to need it. Miss Longstreet's temper seems more riled when you're around. Don't know why. I know ain't none of my business. Just a fact, is all."

Henry pushed Rosalie forward with a gentle nudge. "Go. Be careful going home. Been raining rivers out there. Your road winds quite a bit."

"Well, Mister and me, we're partial to the country. I'll take it slow. I promise."

When Rosalie let the door close behind her, he finished preparing dinner and balanced the trays on his shoulders, then headed upstairs, taking one step at a time. He hitched his breath as he neared the top. With his hands full, he couldn't knock so he whistled instead—out of tune and raspy but a sufficient early warning system.

Sylvia swirled around in her computer chair. "Oh! Good. Just in time. I'm famished."

He put her tray on the table by the window, then found a side chair and settled in, balancing his tray on his knees, and noticed his empty mug. "Oh, dear. I forgot the coffee carafe. Rosalie made a pot before she left." He set the tray down next to Sylvia's and went back downstairs. The doorbell chimed just as his feet hit the bottom step. Why did it have to be the front door? He walked briskly through the parlor, across the sitting room, and into the main foyer, averting any glance into the ballroom.

When he opened the door, Evan North stood on the portico steps. "Henry? You're still here? I stopped by to see Sylvia. She called to say she was stuck at the moment. She invited me over to run a couple of scenarios together. She didn't tell you I was stopping by?"

"No. She didn't."

A voice echoed from the kitchen intercom. "Henry, if that's Evan invite him in. He can join us for supper. Rosalie always makes more than needed."

"Come in, North. Sylvia and I were just having dinner. Apparently, she wants you to join us."

"Don't mind if I do."

Henry averted his eyes from the ballroom as he led the way to the kitchen. Hopefully, the man would forego his usual jibes about his neighbor's ghostly sightings. "Seen any ghosts this time around, Henry?" Nope. Right on cue.

"Ignore him," Higgy would advise. But North's nasally insinuations would rile a lamb.

Once in the kitchen, Henry clicked on the intercom. "North's going to join us."

"Go ahead and fix up a plate for him. I'll bring our trays down, and we can all sit at the counter. There's not enough room in my loft for three."

Well, Rosalie's prayers must have worked. With North there, the likelihood of an argument breaking diminished greatly. Still, he'd have to muster every ounce of cordiality he could. Of the few people in this world he absolutely could not tolerate, Evan North topped the list. However, since North was Sylvia's closest friend, civility demanded decorum in the presence of a lady.

"Coffee, North?"

"Cream, two sugars."

Henry gazed around the kitchen. He drank his coffee black, and Rosalie always put sugar and cream on Sylvia's tray for her. Where would a good cook store the sugar?

North chuckled. "There should be a bowl on the bottom shelf of the second cupboard to your left."

Henry suppressed a growl. The man he most hated felt more at home than he did in this "Hill House." There was something unnatural in North's familiarity, but best to dismiss the thought. Sylvia had better taste in men. If she were going to have an affair, she could do much better than North for a lover. Rumor about town was the scumbag traded grades for favors from his female students and bluffed his way around the University faculty as much as he did his books. How he ever won a Pulitzer was anyone's guess. Yet, the bigger mystery was why Sylvia was utterly devoted to the man.

Henry clicked a disapproving tongue. He'd have to find a place setting for his unwelcomed guest. Once again he twirled, clueless as to where things might be. North laughed again—more like a sinister growl, a failed attempt to cover his derision. "If you spent more time here, Henry, you would know where things are. China's in the pantry."

Pantry? Henry turned in circles as he scanned the kitchen. Where was the pantry?

North zeroed in on Henry's perplexity. "The alcove behind the spiral staircase. Didn't you ever wonder what was behind that door?"

Henry's cheeks burned. Whenever he visited, he spent little time in the kitchen except for Rosalie's coffee and breakfast. Why should he know Sylvia had a pantry?

"Plates are there too. I'm betting Rosalie fixed yours and Sylvia's trays before she left."

Henry pulled out the storage container for the extra chicken veal from the refrigerator and plopped it in front of North. "Since you're so smart, you can heat this up yourself while I find dishes for you. If it weren't for Sylvia, I'd throw you a paper plate. I know where they are."

"I better get my own silverware or else I'll have to eat with my fingers."

Henry snorted as he made his way under the staircase and opened the pantry door. Stacks of expensive china gleamed back at him. He picked out a rose-colored cup similar to Sylvia's and a matching plate. When he returned, Sylvia had inched her way down the steps, placing her tray next to North and Henry's to the other side of the counter. He dragged a stool to his relegated spot. As if to demonstrate his rival's ineptitude, North heated his own chicken veal, helped himself to the creamer in the refrigerator, and retrieved his silverware from the drawer, then sat uncouthly close to Sylvia. Henry moved his stool back to the other side, slid his tray over, and placed his hand on Sylvia's knees. *That'll show North whose wife she is.*

"I'm curious, Henry," North said. "What's your remedy for those roses? I could use a pointer or two. My bushes aren't as plentiful as your gardens, but a rose is a rose ... is a ..."

North threw insults like a challenge to a duel. When it came to landscaping, Henry was using a stick compared to North's sword. "Actually, I've hired a professional. He'll be here tomorrow."

Sylvia glared. "Henry, I could have called someone myself. You promised to see this project through. I don't care how good he is, the work has to be supervised. I know you're anxious to get back to Manhattan, but you'll have to stay until the work is done. Or do you want me to miss my deadline?"

North's gleam seared worse than a rapier to the groin. Sylvia confided in North more than she did her therapist. If divorce was on Sylivia's mind, North would know. Maybe he planned on moving in before the papers were even signed.

True that the marriage had been cold for years, and Sylvia was still an attractive woman. If they did divorce, she deserved an Erik the Mangnificent over a North the Dolt. Maybe giving up wasn't the answer. What if there were some undiscovered embers able to be stoked, some magic potion to rekindle what once was? Or a miracle? He could use one, even if he thought God had lost interest in puny humankind.

Henry held Sylvia's hand in his. Her eyes bulged with confusion. "Sylvia. I made a promise, and Henry Fitzgibbons never reneges on a promise." He kissed her hand. "I'm here for the duration."

North didn't know enough to admit defeat. "So, how's Julie? I hear she recently went on a cruise?"

Did the man also have intimate knowledge of Julie's comings and goings?

Sylvia must have guessed her husband was clueless where Julie's travels were concerned. "I'm sorry, Henry. I forgot to tell you. Julie said she met some nice young man on the cruise. She didn't say much more than she thought he was very attractive."

"And when did she take this cruise?"

North piped up. "February ... according to Sylvia."

Well, if Julie found herself a boyfriend, maybe she'd be safe from North's lustful connivances. She might be a grown woman, but a father still had a prerogative to worry.

The rest of the meal was lost in comments about the ghastly weather and Evan's touting his most recent book, due to be released within the next day or two.

"Henry, would you be a dear and pick up the kitchen?" Sylvia asked.

Could he refuse in front of North?

"Evan and I are going upstairs to work on my book. I'm sure there's a game or something on television. We'll discuss this professional you hired later."

Like a dismissed servant, Henry watched Sylvia lead the way up the spiral staircase with Evan too close behind. He turned and grinned at Henry, as evil a glow as the deriding ghosts in the ballroom.

CHAPTER 7

Tap-Tap.

The noise woke Henry from a sound sleep. Were the guests in the ballroom now tapping at his door? He gazed out the glass door and sighed relief. Only a woodpecker.

Nearly six. He jumped out of bed, tearing off his pajamas, and hurriedly put on a golf shirt and khakis, figuring he could shower after the morning session with Michaels. He replayed the evening fiasco as he brushed his teeth, spitting out the mouthwash with the disgusting thoughts—Sylvia's displeasure at Henry's hiring a stranger and North's unwelcomed, untimely visit, obliterating any hope for Henry's rehearsed speech to Sylvia. "Don't you think it's time we put an end to this masquerade called a marriage?" Maybe not as poetic as she could put it.

But he couldn't divorce her now. Not with a wolf like North sniffing around. His and Sylvia's cackles echoed through the house well after midnight. A decent man didn't stay in a married woman's den with her husband in the house. Henry couldn't sleep until he heard the click of the portico door and Sylvia's soft steps heading into her bedroom.

Well, no matter how much he wanted to go back to Manhattan, he would have to endure this current curse, at least until he could confidently slough off the job to this Michaels guy and shoo North off Sylvia's scent.

Henry sighed. How foolish to think he could escape so early, even if Charlie turned out to be the Ty Pennington of floral makeovers. Henry's only hope of escape rested in an office crisis requiring his immediate return.

Too bad he couldn't come right out and ask Higgy to manufacture an excuse. But Hell was not about to freeze over. Paul Higgins hadn't told one lie since the day they met, even when life and death were in the balance. Henry batted about a few ideas to manufacture some minor glitch, a truth he could stretch to convince Sylvia he must regrettably return to manage things at the office.

No use in trying subterfuge. Sylvia saw through the cleverest of ruses. This indisputable fact remained— Connecticut claimed him for the duration.

Henry strolled out the back door toward the kitchen, sniffing the air in anticipation. He still had enough time to grab one quick cup before Charlie arrived. Most gardeners he knew showed up two hours late if at all. Rosalie's coffee might ease his agitated spirit from getting up so early.

Odd. No aroma yet. Rosalie usually came at five in order to get Sylvia started on her day. He stuck his head into the kitchen, expecting to see Rosalie darting to and fro, scrambling eggs and stirring batter for Sylvia's morning muffins.

No Rosalie.

No breakfast.

No coffee.

He'd prefer not to walk the half mile to the nearest café, and he'd rather down a cup of vinegar than subject his gullet to gas station coffee. If he could muster up the courage to drive himself into town, he still couldn't get back before this gardener was due to arrive. Should he wait for Erik to report or make his own coffee, something he'd never done for himself?

He rummaged through the cupboards for endless minutes before finding the coffee beans. Whole coffee beans. He opened and shut four more cupboards before he found the grinder. Leave it to a woman to store a coffee grinder with a pepper mill rather than the coffee.

Now, how much should he grind? The beans were stored in an airtight bin with no instructions. He filled the grinder to capacity and smiled at the pungent scent. Then he measured six heaping scoops into the thing that held the grounds, filled the carafe to the six mark ... should be enough for a couple of cups ... then poured the water into the reservoir. He crossed his fingers while his effort brewed.

Who said Henry Fitzgibbons could not adapt to something new?

Soon, brown sludge plopped through the maker. At least, he could find his favorite cup since he'd washed it and put it away last night after stacking the plates in the dishwasher. He filled his cup, swirled the muddy water under his nose, and gagged at the unexpected stench.

Oh well. Sometimes invention tastes better than it smells. Henry ventured a sip only to spit it out into the sink. He emptied the carafe and the grounds into the sink, turned on the water and the garbage disposal, not certain if the rumbling he heard came from the sink or the driveway. He switched off the disposal and the water. Nope. Not the disposal. Definitely driveway sounds. Henry looked at the clock as it chimed six times. If nothing else, Charlie Michaels was punctual.

Henry dashed outdoors to steer Charlie away from the circular drive to the cement pad in the rear. Sylvia went into tirades over any commercial van parked in the front visage.

Coffee would have to wait.

Henry held his breath as he raced through the rooms to the portico, catapulting out the door just as a red pickup inched into the forked section of the driveway. He signaled the driver to turn right while he walked behind the man's truck.

Once parked, a towering bag of bones emerged. "Morning. You must be Henry. I'm Charlie." He offered a handshake, and Henry accepted.

He'd expected a short, obese man dressed in navy work pants and a grease-stained cap. Instead, Charlie's shoulder-length white hair set off a goatee and thick eyebrows, his hair capped by a red bandana matching the one that hung from his back jean pocket. Shod in thick tan work boots and buttoned flannel shirt overtop gray thermal underwear, Charlie looked more like a giant, pot-stoned, sixties throwback than a landscape artist. If one imagined him with fewer wrinkles, black hair, and a guitar slung over his shoulder, he could definitely pass for the one-time famous folk star.

Charlie glanced toward the house. "Place hasn't changed much since I was here last." His left eyebrow drooped. "Oh, I'd say about thirty years ago, give or take."

"Could be. My wife's lived here for about fifteen years."

Henry gulped. Should he have clued this man on their peculiar marriage?

Charlie either hadn't guessed or didn't care. "I took a gander at the front as I drove by a few times. Whoever managed the hedges done a good job. I like the way they graduate down the front slope. Nice, how the first row rests below the windows but far enough away so's the roots don't penetrate the foundation. Some folks don't pay no attention to foundations. Yes sir, the front's a masterpiece. Couldn't have done a better job myself. Simple, yet, elegant."

Henry never heard a yard described like a fine wine. His less eloquent description could be reduced to a simple phrase—neatly cropped. "I'm afraid my wife's handyman wasn't much of groundskeeper. He quit over a year ago. Our son David managed to reclaim the front, but the gardens have fared poorly over the years. I'm in Manhattan quite a bit."

"Well, let's take a walk around."

Charlie whistled an off-key version of "My Wild Irish Rose" as he took long strides through the gardens. Henry eyed the man. What kind of lunatic had he hired? Then again, maybe Charlie already downed a cup or two of coffee. He halted at the veranda and gazed toward the hinder portions of the main yards from the house to the retaining wall.

Henry pointed toward the back. "As you see, the retaining walls jut from the shed and run the length of the useable yard."

"Nice to see the walls have stood up all this time. I redesigned these gardens myself. When Trumball built the place, must have had acres upon acres of hedges and rose patches. I managed to refurbish what you see here with the original design. Before Alfred Donner inherited the place, except for the house, the property was infested with weeds and wild sumacs. I replaced the original labyrinth with new cobbles. I see someone's reinforced the walks some and added another section at the west wing. But I can't judge based on previous experience. Soil composition can change over the years. If you want to know what's going on in your garden, you have to have a conversation with it."

Conversation? *Do roses talk? If so, what do they say?*

"Flowers are a lot like people, Henry."

So, he hired a madman after all.

"They don't need to use words to tell you what they want. A child's frown speaks for itself. When a rose droops, it's telling you it needs attention."

"Makes sense."

Without warning, Bandana Man hauled out a compass from his pocket and paced the yard one square foot at a time, marking the surveyed territory with a stick or stone. After squaring off a section, he squatted, scooped up a handful of dirt, and streaked a few mumbled words before moving on to the next area.

The cultivated footage behind the house couldn't be more than an acre. Why did anyone need a compass in the backyard? Was Charlie afraid he'd get lost?

"Is this all the land you own? Mr. Donner had me make some trails through the woods behind the retaining walls for the town folk to use."

"Sorry, I'm not much help on the history of the place. Like I said. I'm not here much. I think my wife owns about four acres beyond the walls and another two on both the west and east sides. Far as I know, Fernando only tended to the immediate area near the house. My wife likes being near the main road but prefers to stay isolated from the neighbors."

Charlie dug into a sandy spot and slid the granules through his palms. His rosy cheeks glistened like a skinny, hippie Santa Claus. "I heard Old Man Donner's heir divvied up the estate. Sold a lot of acreage to developers, I understand. So, I wouldn't be surprised if the trails are mostly gone. He couldn't sell the house for a long time, though, 'cause of all the rumors."

Did the mention of the rumors or caffeine deprivation cause this sudden drained feeling? "My wife tells a few stories now and again at her dinner parties."

"Some folks say the house is haunted. I never saw anything. Old Man Donner swore up and down he'd seen ghosts in the ballroom. He said they danced and teased him every time he tried to go in there. He didn't live here long, only a few years. Some folks think the ghosts got him. I don't cotton to the stories much myself."

So, the ghosts danced for others. If Henry suffered from delusions, Donner shared the same disorder. Sylvia must have known Donner's reports. She tossed the rumors around like a Grimm fairy tale, signaling her husband's sightings as if he alone owned the experience. The fact she derided him with the telling and knew the former owner made the same claims brought new dimensions to his rage.

He recalled Sylvia's gibes to Evan North. "Oh, by the way. Henry saw those ghosts again."

"Don't say." Evan had laughed and picked up his glass of sherry. "Here's to the party in the other dimension." The guests joined in the toast, oblivious to any embarrassment their ridicule caused.

Henry sighed with yet another recollection of how Sylvia shrugged off her flippant remarks when he complained of her ridicule. "Can't you take a little joke at your expense? You're acting like a baby. No one thinks ill of you because you see things. My guests love the stories." With that, she had pecked him on the cheek. "Henry, my dear, your hysteria has upped my social standing. I'm forever in your debt."

How does a man forgive such blatant disrespect?

He forced himself back to the present. While Charlie scanned the yard, Henry wallowed in pretense, occasionally kicking a twig aside, as he huffed to keep in stride with the pole of a man. Their conversation ran the gamut from the latest Yale faculty additions to the ground enrichment rituals of the ancient Babylonians. Henry thought himself an intelligent man, but this aged flower child, barring his syntax, proved to have the greater intellect.

Charlie gazed toward the shed and clicked like a disappointed father reviews his child's poor grades. "The shed's nearly swallowed by those vines, Henry."

He squeaked out an apology. "Yeah. Guess the beds have been a bit neglected. Sorry you have to find all your hard work from so long ago in disarray." His forehead throbbed. "Charlie, I'm going inside to grab a cup of java. Can I get you a cup?"

"Don't mind if I do, Henry. If I take on this job, we'll have to agree on some things. I like doing business over coffee. Keeps things friendly."

Charlie's friendly might very well be a euphemism for expensive. "How do you like it, your coffee I mean?"

"A little milk and one sugar."

"Coming up."

Henry expected to see Rosalie when he came into the kitchen. No coffee and no housekeeper. He trained an ear for any evidence she might be milling around. Unfortunately, the only sound he heard was the *click-clack* of Sylvia's computer.

He hesitated to disturb a writer when in their zone. Shouldn't Rosalie's absence count as a dire emergency? *Get a grip, Henry old boy.* Maybe Rosalie stopped for groceries or needed a morning off. Not like Sylvia ever clued him in on the help's schedules.

First, he'd try his hand at another pot of coffee. With a few adjustments, he might make some he could drink. He corrected his measurements, then held his breath until the water dripped through, expelling a breath of relief when the liquid looked a little less like Dakota mud. He rinsed out his Bubba Watson cup and pulled out another mug from the cupboard.

He prepared Charlie's cup first and brought it out to him. "Here you go. I'll be right back. Need to ask the wife a question. Have a seat on the veranda. I'll be back in a few."

"Thanks Henry." Charlie took a sip. "Ah ... good and strong ... makes your hair stand on end. Just the way I like it."

Henry returned to the kitchen, filled his mug and then poured coffee into a porcelain cup for Sylvia, lining the tray with a paper napkin from the holder on the counter. Best he could on short notice. If he must disturb Sylvia, coffee might help.

He sucked in a breath for courage and started toward the spiral staircase, retreating to grab two Lorna Doones for good measure. He knocked on the wall before he emerged into the loft.

The *clickity-clack* continued at a strong steady pace. "Ah, finally. I'm starved. Not like you to forget me, Rosalie."

"It's Henry."

Sylvia stopped typing and turned to face him. "Henry? Why aren't you with that Charlie fellow?"

He removed his mug, then placed the tray on the table next to Sylvia's computer.

"Thought you might need a break. Rosalie's not here yet. Did you give her the morning off and forgot to tell me?"

"No. I didn't give her any time off, and I can't imagine she'd leave me high and dry with no notice. Rosalie's as dependable as my grandfather's old Chevrolet. Started up in the dead of winter. If she's not here, something's wrong. Did you check to see if there's a message on the answering machine? I thought I heard the landline ring a few times. I don't answer when I'm writing. Rosalie takes my messages and lets me know if there's something I need to tend to right away. I keep my cell on automatic voice mail."

Was he supposed to know all this encyclopedic knowledge of how Sylvia managed her communications? He rarely called Connecticut. "Have you checked your cell yet this morning?"

"No. It's in my room. Be a dear and get it for me?"

Navigating the interlocking rooms from her loft to her bedroom proved more challenging than a carnival fun house. He shouldn't leave Charlie by himself much longer. Henry visualized the man's calculator spinning out of control like a wild electric meter. The longer he sat by himself, the bigger the dollar signs might grow. After four wrong turns, Henry finally found the door to Sylvia's bedroom, snatched her cell from her dresser, and returned to her loft, pleased he found his way back with no misstep. "Here's your cell."

She powered on. "One message. Rosalie's number." Sylvia tapped her foot while she listened, her cheeks whitened with worry. She said nothing and dropped the phone into her lap as she stared at the wall.

Henry took the cell and set it by the window. "Sylvia? What's wrong?"

For a tender instant, Sylvia's eyes moistened. "The message was from Delbert, Rosalie's husband. She had a car accident on her way home last night. She'll be okay, but she's in the hospital with a broken leg and cracked ribs. He doesn't know when or if she'll be able to come back to work."

A loving husband should take control in times like these, sit by his wife, hold her hand, and tell her not to worry. Henry despised himself for his inability to rise to any occasion. Maybe he waffled because Sylvia viewed him as an imbecile, as helpful as a blister on a thumb. A disheartening analogy but true, nonetheless.

In her state of uncertainty, she looked like the rain-soaked waif he'd met at the bus stop so many years ago. He wanted to comfort her in some way.

"What'll I do, Henry? How can I manage without Rosalie?"

"I'm not completely helpless, Sylvia. Let me take care of you for a while."

Sylvia's disparaging laugh singed his already bruised ego. "You're going to take care of me? You can't even make a decent cup of coffee. How do you expect to clean the house, cook, take care of the books, and still tend to the disaster outside?"

She assumed him a flop before giving him the opportunity to prove her right. "We'll find a way, Sylvia." Henry left the tray, grabbed his mug, and stormed down the spiral staircase. Must she always challenge his manhood with flaming darts? He had built a multi-million-dollar business from scratch. A cum laude Princeton graduate, Henry Fitzgibbons was no one's fool, except in the eyes of his wife.

He put the carafe and his mug onto another tray and traversed the cobbled path back to the veranda.

"Sorry I took so long, Charlie. Coffee need warming up?"

He stood and stretched his back, then wiped his face with his pocket bandana. "No, thank you, I'm good." He cocked his head to one side. "Probably none of my business, Henry, but seems rather strange you go around the side to get into the house when there's a door right behind us."

"I take the long way around. Don't exercise enough otherwise." Henry sat in the wicker chair and took a long sip. "Well, then. Suppose you tell me the bad news."

Charlie scuffled and snorted and sat back down in one combined effort. "I'll need to take more soil samples, but I think the yard's salvageable. I'll have to replace about 75 percent of the bushes, though."

Really?

"I'll have to dig up a lot of your yard if I'm going to tame those vines. If so, I'd have to resod. There's the shed too. Probably not in very good shape. Vine tends to rot what's underneath. People like the look of it growing on their houses, but vines ain't healthy for the house."

"How much, Charlie?"

"Can't say till I'm done."

Of course not.

"Well, then, how long?"

"Hard to say. Do you want me to take the opportunity to put in a wildflower rock garden? Up to you. Your house."

No. Not his. Never was. Never would be.

"Sylvia might like wildflowers. Go ahead." He giggled with internal delight. Concerning the affairs of Connecticut, Henry Fitzgibbons had just made his first executive decision.

"I figure I can get things squared away by fall. Then let it ride for the winter."

Henry spewed his coffee. "That long?"

"Henry, a magician couldn't undo this mess in a few days. Thankfully, you called me early enough in the spring. Plants are the most vulnerable during the height of growing season."

A knot formed in his stomach, and Henry groaned.

"You okay, Henry? You look a little gray in the gills."

No, I'm not okay, Charlie.

Henry's apartment could fit into Sylvia's house three times with plenty of room left over. Yet, the mere thought of an entire summer trapped within these walls made him sick to his stomach. "Nothing to do with you or the work, Charlie. I had hoped to go back to the city in a few days. Well, looks like I'm stuck here anyway. Garden or no garden."

"Why's that?"

"My wife's housekeeper is in the hospital. Car accident. Not serious in the long run, thankfully, but won't be able to work for quite a while ... might not be back at all for that matter. Sylvia's on a deadline, so looks like I'll have to take care of things until we can hire another housekeeper."

"Sorry to hear of your troubles, Henry."

"About the housekeeper or that I'm stuck here?"

"Both, I reckon."

"So, when can you start?"

Charlie stroked his chin. "Tomorrow's as good a day as any. Don't normally check in at the store until nine. So, I'll come over here first thing every weekday. Won't work when it rains and won't work on the weekends. Are we set, then?"

Henry nodded, and the men shook hands. He liked the old-fashioned manner Charlie used to conduct business. In Grandpa Fitzgibbons's day, a man's word meant more than gold. As friendly as Charlie seemed, there was something electric in the man's handshake. As though he singed Henry's veneer and left him morally nude.

"See you tomorrow, Charlie."

"Lord willing, Henry ... and I expect he is." Charlie whistled "Danny Boy" as he ambled back toward his truck.

Henry looked at his watch. Eight o'clock. The morning had barely begun, yet he felt the drain of a full day's work.

He gazed up at billowing cumulous clouds, while birds fluttered over the shed in frantic circles. A naturalist he'd never be, but even Henry Fitzgibbons, city bred and country ignorant, knew a storm brewed.

FROM JOHNNY GALLANT

C7

Celeste rubbed the white Angora cat with short, affectionate strokes. For a few minutes, Johnny rolled in the fantasy he was the cat. Odd how his desire for her ran much deeper than the physical, a feeling for which Johnny had no description, the emotion as new to him as a baby's first cry.

He longed not so much for her touch. He envied the cat because she loved it, and it stretched in that comfort.

He must shoo these desires like a buzzing fly. How could he protect her if he became involved—on any level? He'd crossed the line once before. Her name was Henrietta ... he had called her Rita. Older than he by twelve years, she still turned heads when they walked together. He sensed the envy of every man who passed them on the Parisian streets. She spoke only a few words of English.

The relationship, too short-lived, nearly cost both their lives. He had kissed her goodnight and stepped into the shadows while she slipped into her house where Johnny planned to meet her later. Discreetly, of course. Too caught up in the thought of her, he hadn't seen the assailant until his hands were around her throat.

Johnny had pounced on the man who pulled out a Glock and managed to shoot Johnny in the chest. An inch or two more to the left, and he'd have told his tale to the devil. He'd vowed never again to let his unruly male impulses put a client at risk.

If he had failed Rita whom he merely desired, how much more harm could he cause Celeste whom he now knew he loved more than life itself? Remaining cool, calm, and collected depended upon detachment from his client.

He moved beside her and tickled the cat's chin. "What's his name?"

"Jasmine."

"A female, then. Sorry, I assumed ..."

"Assumptions are dangerous, Mr. Gallant."

"I told you to please call me Johnny."

He sensed heat in his gaze. He stared at her hair, eyes, and lips far longer than propriety allowed.

"I'm sorry."

"Don't apologize, Johnny"

She tilted her head, her gaze an invitation, one he could not refuse.

Just a kiss, wasn't it? Johnny Gallant had kissed more women than most men. Why did his knees tremble like a clumsy pubescent boy as his lips met hers?

CHAPTER 8

Sylvia reexamined the last paragraph, pleased with the name she selected for Johnny's love interest. According to her book of baby names, Celeste, derived from Latin, meant heavenly. To Johnny, Celeste lived beyond his reach, like a constellation to be admired and studied, too unattainable to hope for.

Sylvia typed in: *What if one could achieve such heights? Would they find their heart's desire? Or would the ground they so hungrily pursued crumble like frozen snow?*

She leaned back against her chair. Did she write those words for her character or for some lust within herself? Was Johnny Gallant symbolic for Henry—her elusive butterfly? Her marriage was a joke, a flat one, like a half-witted comedian who craves the crowd's roar only to rate resounding boos.

Maybe Henry's frigidity was a mere extension of Lana Longstreet's repulsion. His office staff described her as cold. She overheard Monique telling the accounts clerk, "Henry's wife wears aloofness like a Lana Longstreet imprint."

What others termed offish, Lana Longstreet classified as a mere trait, hardly a tragic flaw. What did she know? She ruled over Sylvia's tenderness, squashing every sort of sensitivity. Like Jason's Argonauts sought the fleece to heal their land, she sometimes cried to a God she'd long forgotten to free her from Lana Longstreet's oppression. But how?

Even if she could change, why should she? Why couldn't Henry accept her for who she was, regardless of which side of her personality made an appearance? True love didn't pick apart the object of its affection like a cruel critique. She refused to pretend any longer ... to play the role of a sugary hypocrite ... like Her Prickiness, Monique ... just to keep a man.

Henry wasn't the man she married, but Sylvia still loved him in spite of his idiosyncrasies. Over the years, he stopped taking chances. The last time he took a risk was right after Julie's birth. He wrapped her tiny finger in his big hand. "Sylvia," he said. "I think we've done a marvelous job with this production. Maybe the time has come for us to start our own publishing company." Sylvia could not have loved him more at that moment.

She loved this current version of Henry Fitzgibbons as much as she loved the man who swallowed his fear and rode a bus across town with her, for the sole reason of getting her phone number. She loved the Henry of yore and the Henry of today for his deep philosophical thinking. Over the years, his generosity challenged her, made her a better person. He still asked questions only an Einstein could answer, and he still gave to others far beyond the necessary.

She regretted her ridicule. Why did she let Lana Longstreet attack Henry's manhood? How sweet of him to offer help, even if the measure was beyond his capability. Henry could not begin to realize Sylvia's dependence on Rosalie. More than a cook and housekeeper, she was a personal assistant. Although Sylvia loved her mother, she loved Rosalie more—faithful servant during the worst of times and best of times. No one could take her place.

Then again, Henry never failed to surprise her. The image of a spatula-wielding Henry donned in chef cap and apron scooted across her mind. How to make amends? He deserved an apology, at least.

She smiled when she conceived the idea. One way to meet their immediate crisis and let Henry retain his pride. She looked at her watch. *Ten o'clock.* She'd discuss her idea with Henry when he brought her lunch, then they could both visit Rosalie at the hospital.

Erik pulled up to meet Henry at the cement pad and parked. Henry smiled at the way the Swede opened the door as if he ferried royalty.

"Thanks, Erik." He stood a majestic posture, a doorman for the king. Henry climbed into the Porsche, hardly the prince. Erik closed the car door with a gentle click, then marched to the driver's side. Yet, for all his pomp, he maintained an elusive air. Henry hadn't gained any more goods on Sylvia's chauffeur than he garnered on the trip to Connecticut.

"You're sure St. Raphael's is only fifteen minutes away?"

"Ja, Mr. Henry. I take I-91 South. Chapel Street, not far. Is gud hospital for Miss Rosalie."

Henry fastened his seat belt and gulped a large supply of needed air. "I'm sure Rosalie's getting the best medical attention possible. Still, I'd like to see for myself."

Erik eased into traffic and picked up the Interstate within a few minutes' drive. Henry finally dared to breathe. If he must ride in a car, he preferred the openness of the freeway to narrow roads.

Conversation eased his fears, made him focus on something else besides war memories, the source of his claustrophobia. Small talk with Erik, however, was sure to read like a *Mission Impossible* logline: *wealthy entrepreneur seduces Erik the Enigma into divulging deep, carefully guarded secrets.*

Most men liked to brag on their families. Henry expected Swedes did too. "How's the family, Erik?"

"Gud."

Brother. Like turning over a dead starter—a little *rumph* with no real result. Time to pry open the fount of knowledge with a few open-ended questions. "What kind of work does your wife do?"

"Like I say before, Martina does housework for elderly peoples."

Henry sprang to attention like a released Jack-in-the-box. Yes. Why didn't he remember? "Do you think she'd like to earn a little extra for a few months?"

"Tank you, Mr. Henry. But Miss Longstreet vill not approve Martina."

Not approve? Why not? Sylvia should jump at a reasonable solution to her dilemma. She needed a temporary housekeeper, and her chauffer's wife seemed the perfect choice. Henry studied Erik's firm jaw line. Maybe Sylvia didn't want to compete with the wife for Erik's attention? Henry dismissed the demeaning thought as quickly as it intruded—a tawdry affair, especially with a servant, far beneath Sylvia, even the impervious Lana Longstreet.

Why, then, did he view His Handsomeness as a threat? Threat to what? A dead marriage, relegated to a business contract—not even *friends* with benefits. If Sylvia were as tired of the pretense as Henry, she should divorce him. She deserved passion and romance—something her husband in name only could no longer give her. He imprisoned her with his uncompromising ways, like a princess in a tower—untouched and unloved. The time had come to give her what she desired most, freedom from any obligation to him—business or marital. But he'd have to wait until after the anniversary party. No reason to upset the kids' plans.

Why they wanted to make a big deal of this one, he didn't know. Maybe they figured they shouldn't wait until the thirtieth … have the big bash while their parents were still a couple. Or maybe the kids hoped making a big deal of the anniversary while Henry was doomed to stay in Connecticut would reignite their parents' love for one another. Whatever the kids' reason, could a father deliberately disappoint his children?

Erik pulled up in front of the hospital. "Everything okay, Mr. Henry? Your face … iz white."

"Hunky, dory. I'll let myself out, Erik. Say, do you want to visit Miss Rosalie too? No reason why you can't." People praised Henry for his generosity, but few knew he gave more from his fears, like facing an elevator alone.

"Ja, I vould, Mr. Henry."

"Go ahead and park. I'll wait for you here."

Rosalie's massive form seemed lost in the array of medication bags strapped to a metal pole. Delbert sat at her side.

"Come on in, Henry. You remember Delbert."

Henry accepted the burly man's firm handshake. "Yes, I do. Good to see you again but not under these circumstances. How's the patient?"

"Now don't go talking about me like I've got one foot in the grave. Don't pay no mind to all them bags, neither. Mostly antibiotics. The nurses tend to put the new bag on and forget to take the used one off the pole. They're a tad busy, but I can't complain none about the care they give me."

Delbert shrugged. "Guess the patient's doing fine. I can't get a word in edgewise half the time."

"Delbert, make yourself useful and plump up my pillows a mite, would you?" He jumped at Rosalie's request and punched all five of her pillows. "Doc says my bones are as strong as a kid's. Drink a lot of milk, don't you know. You two pull up a chair and sit ... that is if you can find one."

A nurse, probably a few years younger than Julie, popped into the room. She held a paper cup in one hand. "Mrs. Grady, here's the pain med you asked for."

Rosalie stuck out her hand.

The nurse smiled gently. "State your name and date of birth, first."

Rosalie winked at Henry. "Ain't changed none since she was in here five minutes ago with my antibiotic. Think she'd know by now."

"It's the rule, Mrs. Grady."

Rosalie rattled off the date and stuck out her hand again. "Did I pass?"

The nurse nodded, gave her patient the medication, and turned to face Rosalie's visitors. "Are all of you family? The rules say no more than two visitors at one time."

Henry flashed his most charming smile. "Not exactly. I'm Mrs. Grady's employer. Erik, here is a friend."

The nurse ogled Erik. "One of you can stay. The other can wait in the lounge down the hall. It's up to Mrs. Grady which of you stays."

"I go in vaiting room. You call ven ready, Mr. Henry." Erik graced Rosalie with a wink and left.

Delbert moved a chair from the other side of the room and motioned for Henry to sit. "You feeling okay, Henry? You look a mite pale."

"I'm fine, Delbert. I'm a little uncomfortable in small places. I won't stay long. Just stopping by to see if Rosalie needed anything."

She sighed then leaned back, closing her eyes. "Shouldn't have to stay in here much longer."

"I feel bad about your accident. I should have insisted you stay until the rain stopped."

"No, weren't no one's fault but my own. Weren't paying enough attention. Anyway, ain't the end of the world. I don't mind doing extry for you and Miss Longstreet. Ain't work when you're doin' things for folks ya love. Why you and Miss Longstreet are family to me. Same goes for David and Julie too. But now, here's the bad part. Doc says I'll have to wear a cast for a few months. Then physical therapy. So, don't look like I'll come back afore I retire. I hate putting you and Miss Longstreet into a pickle like this."

"We'll manage, Rosalie. Don't worry. We've got everything under control."

"About as under control as a California wildfire, I suppose."

"Guess you could say that."

"Couldn't Martina take over for a while? She and Erik could sure use the money what with him goin' to school full time in the fall."

"Erik mentioned his wife does housework. For some reason, he thought my wife might not approve."

Rosalie took another sip of water. "Not her. The kids. Miss Longstreet doesn't cotton to noises when she's working. Miracle she lets me vacuum. The house echoes something fierce, don't you know."

"I do know. I hear her clicking away at her computer all hours of the night. Can't Martina find someone to watch them while she works?"

Rosalie laughed. "You sure are comical, Henry. Babysitters around here cost more than Martina could make in a day. I suspect Miss Longstreet doesn't mind the kids as much as the dog."

"Dog? Right, Thor."

"Big black lab. Hangs right to those kids. Best guard dog I ever saw."

"You've seen him, then?"

"Delbert and I have dinner over there on Sundays sometimes. Hate to tell you, though, Henry. Martina can't cook a lick. Sweet girl but can't follow a recipe if it spoke to her."

Henry visualized a bear-like canine sniffing up Sylvia's house. "I can see my wife's hesitancy." He hated dogs more than Sylvia ever did. He had one as a kid. Fool animal ran into the road and got himself killed. Cats made better pets. They left you alone and didn't care if you ignored them.

He regretted having made the suggestion to Erik. For once, he agreed with Sylvia. He'd have to manage the housework. How hard could it be to run a vacuum cleaner?

Rosalie winced as she tried to sit up straighter. "I'm sure if I suggest Martina to Miss Longstreet, she'll agree, least wise until she finds a replacement. But who'll do the books?"

"Books? We have an accountant for our business."

"Henry. For an intelligent man, you sure don't know much about runnin' a house. Miss Longstreet depends on me for lots of things, not just cleanin'and cookin'. Lot goes into keepin' a big house like hers, don't you know."

No. He didn't know. For the next ten minutes Rosalie ran off a to-do list sure to make the president dizzy. At least, a nation's leader could delegate.

"Don't worry about us. My wife's a capable woman. I'm sure we'll manage just fine. I'm glad you got Delbert to take care of you. If you need anything ... anything at all ... let me know."

Snores came from Rosalie's direction. Delbert took over. "Looks like she's gone back to sleep. Medicine knocks her out pretty fast. I do appreciate your offer, Henry, but Miss Longstreet paid my wife a good wage. I get a fair retirement from my custodial job at Yale. We got some stocks as well as a little savings. Combined with our social security checks, we do okay—and we have good health insurance. Ain't what you call rich, but we ain't exactly poor, neither. Our house is all paid for. When Rosalie gets better, we plan on seeing a little of the world and spending our winters in Florida."

"Just the same, we're happy to help." Henry shook Delbert's hand, then left. He marveled at Rosalie and Delbert. They shared a lifetime together, yet their love seemed more intense than newlyweds.

He found Erik in the waiting room and motioned him toward the elevator. Henry startled when his cell rang.

"Dat iz jest your phone, Mr. Henry. You are jumpy. No?"

Henry refused to share his phobias with an imported law student. "Took me off guard a little."

He looked at the incoming number. Sylvia.

CHAPTER 9

Sylvia slapped a slice of cold ham and provolone cheese onto a piece of wheat bread, then folded it in half. After three bites, she gulped down a glass of milk. Where did Henry go? How dare he leave the house and not tell her. Was there no end to his thoughtlessness? She dialed his phone. He gasped as he let out a weak, "Sylvia? What's wrong?"

"Henry, where are you? I was starting to get worried. You could do the courtesy of letting me know when you're not in the house."

"I wasn't aware I had to get your permission. If you must know, I'm at the hospital. Rosalie sends her love."

Henry's tone smacked of sarcasm, almost accusatory, as if she didn't care about Rosalie. "How is she? I had planned to visit this afternoon, but I guess I won't now. I thought we could visit her together."

"She's feisty as ever. But your fears are right. She won't be back to work."

"I'm glad she's okay. Listen, Henry. I've been thinking, and I may have come up with a solution for our problem."

"Not *our* problem, Sylvia. *Your* problem."

She writhed with ire. Closing her eyes, she willed a present calm. "Okay, *my* problem. Remember, you did offer to help. I'll need your cooperation if my plan's going to work."

"I'm listening. What's your plan, Sylvia?"

"Martina, Erik's wife, does housework on occasion. I don't think she can cook, though. Rosalie's had dinner at the Hagstadt's home and complained about the food. We can manage with takeout or frozen dinners for a few months."

"You've never tasted my pancakes, Sylvia."

From his monotone, she couldn't tell if Henry made a joke or a serious offer, his humor as difficult to read as a Thomas Hardy novel, volumes of description before the meat of the story. A person's eyes often revealed true motive. Not Henry's, though—dead and dull. After more than twenty-five years, a wife should understand a husband's subtle ways. If only she could. Henry used humor like a cloak—a means to hide his soul. If she lived to age one hundred, she'd never understand the man she married.

"What about the bookkeeping? Rosalie says she tends to the household accounts. I'm no better an accountant than I am a chef."

Sylvia smiled. Henry was toying with her. "I'll do the books. I've seen the way you add."

"Look, Sylvia. I don't relish the idea of little kids and a big dog under our feet. But, then again, the diversion might prove interesting."

She'd never tell Henry she always wanted a dog—a big black cloud of a dog that slinked through the shadows unnoticed yet was always by her side. A girl felt safe with a big dog. In her fantasies, she named the dog Macabre.

Mother nixed having a dog because of allergies. When Sylvia moved to Connecticut, she thought about buying a Newfie. But Henry despised them. He didn't need another excuse to stay away. Not fair to put all the blame on him. Lana Longstreet didn't want the distraction, and her decision ended all debate on the matter.

Well, desperate times called for desperate measures. "I don't think we have any other options. We'll ask Martina to clean three days a week. You'll have to manage the other day-to-day operations. I promise, as soon as I'm done with *Johnny Gallant*, I'll hire Rosalie's permanent replacement, and you can return to Manhattan ... if you want."

"If you can put up with my incompetence, I guess I'll give it a whirl. Why don't we tell Erik we'll need Martina on Mondays, Wednesdays, and Fridays. May I take off Sundays to play golf with David?"

"Agreed." Sundays might as well be as lonely as the rest of her life.

"Don't forget, Charlie Michaels comes in the mornings Monday through Friday, unless it rains. We'll hardly have any time to ourselves."

Time for what, Henry?

Silence scraped between them.

"So, what do you want for supper tonight?"

"Pancakes sound great."

"Pancakes it is, then."

She placed the receiver in the cradle and settled back into the chair. Rain spat at the windows and trickled down the panes. She secured the kitchen shutters first then walked through the downstairs to make sure all the shutters were closed. When she came to the ballroom, she discovered the veranda doors were open.

Strange.

She could have sworn they were still closed from earlier. Maybe Henry left them open for some reason.She closed the doors, this time latching the bolts.

A faint breeze blew against her legs. In the glass mirror over the mantel, she caught the reflection of a dark cloud as it scurried toward the fireplace. A chill ran the length of her spine as a foul odor, like rotten eggs, filled the room. She'd have Martina start with the ballroom first thing—a thorough scrubbing from top to bottom.

Sylvia sped from the room, glad Henry wasn't around to witness her hasty departure. He needn't know how much the room frightened her at times. She was unable to completely disregard his stories.

Returning to the kitchen, she exhaled ... slowly ... deeply and braced herself against the counter.

"This is Henry's fault—his overworked imagination. Now I'm seeing things and carrying on this stupid conversation with myself. Enough of this insanity." Lana Longstreet willed the experience to the well of Sylvia's forgetfulness.

Henry crept up the spiral staircase with all the stealth of a Longstreet private detective. Not to spy. He didn't want to disturb Sylvia. No telling what screeches she might hurl if startled. He heard no computer sounds, but silence proved nothing. Sylvia said she often napped or read in the late afternoons.

He stopped at the landing. According to Rosalie, when Sylvia didn't want to be disturbed, she left her empty tray outside the loft. Seeing no signals, he ventured through the loft archway. She sat with her feet curled underneath her, her eyes glued to a book. He knocked on the wall.

The soft light caught her dark brown eyes as she raised her head. "Yes?"

He stepped into the room. "Just checking to see if you needed anything else. I'm going to clean up the kitchen, then call it a night."

She rose from the chair and handed him her tray, her dishes empty. Either she'd been hungry, or she'd dumped the pancakes down her toilet. She tossed her hair as she speared a suspicious glance. "Henry, those were the best pancakes I've ever eaten. Have you been keeping secrets from me? Where did you learn how to cook?"

How could he tell her Monique gave him the recipe without Sylvia pushing the tray into his face? Any mention of how he learned to make them would also involve confessing the overnight stay at Higgy's camp following an employee retreat. Monique's car broke down, and she stayed the night, making pancakes for the three of them. Perfectly innocent. She was, afterall, his transportation back to the city.

"Last New Year, I decided I should learn to cook. I started with these pancakes. Unfortunately, I haven't tried anything since. A short-lived resolution, I'm afraid."

"We all get set in our ways as we get older. Face it, Henry. You never could adapt to change."

Barb aside, Sylvia accepted his explanation. Not exactly a lie. Henry did make pancakes once when Monique stopped by with letters for him to sign. If he told Sylvia, she'd turn his confession into something obscene.

So what if he enjoyed Monique's attention? She never ridiculed his predictability like Sylvia did, and Monique complimented his knowledge of history. Nothing wrong with keeping company with her. Besides, she seemed more like a daughter. He wished he and Julie got along as well as he and Monique. No, Monique was simply a young friend, albeit a friend who could charm the socks off any man.

A thought sparkled in his mind like a July Fourth firecracker.

His face must have shown his delight. Sylvia smiled. "What's the look for?"

"Oh, nothing. Unless you need something, I'll take these plates downstairs now."

"No. I'm good. Well, good night, Henry." She stretched and pulled her long tresses up, then shook her locks free again, letting her strands fall to her shoulders. Did she do this on purpose? Did she even know how such a simple maneuver rattled his senses? Before he could say a word, she spoke. "Be sure to turn off all the lights downstairs." She picked up her book and resumed reading.

Whether by accident or on purpose, she'd rejected him again. Henry retreated to the kitchen to face a more winnable challenge. He returned to his interrupted inspiration. More than likely, Rosalie kept a recipe box or files somewhere. He might not know the difference between a spatula and a whisk, but he could learn. For the next few hours, Henry made himself acquainted with the kitchen inventory, scavenging every nook and cranny, and comparing unidentifiable utensils with images from the internet.

He'd struck gold—a small notebook containing at least fifty of Rosalie's mouth-watering favorites. He thumbed through them, checking the ingredients and jotting down a list of any missing supplies. Then he sorted them according to complexity. He'd start with something relatively simple. No soufflés yet.

Luck found him again—her prize meatloaf. He'd also found a recipe for baked chicken casserole and one for spaghetti sauce. For the next hour, Henry rearranged kitchen contents to his liking, then drew a map of the kitchen, labeling each cabinet and nook.

"There. Now this room is functional."

Finally, he turned his attention to the mound of dirty dishes on the counter. He'd never run a dishwasher before in his life—not even in his own apartment. As he lived alone now, he ate out most of the time and rarely had company. When he did eat in, he used disposable products.

Tomorrow, he'd ask Martina to show him how to operate the machine. He didn't dare leave the mess until the morning—he'd have to tackle these by hand. After squirting a hefty amount of dish detergent in the sink, he turned on the faucet, gagging on the sudden burst of flower-scented bubbles. Soon, they rushed to the surface, a few breaking free and spotting the air, challenging the little boy in him to blow away the sudsy wonder, wishing he had a wand to swish them with.

The last piece of silverware rinsed, wiped, and stored, Henry sat on a stool and breathed a heavy sigh, proud of his accomplishment, yet embarrassed over his privilege. Wealth had spoiled him, had made him take coffee and clean dishes for granted. Nor had he given any thought to the investment of labor to provide him with so many luxuries. Given the challenges ahead, what other facets of his pampered life were doomed to surface?

He found a container of iced tea mix and sat to read the directions. Rolling his head to one side in a can-do maneuver, he filled a pitcher halfway with lukewarm water, put in the required amount of mix, gave it a hearty stir, then filled the pitcher up to the top with ice. He poured his creation into a tall glass, sipped, and cooed with self-satisfaction.

He yawned as he looked at his watch. Only eight o'clock—too early to go to bed. He could catch a game on ESPN, he supposed, or he could see if Sylvia wanted to take a stroll. The *click-clack* coming from the loft signified she'd returned to her writing.

How does a bored man while away a long, lonely evening? With a deep sigh, he stepped outside and walked through the garden. The moon, at the birth of ascent, cast a mellow light on the yard, mixing its silver with the orange glow of the setting sun. He noticed yellow buds on a few bushes. Once more, Henry's ignorance took center stage. Why had he never learned the names of these beautiful roses? Charlie would know them, and certainly there were books dedicated to the various classes and category. Guilt raised its heels. These roses had provided Henry with years of comfort as he swaddled in their beauty like a warm blanket—and yet, he referenced each colorful spray with no more regard than a stray, unnamed alley cat.

New determination gripped him. Even if the process took the entire summer, he'd learn both the common and scientific classification of every flower bed and bush on the estate.

He left the garden by the west wing path, entering the house from the hall door rather than going directly into his room. Prompted by a sudden compunction, he went into Sylvia's library containing the whole of her literary career—including all the books contributing to the success of Fitzgibbons & Associates. He blushed with the shameful realization—he hadn't read a single title. An omission he could now rectify. He thumbed through the spines until he found Sylvia's first book, *A Life Gladly Sacrificed*.

He tucked the book under his arm, went back to his room, undressed, slipped into bed, then scrunched the pillows into a makeshift cushion. Setting the book on his knees, he began reading:

One might class him as quite ordinary, a man of no distinctive occupation or community standing ...

Sylvia called the first few lines of her books, hooks. If so, Henry had been caught, all right, losing himself in the world Sylvia had created. He cheered for Harry, wanting him to win the heart of the beautiful widow, Priscilla. the perfect father for her impish children. Did his disfigurement repulse her? How blind Priscilla must be.

Henry read into the morning hours, enjoying the book like a full course meal, waiting for the culminating burp. Did Harry survive the fire when he pulled Priscilla and her children to safety? Why did he risk going in to save the foolish dog? Oh, rats. The vain Priscilla hardly grieved.

Monique said Sylvia's books took the reader on an emotional roller coaster. Henry secretly prided in his tears, their salty evidence his emotions had not been completely eroded by his Gulf War experiences.

He switched off his light and let the day's events tumble in his mind. Soon, peaceful sleep came over him until the alarm jolted him awake.

FROM JOHNNY GALLANT

C 10

The boom cracked like a jet breaking the sound barrier. Johnny jumped from his bed, grabbed his revolver, and checked the security camera. Nothing but snow. Either the blast destroyed the feed or his equipment had been sabotaged.

Celeste.

He looked down at his half naked state, clothed only in his boxers. He headed back to his bedroom, slipped on his sweats, and stuffed his revolver into the waistband. The unmistakable shuffling of feet came from the living room ... light ... but hurried. Johnny reached for the doorknob.

It turned, not by his doing.

He pushed hard to catch the intruder off guard. When he heard the thump, he shoved the door the rest of the way, reached for his weapon and then aimed at a white lump in the middle of the floor. He pulled back the trigger ...

"Johnny, it's me, Celeste. Don't shoot!"

Gasping at what he'd almost done, Johnny slipped his gun back into his waistband and helped her to a stand. "Sorry. I thought you were an intruder. Are you hurt?"

"Might have a slight bruise on my tush is all. I landed kind of hard."

"Yeah, well, I work out."

She snuggled up to him and squeezed his biceps. "So, I see."

The situation might have proven to be funny if he hadn't almost killed the woman he loved. "I told you to stay in the house. When are you going to listen to me? I could have shot you."

"I heard an awful noise. I was worried."

"You crazy, beautiful, darling woman." He outlined her lips then owned them with his own. If possible, her lips tasted sweeter with every kiss.

She pulled from him too soon. "What do you think that blast was, Johnny?"

"Don't know. And until I find out, you'd better stay with me. The security system is knocked out. I can't have you traipsing around by yourself."

Johnny went to the light switch by the living room door. Nothing.

A gust of wet wind followed Stan Marshall as he burst into the room from the kitchen. "Did you hear the whirlwind, Johnny? A microburst whipped through here a few minutes ago. Never saw anything like it. Looks like it uprooted a couple of trees, Miss Robinson, but the main house appears undamaged. Won't know for sure until daylight."

"Slow down, Stan. So, there's been no sabotage? Only a weather-related power failure?"

Stan glanced back and forth between Celeste and Johnny. Stan was a good man. A little slow to catch on at times. "Did I interrupt something, Johnny?"

In the darkness, Johnny couldn't be certain if Celeste blushed, though her heated tones evidenced anger at Stan's insinuation. "Most assuredly not, Mr. Marshall."

"Sorry, Miss Robinson. I didn't mean to imply ..."

The light flickered in time to see Stan's face turn mixed shades of red. Johnny laughed. "Shut up, Stan, before you put both feet in your mouth."

"Good advice, Johnny. By the way, if you're wondering what the crash was ... looks like a tree limb went through the guesthouse kitchen window." He glanced downward at Johnny's bare feet. "Be careful if you go out there. Glass all over the place."

"Thanks for the warning."

"Welcome, Johnny."

Celeste reached into her pocket, took out an elastic band, then with trembling hands, scooped her hair into a ponytail.

Stan turned back toward the door. "You two go back to whatever it was you were ..."

Celeste glowered.

"We'll have the security up and running within a few minutes, Johnny. Don't worry, none, Miss Robinson. We have all kinds of back up. Then there's Johnny's instincts. His gut never fails him."

Celeste's eyes followed Stan as he went out the door. "Well, guess we worried over nothing."

"Just the same, I'm walking you back to the main house."

She blushed. "I'm sure I'll be—"

"I insist. You told me I get to call the shots. So, no argument."

She let him hold her hand as they walked the five hundred yards to the back entrance, where two of his men watched the rear. When he saw them approach, Dan Grayson scratched his head. "How did you get past us, Miss Robinson?"

Johnny shook his head. He thought he had assembled the most professional team money could buy. Instead, he'd rounded up a batch of morons. Would he have to stand sentinel himself? Celeste's eyes met his, and their laughs harmonized.

Johnny waited until she slipped up the stairs out of sight. He put his hand on his revolver for emphasis.

"Listen, you two numbskulls. I'm holding you personally responsible to see this fiasco doesn't happen again. You slipped up. You guys were former FBI agents. You've guarded presidents' wives, for crying out loud. I hope you showed more diligence for our national security than what you showed Miss Robinson tonight. I won't tolerate another screw-up. Understood?"

"Understood, Johnny. Won't happen again."

"Glad we're clear. Good night."

As he returned to the guest house, he contemplated his idiotic wisdom in moving into the guest house. Her idea, which he readily accepted. He should have known how her proximity would eat at his senses. To be so near her drove him wild, clouded his judgment.

Now, she'd fallen for him; and he had encouraged the feelings. How could he protect her? Not from the threats on her life but from a far greater risk emerging—an eternal evil, the monster within him certain to devour her soul.

CHAPTER 10

Sylvia paused. Should she leave the chapter here?

A loud thud followed by muffled voices broke into her concentration. What earthquake dared disturb Lana Longstreet? She pulled back the curtain and opened the window. Henry conversed with an aged hippie she took to be Charlie Michaels. The two men pushed against the old shed.

She opened her window so she could snatch some of their conversation. What kind of man had Henry hired?

"The foundation's crumbled pretty bad." Charlie said as he backed away and tugged at his red bandana, his words conveniently carried by the wind, his tone a baritone quality like one who was used to projecting their voice.

As he walked in circles along the interior labyrinth, Sylvia was drawn to the man's appearance. She reached into her desk drawer and pulled out her binoculars, viewing the scene as if a video played especially for her amusement.

Charlie came back toward the shed, jiggled the doorknob and then backed away. "What's in there, Henry? Don't look like the door's been opened in over a century."

About right. She never used the shed, and Fernando and David had supplied their own equipment. She doubted Alfred Donner stored anything of value in there, either. She'd entertained occasional thoughts of demolishing the useless structure. She would have if not for the favored postcard image—a snapshot of yesteryear half hidden beneath shiny vines. She imagined the picture as a cover for her next book superimposed with Johnny and Celeste in a romantic embrace.

Charlie had better not destroy her vision.

Her focus disrupted, she saved her manuscript and minimized the document. Might as well join them and warn Charlie to keep her shed intact. Besides, this Charlie deserved closer scrutiny—a fascinating character study for a future book. Not as a love interest, though ... more of a symbol, an archaic fixture in a modern world, as outdated as the stone walls surrounding the gardens. Or she could have Johnny Gallant hired by a similarly mysterious man. Only, she would make him a washed-up rock musician, and he'd wear leather jackets instead of a flannel shirt.

The veranda could be reached quicker by going through the ballroom, and she never tired of the fantasies she conjured as she took the grand staircase. Every time she rubbed the cherry banister, she felt transported back in time. She imagined herself a guest at one of Trumball's galas, arenas for strategic Revolutionary War plans.

She stopped to perform her ritualistic rub, drawing her into an imaginary world where clocks and calendars failed to rule over important matters. She imagined Ethan Allen and Patrick Henry descending the stairs, passing through her on their way to a clandestine meeting.

Trumball's world revolved inside her writer's kaleidoscope. Unlike Henry's reports, her fantasies exhilarated rather than frightened, her heart racing with possibilities—images of gathering colonists floating through her playground of ideas.

Lady Ewing curtsies to the flamboyant Stephen Trumball, a fourth cousin to then Governor Trumball. He proffers his hand for a waltz. She coyly accepts. While they twirl to the violins' purrs, she whispers Loyalists' secrets in his ear.

"Fortunate for us, Connecticut has been spared the worst of the fight," Trumball says.

"Oh, but Lord Trumball," Lady Ewing says, "there is a fierce battle brewing. The British will raid New Haven within the next few weeks. The colonists must prepare."

Lord Trumball bows and kisses her hand, then Lady Ewing slips from the ball. She boards her coach and hurries to the home of her betrothed, Ambassador Morris. There she mingles with loyalists to ferret out more secrets for the patriots, panting with duplicity. Is she a Maid Marion betraying the royal family in passionate belief for the rebel cause, or does she trade her secrets like a sot craves cheap wine?

Tap-Tap.

Too loud for a woodpecker ... though the intrusion seemed just as effective. Now she'd never know how Lady Ewing might resolve her inner conflict. Sylvia leaned over the balustrade to scan the foyer. Nothing alarming. A low, resonant hum came from the ballroom. Drat that Henry. Now her own imaginations had become riled. Or maybe the noise came from her psyche as she imagined Lady Ewing's hasty escape. Sylvia shook her head and smiled to herself. Lana Longstreet often dreamt noises while in the throes of pleasant plotting.

When she neared the bottom step, she swiped off a trail of dust from George Washington's portrait. She'd have Martina go over every picture in the house, starting with this, her favorite. Sylvia hoped perhaps the well-rested George actually slept in one of Trumball's rooms.

She should have paid more attention in her American History courses. The house—her house—may have played a key role in shaping a nation's future. Although she hoped to lure Henry with the estate's historical significance, she bought it more from sentiment than curiosity. From the moment she touched the grand staircase and walked the upstairs promenade, the house wooed her like a persistent lover.

She'd have paid whatever exorbitant price the owner asked. That she obtained the property at a bargain didn't matter. She thought Henry would be delighted with the transaction. Hope reigned when she rushed back to Manhattan with the news she'd bought the place. His first weekend in Connecticut was spent in heated dispute. He railed obscene suggestions at her. Never before or since had she heard such filth come from his lips. Lana Longstreet gained a house, but Sylvia Moore Fitzgibbons lost a husband.

She stopped short when she entered the ballroom. An odor like rancid butter stole her breath, and her arms numbed from a sudden chill. She rubbed them while a thin mist formed from her exhales, then she crossed toward the heavy doors that opened onto the veranda, miffed to find them open again. Henry must have given Charlie the cook's tour and forgot to close them.

The air thinned, and she felt squeezed, as if something sucked out all her air. Some aura engulfed her, tugged her away from the veranda. She struggled as if caught in an invisible web, flailing her arms in protest, the web tightening all the more.

The room darkened as she spun involuntarily.

So, this is what death feels like.

Forcing a desperate gasp, she sucked in the putrid air, then was suddenly flung across the room by some furious wind, her last cognition that of her own terrified scream.

An ear-splitting scream rifled the air, one signifying horror.

Henry lifted his head, and Charlie dropped his shovel.

"Sylvia!" Henry galloped toward the veranda. As he approached the opened doorway, wispy caricatures pranced around the fallen Sylvia. He fought to enter, but they sneered and rushed him, tackling him to the floor and like a vaporous tsunami, sweeping him back outside. Henry scrambled to his feet and tried in vain to reenter.

"God in heaven. Do something. They're killing her!"

The prayer came from somewhere within him, taking him more by surprise than the spirit barrier.

Charlie pushed past Henry, entering unhindered, then knelt by Sylvia's side. The mist dissipated as if Charlie's presence commanded them to. "You okay, Miss Longstreet?"

The barrier gone, Henry jumped up and ran in, joining Charlie next to Sylvia's prone body. He helped her sit up. Indomitable, even in this undignified state, she stood and shook the dust from her slacks. Her ashen face belied her demure posture. "I fainted. Probably from that horrible smell."

Charlie sniffed the air. "Smells fine to me, Miss Longstreet. I've got a pretty good nose. Might want to see a doctor, though. Sometimes folks have olfactory sensations before they come down with a bug. My wife thinks she smells burnt rubber right before she has a migraine."

"Nonsense. I'm not sick, and I'm not about to have a migraine. Henry needs a doctor more than I do. He thinks there are ghosts in here. Do you see ghosts, Mr. Michaels?"

"No, ma'am."

"Are you satisfied, Henry?"

He scanned the ballroom. "Whatever or whoever tried to hurt you is gone now. Believe what you want. I tell you I saw them as plain as day. They disappeared when Charlie came into the room."

Sylvia laughed. "Mr. Michaels, I apologize. Seems I've married a madman." She spun around three times. "See?

I'm right as rain. Now don't let me stop you gentlemen from your business."

Charlie squinted as he surveyed the room. "Sure you're okay, Miss Longstreet? By the looks of the dust on the floor and your clothes, appears cinders got dumped in here somehow. Maybe a wind blew stuff from the fireplace?"

To Henry's knowledge, Sylvia never used the fireplace.

She dusted herself off. "Guess my pants are a bit smudged, but I assure you I'm fine."

She waved him off like a queen shoos a subject. Charlie deserved a little extra in his paycheck for putting up with Sylvia's snide remarks. Henry dusted his palms. "If you're sure you're okay, I should give Charlie a hand with the old shed. Why don't you rest, Sylvia. I'll bring you tea when we're finished."

"I'll rest later. Right now, I want to see what's going on with my shed." She followed the men onto the veranda, closing the doors behind her, then sat on one of the wicker rockers. She crossed her arms as if to emphasize her regal position in matters concerning her Connecticut estate.

While he and Charlie walked to the shed, Henry could not rid himself of worry. This time whatever lurked in the ballroom had targeted her. Why now after fifteen years?

Charlie walked the length of the shed, tapping the stone walls here and there with a hammer. "Old Man Donner never went near this shed as far as I know. I'm guessing from the way it's constructed, it might be as old as the house."

Sylvia leaned back, poised to mock. "Right about that, Mr. Michaels."

"Prefer the name, Charlie, Miss Longstreet." He approached the front of the shed and tugged at the latch. "It's stuck pretty good."

Henry sidled next to Charlie. "Here, let me help you."

They yanked and huffed until the door sprung from its hinges, hitting Henry on the head, sending both men to the ground. A thin, warm stream of sweat trickled down his face, the least of his worries. A horde of hairy creatures stampeded from the decayed shed, trampling over his sneakers, and scampering toward the retaining wall.

Charlie sprung to his feet, brushed off a dozen or more stragglers, and helped Henry to a stand. "Did they bite you, Henry?"

He performed a cursory examination of his arms and legs. "Don't think so. In too much of a hurry, I guess. Or maybe they mistook me for a log."

Sylvia rushed from the veranda to his side. "Those spiders could be poisonous."

Henry took her hand. "You're trembling. See? They're gone, now. The shed's empty."

Charlie kicked off one remaining spider from his boot. "Well, not exactly true, Henry. There're still hundreds left in there. These that took off are wolf spiders. I expect we'll find a few hundred funnelwebs hid in the crevices. I don't think this here shed's salvageable. We should level this one and build you a new one. Spiders are good for gardens, but seems you got a thousand or so more than what you need. I can arrange for an exterminator if you'd like."

"Yes ... as soon as possible."

Sylvia nodded as if in agreement, then snatched her hand from Henry's grasp. "I think I'd like to go back in. Do whatever you think best about the shed, Charlie. I'll leave you gentlemen to your work."

Henry took Sylvia's arm. This time she didn't resist his help. He led her down the path to the kitchen. If only she wouldn't pretend to be so all-fired independent. For these few privileged seconds, he was her knight, she his damsel in distress.

Once her body stopped trembling, she pushed away, fracturing the momentary illusion she might need him. "I'll take it from here, thank you."

No. She needed him like she needed an anchor around her neck. She was not about to admit she'd been attacked. Still, whatever evil habited the ballroom was now more aggressive than ever.

When he returned to the shed, Charlie waited for him. "Do you see anything interesting in there, Charlie?"

"A few old-fashioned tools. Rusted almost to dust."

Henry picked up the dislodged door and leaned it against the wall. "Too bad we have to tear the shed down. I liked the look. I sometimes imagine myself sucked back in time."

Charlie's sympathetic eyes warmed like a pat on the head. "Not to worry. If you want, we can make a replica, only without the spiders."

"Great idea. I think Sylvia would agree. Oh, and we'll need to figure out some safety features while we're working. Erik's wife is going to be doing some housekeeping for us and will have to bring her two youngsters from time to time."

Charlie smiled. "Kids don't bother me none. I'll put up meshed wire around our work areas so they can play in the yard."

"Thank you." Henry remembered how Julie once trampled his favorite bush, the velvety pink ones with white tones on the underside of the petals. He could almost see her as she played a game of kickball with her friends, running carelessly into the rose beds. Henry had scolded her like an errant nymph. She cried, ran into the house, and never played in the backyard again, at least while Henry was at the house.

Charlie threw the decayed tools into the back of his truck. "By the by, I examined those soil samples I took yesterday. The pH values are slightly below par, but nothing a little mulch fertilizer won't fix."

"Do you need me to get some for you?" Henry gave himself an imaginary ping on the forehead. S*tupid. The man works at a garden supply store.*

"Thanks for the offer. I prefer not to use commercial fertilizer. I get my manure from a farm up the road. They let the stuff age about eight months. Good and ripe."

"You're the expert. I trust your judgment."

Charlie took out a pad and scribbled a list. "I'll need these here tools. Do you want me to pick them up from my store, or do you want to buy them yourself? I'd bring stuff from home, but I figured you'd want to have these on hand for future reference."

Yeah. Right. Was there a future here? Not for Henry. David might be able to use them next year. Or maybe Sylvia would hire another handyman by then. "Let me have the list. I'll have Erik pick them up later today."

"Say, I have an old antique wheelbarrow hanging around the store. Don't need it, and it might make a nice decoration. Yours if you want it."

"My wife might like that, I think. Sure. Go ahead. Thanks."

"I'm done for today. Not supposed to rain until tomorrow evening, so I'll be by same time in the morning."

As Charlie turned to leave, Henry reeled in unaccustomed loneliness, already missing Charlie and wishing Erik were nearby. Odd he should crave male companionship, even a drop-dead hunk of Swedish manhood. With the exception of a duel of wits, Henry was literally outmanned by Erik. Not to be arrogant, but Henry might have it over Charlie in the handsome department at least. "Got time for a quick cup of coffee? You still have an hour before the store opens."

"Don't mind if I do."

Henry shuffled to the kitchen. He took down the mugs Erik had picked up for him the day before, filled them both with coffee, poured cream and sugar into one for Charlie, then walked briskly back to the veranda. He clocked the return trip at one minute, twelve seconds.

Charlie sat on a wicker chair. "Weather Channel predicts a muggy day. Warmer than usual for May." Henry handed Charlie his cup. He took a sip then held the cup up as a token of praise. "Did you make this, Henry?"

He pulled up a chair and sat next to Charlie. "Guilty."

"It's good. Some better'n yesterday."

"You know what they say about practice. I went through eight pots before I got the right combination of water and grounds. Say, Charlie, just occurred to me we never discussed how often you'd like to get paid. Once a week, okay? How much per hour are we looking at?"

Charlie chortled as he placed his mug on a stand, although his snorts were far from offensive. "Sorry, Henry. Didn't mean to laugh. Guess you didn't know."

"Know what?"

"I don't charge for my work."

"Excuse me?"

Charlie's sip irritated like an ill-timed commercial, exasperatingly long. "I only expect reimbursement for the supplies I buy. Labor's free."

Was Charlie an illegal immigrant or something? A fugitive? Not wanting a financial record of his labors? Should he take the risk or fire Charlie? At least, Charlie acted like he knew what he was doing, and Henry knew he'd never get back to Manhattan before fall without some help. Still, only a weirdo worked for free in these economic times. What was the man hiding? "I don't understand. You can't afford to work for nothing. The store can't pay much more than minimum wage. I can give you cash. No records."

"Oh, that cut deep, Henry. You see, I'm the owner and pay my help a good wage."

"I hired the owner?"

"I own the whole chain. You see, Henry, I'm already a wealthy man. I don't do this for money."

"If you don't need the money, then why accept the job? You could have asked one of your men to do the work."

"You're right. I could have sent Jerry. He's a regular Rembrandt with landscapes. I have special reasons for coming out here myself."

News Alert: Famous author and husband slain by crazed gardener. Stay tuned for complete details following tonight's Murder Mystery Playhouse.

"Reasons, as in plural?"

"First off, you sounded pretty desperate."

"I *am* desperate, Charlie. You've met my wife."

His laugh tickled the senses like dew on bare feet.

Exonerated.

"The other reason has to do with Old Man Donner. I told you before, I used to work for him. See, I'd just started out in business in those days. He backed a loan for me. Didn't know at the time, but he wrote the loan off in his will. In a sense, I owe him. He loved these roses like a parent loves a child. Said they were God's gift to him. So, if I can save some of them, be sort of like doing him and the Lord a favor."

Henry's head drooped from the weight of his shame. He had treated Charlie like a commoner. Kindly, of course. Henry Fitzgibbons was nothing if not affable, and Sylvia often criticized him for being too generous. However, if the truth were known, his random philanthropic acts were no more than baskets thrown to the wind gods, a tribal ritual in search of forgiveness. Yet, peace eluded him no matter how much he gave away.

Next to him sat a man, one with the earth, who could buy Henry three times over. Maybe Charlie's sins even outweighed Henry's.

FROM JOHNNY GALLANT

C11

Thud.

Someone's in the kitchen, and Dinah was nowhere around. Johnny retrieved his revolver from the nightstand, removed the safety, then crept toward the pitter-patter of hurrying feet. He pushed the door open, poised ready to fire. There, on its haunches, sat a satisfied squirrel with a marshmallow stuffed in his jaws, surrounded by the remaining shards of glass from last night's wind damage.

Johnny pulled the trigger, aimed and then thought better of killing the poor critter who wasn't to blame for doing what nature taught him to do. Instead, Johnny fired into the tree, scaring the squirrel who scampered away, but not without his treasured marshmellow.

Johnny twirled his revolver around his finger like a gunslinger in a B-rated western. Suddenly feeling hungry, he opened the refrigerator, the blast of cold air signaling him to put on a robe. He returned to the bedroom, slung on the terrycloth one Celeste had bought him, and started back toward the kitchen. A winded, pajama-clad Celeste and a beet-faced Stan Marshall tumbled in through the living room door.

"Sorry, Johnny, I tried to stop her."

Celeste threw Stan a scowl. "I heard a gunshot. Are you okay, Johnny?"

The sight of her in white satin made his heart stop. At this eternal moment, with no makeup and uncombed hair, her smile muted the Mona Lisa. Let Stan cluck his disapproval. Johnny rushed to her intending to declare his love for her and envelope her in his arms. Not one word melted from his frozen tongue. All he could do was stare at her—drained of all free will.

There are moments in a man's life, like this one, he wished he could freeze frame. In this ethereal instant, Johnny knew his heart was hers forever to command.

CHAPTER 11

Sylvia leaned back to contemplate her own life. Here in this loft, she felt free to question her existence, argue with the deity so many claimed to be in control of this world, and to ponder the meaning of life; while elsewhere, Lana Longstreet allowed no one to brand her a philosopher, especially Henry.

Didn't everyone wish they could freeze some special moment in their life? If she could, which memory would she want petrified for all eternity? She played her memories through the viewfinder of her heart, stopping on the day Henry proposed.

He had exuded all the sophistication of a James Bond in his new white tuxedo, a stark contrast to his then dark hair. He had played a lot of golf that summer—his tanned complexion added to his mystique. They planned to celebrate Henry's promotion to senior editor of *Sports World Review.*

Since the day they met, Henry avoided social gatherings ... but how he could dance, and she was pleased when he suggested a night on the town. They dined on pheasant and danced until midnight. After their last tango, one rivaling Fred and Ginger, they returned to their booth, then Henry waived at the orchestra. A soft piano began playing, and Henry serenaded her with, "You are the Sunshine of My Life." Who knew he could sing? Then he slid to one knee, pulled out a velvet box from his pocket, and showed her the delicately set diamond ring as he cleared his throat. "Sylvia, you are an amazing woman, and these months with you have enriched my life beyond what words can express. I can't imagine my life without you. Will you marry me?"

Overcome with emotion, she nodded her answer, then he slipped the ring on her finger during the piano reprise. He'd hired a hansom cab, and they rode through Central Park until the morning light broke over the horizon.

Fondling her engagement ring, she lolled in happy memories, until a harsh bark blasted them away, pulling her back to today. Martina must have arrived with the children and Thor.

A woman scolded, "Bad dog. No barking in Miss Longstreet's house."

Then, as abruptly as the hubbub began, silence returned. The quiet distracted her more than the yelps. Sylvia had left instructions on the kitchen counter, but what if Martina couldn't read English? Erik's command of the language was barely functionable.

Sylvia hurried down the spiral staircase and found a buxom blonde reading the list taped to a cupboard. "You … must … be … Martina?"

"Yes, I am." Her blue eyes sparkled while a halo-like ring reflected from a crown of yellow locks. She grabbed a broom and picked up the list from the counter. "No need to tell me who you are, Miss Longstreet. I've read every one of your books. I'm a big fan. I'll dust off those pictures for you and then get right to figuring out what's stinking up the ballroom, though I didn't notice any odor when I stuck my head in a minute ago."

The girl bubbled more than champagne and with no hint of an accent. "Erik never told me you weren't Swedish. I assumed you were."

"I am Swedish. My parents both came from Stockholm. My father was a groundskeeper for Yale. I was born in New Haven and have lived here my whole life. Erik and I met when I did housekeeping for one of his former employers."

"Where are the children? I thought I heard them come in with you?"

Worry marks stretched across Martina's face. "I hope we didn't disturb you, Miss Longstreet. Henry said you like quiet while you work. The children are in the back. Henry's showing them where they can play."

Martina's contented servitude blended with an aura of personal confidence. The two seemed incongruous and piqued Sylvia's curiosity, drawing her to the girl. She suddenly bristled—Lana Longstreet would never be friends with hired help, no matter how engaging they might be. "Okay, then. Go on about your business."

With a half curtsy, the girl bolted toward her given assignment.

Sylvia opened the kitchen shutters, turning her attention toward the gardens. She'd like to think nostalgia pulled her into the scene, and she sifted through the albums of her mind for one happy memory associated with the roses. To her, they serviced, like plates and pictures, commodities with which Lana Longstreet impressed her guests. She had never taken the time to appreciate their natural beauty. Shame eroded her defenses, their neglect yet another sin. She lifted her head heavenward, vowing to devote a few minutes of each day to enjoy the gift.

Sylvia walked the long path into the back where Thor was chained against a makeshift post. Henry tossed a rubber ball to two impish mop heads, his snorts mingling with cherub giggles.

Henry's having far too much fun.

Although mired in the present, her memories fled back to Central Park. She sat on a plaid blanket, unpacking fried chicken and grapes from a hand-woven picnic basket while Henry played soccer with David and Julie.

The memory singed her heart with realization. Henry had been a good father until she moved the children away from him. Had she been guilty of forcing him into part-time fatherhood?

No! Lana Longstreet shooed the guilt. Henry chose to stay in Manhattan. She refused to bear the blame rightly belonging to him.

"Sylvia. Here. Catch."

A white blur hit her on the nose.

"Sorry, Sylvia. You okay?"

She laughed as Sven and Gunnar froze in horror. She wiggled her nose, and they relaxed. "See, nothing's broken." On a whim, she shooed Lana Longstreet to the back of her mind, picked up the ball and tossed it back with far more gusto than required. *Quid pro quo.*

Sven and Gunnar joined in chorus. "Will you play with us, too, Miss Longstreet? Please?"

Why not?

"Okay, But only for a few minutes. I need to get back to work."

The minutes melded into an hour and blended into one glorious afternoon.

Henry had enjoyed his time with the Hagstadt urchins. Of course, he couldn't devote every day to their attention—however, the sounds of happy children were a welcomed diversion. Martina's mother planned to care for the children most days. When her mother was unavailable, she promised to bring the children's favorite books and movies. Apparently, the twins were good medicine for

Sylvia, despite her insistence she required absolute silence in order to write.

Whatever her faults, she'd been a good mother, a far better parent than he could have hoped to be. He saw her today as she had been an eternity ago when they took the children to Central Park for an afternoon romp. Days lost forever.

Regret could not bring back his children's youth. He had missed their teenage years, unjustly blaming Sylvia. He should have swallowed his inhibitions. Instead, he chose the role of mostly absent father.

Sure, he visited for the big events like Christmas and graduations. He condoned his disinterest, blaming his claustrophobia. In truth,his stubbornness was why he had missed Julie's first prom and David's winning touchdown propelling his team to regional playoffs.

David, thankfully, emerged from fatherless days less scarred than Julie. Henry blamed her long hours at the canvas. So much like her mother, lost in her creative passions—withdrawing into a cocoon of make-believe. At least, he'd endured the occasional flight to attend some of her art exhibits.

Pop equated pride to sin. If so, Henry Fitzgibbons had much sin in his life ... for he took enormous pride in both his children, even if he could take no credit for their accomplishments. Were the children resentful for his long absences? Neither of them complained. David called often, and they would rehash a football game or PGA tournament over the phone for hours. Julie, however, lived outside his emotional reach. After her move to California, the breach widened.

The timer's ding meant the meatloaf was done, but Rosalie's recipe suggested a cool-down of ten minutes before serving. Henry lifted the lid on the boiled potatoes, reciting Martina's instructions on how to mash them. "Pour in a little milk and drop in some butter," measurements as precise as a dollop of whip cream.

He tipped the pot over, using the lid to drain the liquid. The hot steam burned his hands, causing him to drop the pot and lid into a sink of dirty dishwater. Now what could he do? He couldn't, wouldn't confess this fiasco to Sylvia. How to cover up his mistake? He'd have to settle for tasteless instant.When the water boiled, he followed the instructions on the package, then placed the pot to one side.

As he examined the contents in the refrigerator, the idea sprang at him like a plucked rubber band. Why not enhance the instant with sour cream? He measured a quarter cup into the hot mixture. "Even looks creamier." He filled the kitchen with praise unto himself for his culinary craftiness.

Now for a side dish.

He remembered spotting a few oranges and kiwi fruit on the bottom shelf of the fridge, but he'd forgotten where he'd moved the cutting boards. He searched cupboards with frenzied urgency, then checked the map on the refrigerator. Ah. Yes. The narrow cupboard next to the built-in dishwasher. He sliced a banana in two then put each piece into a goblet along with the sliced fruit. For good measure, he splashed the contents with grenadine.

He found a kitchen ruler on top of Rosalie's desk and sliced the meatloaf into uniform pieces, arranging them into a circular pattern. With all the pizzaz of a Gordon Ramsay, he topped the arrangement with a sprig of parsley.

He puffed a self-satisfied, "Good job, Henry." So what if he'd copied the presentation off a recipe card? That he replicated it to perfection deserved some praise, didn't it? His hopes for the evening depended upon a happy wife. He scooped the potatoes into a porcelain serving bowl, indented the mound with the backside of a wooden spoon, then filled the valley with melted butter.

"Henry, you've outdone yourself. That's what she'll say." Now, what should he use for dishware? His genius deserved Sylvia's best. He sashayed a moon dance into the pantry and selected what he assumed was her best china. At least, the service she used for her soirees.

He stacked a wooden tray with food, dishes, salt and pepper, linen napkins, and any other useful item he could think of—hardly with the precision Rosalie would use—but appetizingly arranged. With a hopeful heart, he placed a purple rosebud on top of the heap and then ascended the spiral staircase. Would Sylvia invite him in, or would Lana Longstreet send him back down the steps with a curt dismissal?

Sylvia squealed when he entered the loft. "Henry, you remembered how much I love meatloaf."

He stifled a relieved whistle. *Thank you, Rosalie!*

He shouldn't have taken the credit. However, confession would only spoil the mood. "I'm glad you're pleased."

He set the tray on the side table near the window. "How's the book coming along? I'm sorry for all the interruptions. Tomorrow should be quieter."

"I managed to get quite a bit done today, all things considered. I planned on quitting for the night when you brought supper. No need for you to eat alone. Will you join me? There's going to be a spectacular sunset tonight."

"I hoped you'd ask me to stay. See?" He pointed to the extra place settings. Drawing up two chairs, he motioned for Sylvia to sit. "After you, m'lady."

"You did this?"

"Guilty."

He waited for her to take a bite. "Well?"

"Good."

He took a bite for himself. It *was* good. Perhaps miracles happened after all, even for heathens like him.

What could they talk about? The silence between them loomed like a cavern. "Nice afternoon, wasn't it? Especially after the crazy morning we had."

"I enjoyed playing with the kids. Brought back a lot of memories."

Red streaks dispelled the clouds. "Sure is a beautiful sky, Sylvia. Tomorrow promises to be just as pleasant, weather-wise."

When the room thickened with the night, Sylvia lit a candle. They talked beyond the moon's ascent, careful to avoid the touchy subjects, like Evan North and the garden project. He explained why *The French Connection* was his favorite movie. How he liked Popeye Doyle's character because he was as clever as he was forceful. Sylvia confessed the temporary paralysis she experienced each time she started a new book. How she feared a flop more than a python. Every revelation given and received stoked dying embers to life. For Henry, this woman with whom he dined, with whom he shared intimate secrets, bloomed before him like a rose at maturity. He stood and extinguished the candle. "I suppose I should clear these dishes. Let you get your rest."

She clutched his hand. "Don't go, Henry. Stay with me tonight?"

Sleep—restful and wonderful—overtook him, until Sylvia pushed him. "Henry, wake up! I hear something."

"What?"

"Shush. Listen."

He roused, training an ear toward the hardwood flooring.

Tap – tap. Tap – tap.

Rhythmic thuds shook Sylvia's bed.

Henry threw on his pants and switched on the light. Grabbing a large book from Sylvia's shelf, he followed the sounds to the main stairwell, then hesitated. Within seconds, Sylvia caught up to him. "Aren't you going to investigate?" He couldn't tell her he preferred to tumble to a premature death than confront the ballroom in the darkest part of the night.

Sylvia snatched the tray from his grip. "Never mind, Fearless. I'll take a look myself." She took the steps two at a time.

Tap – tap. Tap – tap.

"Henry, get down here. I can hear something or someone moving around."

"Shouldn't we call the police?"

"Nonsense. I don't even lock my doors. It's probably just a squirrel come in from the fireplace."

Feeling more like a frightened pet instead of a protector, Henry caught up to Sylvia where she waited in the foyer.

Tap – tap. Tap – tap.

An eddy of dust and suffocating wind trapped them, tearing at their clothes while screams like howling hyenas bounced from the walls.

Then a calm silence.

Henry's voice cracked as if parched. "I'd say we should get out of here, now. Don't you agree?"

Sylvia squeezed his hand. "Good idea."

CHAPTER 12

In spite of the pre-dawn intrusion, Henry awoke invigorated and rebuked the spontaneous whistle. Thankfully, he hadn't disturbed Sylvia, whose sleeping snorts pinged the morning. He looked out the window to admire the morning glow on the rose bushes. What time was it? He couldn't find a clock. Faint digging sounds emanated from the backyard, most likely Charlie.

He dressed, then went through the loft, taking the spiral staircase like a buck teenager. After starting the coffee, he strolled outside to join Charlie who had already dug a wide berth where the shed once stood. Tangled vines lay atop piles of crumbled brick. "Morning, Henry. As you can see, the shed's gone. Fell over during the night. Don't know how it stood up as long as it did. See those beams? Rotted to the core. We must have unloosed whatever held it up."

Henry stepped back as a colony of wolf spiders paraded from underneath the piles. One of them crawled up Charlie's pant leg, but he brushed it off like a fly. "I called an exterminator like I promised—will be here this afternoon. Got a work crew coming Monday to start on the replica. You told me not to worry about the cost."

"Yes. Of course. I want the best."

"That's what I told the contractor."

Henry glanced at his bare wrist. In his hurry, he forgot to put on his watch. "Sorry I wasn't awake when you got here. What time is it, anyway?"

"Quarter to eight. Almost done for the day. Just need to clean up this debris." He grabbed a shovel, scooping up what was left of the crumbled shed into a large, wheeled container, piling the vines on top of the heap. "I need to burn all this for a bit."

Didn't make much sense. "The stones too? You can't reuse them?"

Charlie snickered, kindly, of course, at Henry's ignorance. "Vines re-root easily, even in the rubble. And burning will take care of any spider eggs."

Useless in this scene, Henry gazed at the ruined remains of the past. "I did get those tools you wanted." He pointed to the veranda. "I put them there after the Hagstadt kids left. Any idea where we should store them until the shed's built?"

"I've got a tall storage bin I brought for temporary use. I'd appreciate a hand unloading it, then I can wheel this container onto the truck and haul it away. I have a furnace at the store for these types of jobs."

Henry whistled as the two men walked to Charlie's truck. He slid out a ramp from underneath his truck bed, then they jumped onto the truck and eased the bin to the ground. Once the shed was unloaded, they pushed the container onto the truck.

Charlie gazed toward where the shed once stood. "Where do you want this, Henry?"

What did he know? "Maybe in the corner by the retaining wall?"

Charlie nodded approval, and the men walked the bin back the length of the yard to the designated spot. Charlie leveled the bin, then slapped his gloved hands, releasing a cloud of dust. "That should do it. Now let's load her up."

Henry hummed to Charlie's whistle as they walked back toward the house.

"You're chipper this morning, Henry."

"It's the strangest thing, you know. But I think I'm beginning to feel at home here. Except for the ballroom."

"Miss Longstreet's fall put a scare into you sure enough. I didn't sense anything wrong in there, but that don't mean there weren't something odd. There are a lot of things in heaven and on earth can't be explained on the Discovery Channel."

"My wife insists I'm either insane, or I have a highly evolved imagination. Frankly, I'm not creative enough to make up something like ghosts. Sylvia's the writer in the family."

Charlie didn't seem like a cleric, nor act like any clergyman Henry had known, including his father. Yet, confession after confession rolled off Henry's tongue as they walked. "You know. I can't explain why I suddenly feel attached to the place. I've only been here a few days, but already I've stayed longer than ever before. I'm thinking I should retire, move in on a permanent basis, and give up the Manhattan apartment."

Charlie smirked as he took off his gloves. "You don't say?"

He hadn't asked what drove a husband to live apart from a beautiful woman like Sylvia. Yet, Henry babbled on like a penitent sinner at an altar. "Time I owned up to the truth. It's true—I hate the commute, and I avoid taxis and trains too. The real reason I stayed away goes much deeper than claustrophobia. I never forgave Sylvia for moving here against my wishes. Maybe the ghosts aren't real, and I unconsciously conjured them up as a convenient excuse. The more I stayed away, the easier to believe I *should* stay away. I'll tell you, Charlie, I'd sell my soul to have those years back. Things might have been so much different if I'd swallowed my pride and moved here when Sylvia did."

"Nothing's worth selling your soul for, Henry. If you want my opinion, it ain't healthy to get your nose all bent 'cause of something you can't change."

Charlie retrieved the tools from the veranda, handed over a few for Henry to carry and led the way back to the bin. "No sense beating yourself up over the past. We all have regrets. Maybe we can't change yesterday, but with God's help we can do something about today. Rehashing sins only serves to keep us mired in 'em."

As Henry helped store the tools, he realized how much he'd enjoyed Charlie's company, a man he felt he could trust. "If I'm going to retire, I'll need a hobby." Henry winked. "Like gardening. You've taught me a lot, Charlie."

"Now I know you're kidding me."

"You're right, of course. I should consider all the ramifications before I do anything quite so drastic. For now, though, the idea has a lot of appeal."

"Gardening or the move?"

"Both."

A gnawing ache crept across Henry's forehead. "Coffee?"

"Sure."

"I'll meet you on the veranda, then." Henry jogged back to the house, poured two cups, one with cream and sugar, then returned without spilling a drop. Charlie clicked the timing feature on his watch. "One minute flat, Henry. Not bad for an old feller."

The men rocked in the wicker chairs like two old friends, familiar with one another's company as they sipped on their coffee. Strange he should feel so comfortable around this odd man, a mixture of backwoods charm and uncanny insight. How could a simple gardener see into a soul like Charlie did? The man's syntax scraped the brain like wanton fingers on a blackboard, yet he possessed enough knowledge to fill a couple of libraries.

"So, I'm curious, Charlie. How did you come by your horticultural interests?"

He set his cup on the table, stretched out his legs as he leaned back, then stroked his beard as if calculating a response. After a few seconds, he spewed his answer. "In prison."

Interesting. Would he have hired Charlie knowing he was an excon? Maybe. Oh well, if he were a scoundrel, at least he was a rich one.

"I don't want you to think ill of me, Henry. Since you asked, I won't hide the truth. You see, I don't just look like Charlie Michaels the folk singer. I *am* Charlie Michaels the folk singer."

Henry was in the middle of a swallow when Charlie dumped this piece of information, and the hot liquid went down the wrong way.

"Easy, there, Henry. Didn't mean to startle you."

Finally able to swallow, he wanted to know more of Charlie's story. "What happened? I mean you had three number one hits in a row. Then, nothing. Like you fell off the face of the earth."

"Drugs, Henry. Ruined my music. Couldn't write or sing anymore. When I couldn't afford to buy my stash, I sold pot to kids."

So, the man did have secrets. Criminal ones. "Forgive my surprise, but you don't seem the type, Charlie."

He reclaimed his coffee cup. "Is there a type? I was in prison a lot of years. Don't know that there's a type."

Henry's face burned with embarrassment.

"Don't fret none, Henry. You see, God got a hold of my life in jail."

If Henry didn't know better, he'd accuse Higgy of sending Charlie here. Common sense said to have nothing to do with the man, but Charlie was an enigma Henry wanted to solve. Besides, compared to his own sins, this hippy's past was mild.

After the Persian Gulf, Henry convinced himself God didn't exist … or, if he did, he didn't care a hoot for the helpless. And if God were as righteous as Pop preached, he'd want nothing to do with a murderer like Henry Fitzgibbons.

So how did an aged Mary Jane freak find religion in Hell's Belly? "It's none of my business really, but sounds like an interesting story." Henry laughed. "Maybe *you* should write a book."

"Not much to it, really. A lot of inmates attend religious services, mostly for something to fill their time. Some are sincere when they give their lives to Jesus. Trouble is, for a lot of inmates, once they get back outside, they forget how much God loves them."

Henry understood foxhole religion and supposed the same principle held true in prison life. Luke Barrington had cried out to God seconds before he died. Other soldiers begged to be saved and were miraculously spared. Then their lives were no different once they returned stateside. "Didn't you find religion inconvenient outside of prison?"

"At first. God spoke to me in the middle of a drug deal. I heard his voice as plain as yours, though not as loud. Came from my own soul, I guess. I threw the money on the warehouse floor and walked out a changed man. Kind of surprised I wasn't whacked. That gang didn't take too kindly to desertion. I figured God must have protected me for some reason."

Henry stretched his legs, waiting for the punch line. None came. Was Charlie serious?

"I had no money, no home, and no education, 'cept the horticulture classes I took while in the joint. One day, I saw an ad in the help wanted section for a gardener. Turned out to be Alfred Donner."

Coincidence? Henry had seen a lot of them over the years. "So that's how you met him." He suspected there was a lot more to Charlie's story. Something more than sheer will brought a destitute man from his knees to a multimillion-dollar enterprise.

"Alfred Donner gave me a chance when everyone else despised me. I worked for him until he died a few years later. Married his housekeeper, and gradually, I built a respectable life. Mr. Donner lent me the money to start up my own business. Now you know why I owe him so much."

Henry leaned forward in challenge. "Tell me, Charlie. Do you still believe in Jesus? A rich man doesn't need religion." Henry regretted his sarcasm. "Sorry. I didn't mean to be so rude."

Charlie shrugged his shoulders. "Lots of folks have a similar opinion. To tell you the truth, I need Jesus more as a rich man than I did as a criminal. I go to church every Sunday, but church don't make a man a Christian. Jesus does the work. I go so's God can remind me where I started from. He's forgiven me of a lot ... not just my past. I slip up some way or another most days, and he still forgives me."

He glanced at his watch. "Guess I should get going. Thanks for the coffee."

They shook hands, not as employer and gardner but as friends.

Sylvia greeted the morning with uncontrollable giggles as Henry approached, jostling a breakfast tray and whistling like a Disney dwarf going off to work. When he set the tray on the bed, a small amount of juice spilled onto the tray.

"Careful!" She took the napkin and dabbed the small pool, cackling like a college coed.

Henry kissed her and combed her hair with his fingers. "You slept well, apparently, even after our rude awakening."

Her gaze fell to the solitary plate of muffins.

Henry stroked her cheek. "I had toast earlier."

For the moment, she needed him near her more than breakfast. She'd gladly bid Lana Longstreet farewell if she could be Mrs. Henry Fitzgibbons once more—if Henry asked her to. She studied his quirky smile, full of love. Did a bud burst with as much joy when the sun called it to bloom?

He rubbed her feet. "You know. I'd like to spend more time here, Sylvia. What do you say to turning over the business entirely to Higgy? I could retire."

She placed the tray on the nightstand, then threw her arms around her husband's neck. "Are you serious? Don't toy with me, Henry. I've waited years for you to say you wanted to be here with me—for you to call this house your home."

"Let's see how the summer goes. Yeah. Retiring and moving here is entirely within the realm of possibilities."

Tap – tap.

Again?

The bed rattled, then hopped across the floor.

Henry's face paled. "Sylvia, get out of the bed. Now!" He managed to pull her off before it turned over. She nestled against Henry's chest as he lifted her chin and gazed into her eyes, his filled with worry. "I can't explain it, Sylvia. I get the feeling something doesn't want us to love each other."

She pushed him, albeit playfully. "Henry, you're getting all weird again. I'm sure there's a simple explanation. The front of the house is fairly close to the main road, and there has been an increase in the number of large trucks going by. Could be this is nothing more than vibrations."

He loosened his hold on her, his voice a whisper. "Think what you will, Sylvia. I've never seen vibrations turn a bed over."

She shoved him a little harder, grabbed a hairbrush, and vented her frustration with each stroke. "Henry, stop being an alarmist." The present mood obliterated, Sylvia looked to the future. Maybe later they could find another opportunity to talk about Henry's sudden desire to move to Connecticut. Why now? She swept her hair up into a twist, securing her do with pins. "I'd better get to work. I've got a lot of word count to make up. Forgive me if I hope for a dull day?"

Henry kissed her hand. "Fair thee well, My Lady Love." He righted the bed. "If this moves again, get out of the room. Immediately. Promise me."

She surrendered a brief kiss. "I promise. Now, Sir Galahad, if you'd kindly leave me to my work."

Henry's petulant stomps against the cast-iron steps echoed through the house like those of a hot-tempered two-year-old. As much as Henry's surliness repelled Lana Longstreet, Sylvia adored his little boy antics. She loathed this perpetual tug-of-war between her two personalities and Lana Longstreet's dominance.

The ring, sounding like the cheer at a baseball game, echoed into the loft. Henry's cell. She stood at the top of the spiral staircase to listen, hoping Monique hadn't called to lure Henry back to Manhattan.

Stop being so suspicious, Sylvia!

Monique was probably entirely innocent. Still, she doted on Henry far more than a girl her age needed to placate a boss. The call was probably from Paul. What could he possibly need on such a gorgeous day?

She showered, then dressed in a red blouse and black skirt. Henry said the colors were symbolic of her split personality. "The combination flatters both of you," he'd said. A backhanded compliment to be sure, albeit accurate. As the years passed, her Lana Longstreet persona surfaced more and more, dictating what Sylvia ate, how she dressed, and what she said. The more Sylvia had resisted Lana Longstreet's control, the stronger her hold became, until Sylvia shriveled into a shadow of herself. Over the last few days, with Henry trying so hard to please her, she wanted Lana Longstreet gone. Only then could Sylvia Fitzgibbons be the woman she once was.

Sylvia yanked out the pins and let her tresses fall over her shoulders, the way Henry liked her to wear her hair. "Take that, Lana Longstreet."

She wanted to please Henry, when she knew what he liked, that is. He rarely said, "I like that" ... or ..."I wish you would ...." Lana Longstreet blamed Henry for the failed marriage, her admonitions loud and clear. "Henry's never loved you."

Lana Longstreet had lied all these years. Hadn't he clearly shown his love this morning? Willing to finally move to Connecticut, no longer an infrequent visitor?

Henry should know how much she wanted to vanquish Lana Longstreet forever ... be just Sylvia Moore Fitzgibbons once again. She'd need help if this constant pull were to end. Maybe Henry would understand the war between the woman Sylvia and the writer Lana Longstreet.

She scurried down the spiral steps, anxious to spill her heart. Henry sat in a chair, his body rigid as if in a stupor.

"Henry?" She embraced him, but he still didn't move. "Was that Paul?"

He nodded.

"What did he want?"

Henry gripped her hand. "Sylvia, I've got to go back to Manhattan."

Dread robbed her of hope."Oh, Henry. Not now. Didn't you just say—"

"We're being sued."

CHAPTER 13

Like a medieval melodrama, he was trapped … compelled to stay in Connecticut to protect the woman he loved, yet forced to leave her side in order to save her from the mythical dragon.

Henry brushed his lips against hers as he readied to leave. "I don't want to go, Sylvia. Not this time."

She stood at the door, a picture of self-reliance. Of course, she'd manage without him. If the company did go belly up, other houses would clamor for her talent. He might as well face the truth. Henry Fitzgibbons was excess baggage in Lana Longstreet's life. With the exception of Charlie's accidental but fortuitous hire, Sylvia solved her problems without Henry's input, though he'd enjoyed the illusion of one in charge. Years ago, she needed him, before fame elevated her and revealed his uselessness. He found her strength an intoxicating lure. Yet, Sylvia's need of him had always been a more portent enticement. He despised the contradiction within.

When Erik opened the passenger door, Henry crawled in, grateful Sylvia's chauffeur preferred silence. The quiet let Henry think, sort through new truths, painful revelations shattering previously nurtured delusions. He pondered the last few days—a glimpse of a possible future if they could demolish the barriers separating them, real or imagined.

An embryonic promise had been conceived last night. A few days ago, he'd wished for a calamity to whisk him away. Fickle fate forced him to leave when he most wanted to stay.

As Erik pulled up in front of his apartment building, Henry grabbed his computer tote from the backseat. About to exit, he glanced toward Erik, stiff as ever. "I need you to get back to Connecticut as soon as possible. I'm worried about Mrs. Fitzgibbons. You *will* watch out for her, won't you?"

"Ja. Martina und I vill do all we can. Und vee vill pray for her und for you too."

Conspiracy inundated Henry's world. "Don't tell me you're religious too."

The Swede relaxed, as if truth freed him. "Ja. Vee are Christian, Martina und I."

"Why the big secret until now?"

Erik blushed. "I do not tell you before. Dr. Gordon did not like my talk of Jesus und fired me. I cannot afford to lose dis job. But now I see you need Jesus. So, vee pray for you."

"Thank you, I guess. I do appreciate your prayers, though I don't think God wants anything to do with the likes of me. I'm not the man you might think."

Erik got out and marched to the other side to open Henry's door. "None of us are who vee seem."

Henry stepped onto the sidewalk, his thoughts still in a jumble, realizing he hadn't thanked Erik for working overtime to drive him into the city. By the time Henry turned around, Erik had already disappeared into traffic. Across the street, the First National Bank's sign flashed the time: seven-thirty. He still had a whole night to whittle away before the morning meeting.

He missed Sylvia.

Oh, well. Higgy was a genius at straightening out messes and would likely have the whole thing ironed out by the meeting. "Sorry to drag you in from Connecticut," he'd say. Then Henry could be back in Sylvia's arms by lunch tomorrow. Maybe they could have dinner at Regina's to celebrate another disaster averted.

Sylvia waited until Henry was out of sight before releasing her tears. He'd be back soon. He'd promised. Something bound them anew—something more than business or corroded vows.

Since the evening held no prospects to lift her spirits, she grabbed two Lorna Doones from the opened package and slid them onto a plate. Then she put water on for tea. She heard faint snatches of conversation coming from the back hall. Had Henry left the television on? She should check.

When she came to the ballroom, she hesitated, and sniffed the air. A pungent but pleasant smell. Lilacs? She should thank Martina for her cleaning efforts. Sylvia stepped into the room, grateful for the absent chill. Not surprising. The temperatures had stayed above average for the past few days. When she came to the hall, the whispering stopped. The voices must have been only her imagination, fueled by the craziness since Henry had come home. As she returned to the kitchen, the flowery air seemed to trail behind her.

With Henry gone, calm had returned. Yet, she'd give up all her quiet nights to have him with her. She popped her lips with sudden realization. The scent was the same as the candles she'd lit last night. The aromatic mists must have seeped through the floor crevices into the ballroom and through the downstairs.

She steeped a peppermint tea bag, dunking it four times, and the mingling aromas produced a smile—Henry would've laughed at the fragrant juxtaposition.

How had Henry managed on his ride back to Manhattan? She'd worried for him. She'd tried to pry the details out of him, but he had refused to answer any of her questions, saying only, "The less you know the better." His ashen face meant the threat was serious enough. What if they lost everything? From somewhere in the recesses of her soul, she breathed a prayer they wouldn't. Funny how the desperate turned to God, a God she'd forgotten until Henry came back. Once her faith in God was important to her—a long time ago when the impossible seemed possible, when magic stemmed from a child's imagination.

She worried for Henry. Scented candles, peppermint tea, or Lorna Doones could never soothe the ache in her heart. What if he never came back? She climbed the spiral staircase like a drone to the mines.

CHAPTER 14

"Talk to me, Higgy," Henry said as he rushed into the conference room. "Please tell me I came here for nothing."

"Simmer down, Fitz." Higgy handed Henry a cup of coffee. "Maybe this will help. I'm guessing you haven't eaten anything this morning either." He picked up a gooey treat. "Here, have a turnover."

Henry took a sip of coffee, then raised his cup in gratitude. "Good coffee, but I'll pass on the turnover. Look, I need an explanation. I know you couldn't say much on the phone. Now, tell me why Evan North wants to ruin us?"

Higgy gestured Berkowitz to take over. "I'll let Berky explain. Mr. North seems to think one of our authors stole his work."

If he needed to give up his law practice, Berky could find a lucrative career as a sideshow attraction with a carnival. As short as he was stout, even standing, only his upper chest and head showed above the table. "I'm afraid this one isn't going to disappear quite so easily, Mr. Fitzgibbons."

Henry's fist fell hard against the table. People often described him as calm and collected during meetings. Not today. Today he could strangle a rhinoceros if it dared cross his path. Only Evan North could bring Henry Fitzgibbons to this level of bestiality.

He learned to quell his emotions after the Persian Gulf incident, refusing to react to fear. However, a fraudulent, fifty-million-dollar lawsuit made Henry's blood boil. Berky's worried face did little to amend Henry's predilections that Fitzgibbons & Associate had been wielded a potentially lethal blow.

"Why *can't* you fix this, Berky? So what if we acquired a story resembling a North epic. These things have happened before. Ideas are rarely unique, and North knows this. Are you implying he won't consider a settlement?"

Higgy cleared his throat. "I'm afraid North's attorneys have a viable case."

He scanned a mental roster of his authors. Not one of them seemed likely to intentionally plagiarize another author's story. Not even the atheist, Stanley Brewl, whose claim to fame was his strategic placement of foul language.

"Who's the author in question?"

"Fitz. You'd better sit down."

Henry took a swig of coffee. "Just tell me, Higgy."

"Lana Longstreet."

The hot coffee burned Henry's lips as he spat it out. He wiped the dribble with the back of his hand. "Tell me this is all a mistake. Sylvia doesn't need to cheat. She's far more talented than North ever thought he was. If by some stretch of the imagination she doubted her genius, she would never jeopardize North's friendship. He's her hero. Evan's books take up more shelf space in Sylvia's library than any other author, excluding Lana Longstreet, of course."

Henry searched Higgy's eyes and found sympathy. "Henry, I've known Sylvia nearly as long as you have. I don't believe for one minute she'd do something like this either. She's too careful to have plagiarized by accident. Even so, the evidence is pretty strong."

Higgy tossed Henry two books: *The Gathering Flock* by Lana Longstreet and North's *Fowl Weather*. "Read them both, Fitz. You'll see our dilemma."

Henry thumbed through the pages. Nine hundred total. Did Higgy expect they could both be read in one sitting? Henry tucked the books into his briefcase. "Berky, what's our current defense strategy?"

He flipped through a stack of papers and shoved a legal brief across the table. "I'm trying to buy us a little time. I've submitted a motion to dismiss, citing the lawsuit is frivolous. I doubt the court will throw the case out, but Judge Levine owes me a favor or two. I'm sure he'll postpone the preliminary hearing for as long as discreetly possible. However, unless we can prove Miss Longstreet's innocence, we're merely delaying the inevitable."

Higgy swung an arm around Henry's shoulder. "Fitz, Sylvia needs to know about this. Right away. I thought we should bring you up to speed first. Do you want to tell her or should I?"

"How? You've seen her temper. She'll find some way to blame me."

"She has to know, Fitz. Her integrity's on the line here. I know things haven't been the best between the two of you. Maybe she'd take the news better from me."

Maybe Higgy should be brought up to speed on his partners'improved relationship. No, wait. A pending reconciliation might complicate legalities and implicate him as well. The whole office knew Henry and Sylvia rarely spoke except to argue. Their estranged situation could provide a defense. As CEO, shouldn't he do all in his power to protect his company? If the accused were lesser known, North's complaint would have been reduced to a brief note in the tabloids. With the name Lana Longstreet as American as Noah Webster, the news media was certain to gobble up the story like piranha. If the world learned how much Henry loved his wife, collusion charges could strengthen North's accusations and bring further damage to Fitzgibbons &

Associate's credibility. He had other authors to protect as well as Sylvia.

He should stay in Manhattan until the issue was resolved. "I'll tell her, Higgy. She's still my wife. She'll be in Manhattan on Wednesday. No need to upset her until then."

Higgy shrugged his shoulders. "We'll do everything we can to keep the media hounds away from any scent about this business. Just don't wait too long, Fitz. Stories like these get leaked faster than you can say bankruptcy."

Henry walked toward his office through the cavalcade of cubicles where his few remaining in-house editors poured over manuscripts. For most of his staff, working from the comfort of their homes proved to be both convenient for his workers and financially beneficial to the company. Still, he missed the camaraderie of those early years before the industry changed so drastically. Sadly, within a few years, his company would be managed completely online.

Though Fitzgibbons & Associate still managed to operate in the black, the increase in smaller, computerized publishers had cut into sales. Not to mention the decrease in readership. If North's suit held, the business could not survive this large a payout, even if they settled out of court.

He walked past the few remaining desks, aware of the glares at his agitated clip.

"Hello, Henry."

He turned to meet the sultry voice tinged with a British accent.

"Hello, Monique."

"Shame Mr. Higgins had to drag you away from Connecticut."

Henry feasted on Monique's words—her savory voice as delectable as fine wine. His cheeks warmed. "Any messages?"

"You have quite a few piled on your desk. Mr. Higgins took care of the ones requiring an immediate response."

If he could fool Monique, he could fool Higgy. "Time I came back anyway. Miss Longstreet has everything under control in Connecticut."

"How's her newest book progressing? Sounds fascinating. Your wife is massively talented. Her characters jump off the page."

Henry caught himself paying more attention to Monique's blue sweater than her words. The tint matched her eyes. He loosened his tie, fearing he would expose his inner blush. "I'm sorry, Monique. My mind went away for a second. You were saying?"

"I wondered how Miss Longstreet's book was coming."

"Good. I guess. I haven't read any of it yet."

Monique's laughter rang like church bells. "Henry, you haven't read *any* of them."

How well she knew him—too intimately for propriety's sake. "You're wrong. I read her first published manuscript this week. Great book ... historical fiction. I couldn't put it down ... even brought a tear to my eye."

Monique peered at him, and he examined her stare, barely cognizant of Higgy's approach until Monique stepped back a few paces, her soft coo exchanged for robotic tones. Higgy handed her a stack of files. "Will you put these back, please?"

"Right away, Mr. Higgins. Anything else you need, Mr. Fitzgibbons?"

Henry re-straightened his tie. The tug reminded him of his renewed pledge to Sylvia. He'd never admit his sinful lust to anyone, and certainly he didn't want to admit Sylvia's jealousy was based somewhat on reality. True, he'd entertained fantasies about the prettiest secretary a man was privileged to have. He was human, after all, and Monique dripped sensuality like melted butter on a corncob. Thankfully, he'd never acted on those thoughts. If he betrayed his vows, he'd betray himself. Pop always said the thought equaled the deed. If that were true, Henry stood morally guilty. He had become the kind of old man he most despised—one who craved the illicit yet lacked the courage to pursue.

Henry examined Higgy's scowl. Perhaps Monique's flirtations, as well as Henry's appreciation for them, had not gone unnoticed.

"Mr. Fitzgibbons? You've drifted into your thoughts again. I asked if you needed anything else."

"No. I'm set, Monique. Thank you. Take the rest of the day off. The hurricane hasn't hit yet. Right, Higgy?"

He nodded as his glance followed her sashay toward the file cabinets. Did Higgy fantasize too?

"Higgy, they don't build secretaries like her anymore, do they?"

"Of course, they do, Fitz. But we're not supposed to notice. If we do, we're supposed to keep our appreciation to ourselves. The work place isn't what it used to be. I say, good for the gals. They deserve our respect, not our ogling."

"Politically correct as always, my wise friend."

Normally, the two of them engaged in winded philosophical discussion about temptations in the workplace, how women's styles made avoiding impropriety more difficult for their male counterparts. Instead, Higgy's weighted hand on Henry's shoulder implied they'd be discussing something else. "More trouble?"

"Look, Fitz. It's only fair I warn you. Berky just told me the local news found out about the lawsuit. He's trying to keep a lid on things, but you'd better get hold of Sylvia right away."

"You're right, of course. I'll call her. I don't want to drop this on her over the phone, though. I'll see if I can convince her to come into the city, break it to her over a nice dinner. Her tempers are more controlled in public places."

"Before Wednesday? Good luck."

"You might be surprised."

"For your sake, I hope so, old friend."

FROM JOHNNY GALLANT

C14

Johnny glanced about his cramped one room apartment. How he missed the guesthouse and Celeste's Olympic-sized pool. As much as he yearned for the spacious lawns, he longed for her more—to walk the garden paths with her, to stop below the moon's crescent and kiss her lips. He pined for the strawberry scent from her freshly shampooed hair.

He imagined he held her close and fantasized her head on his shoulder. In his dream, she confessed her fears as she did that night.

He had recognized the frightened girl subdued inside the confident actress, and they talked from dusk until dawn. Until then, Johnny supposed the glitter of Hollywood to be an intoxicating elixir for anyone.

Many celebrities had hired Johnny's team for a host of reasons. Most of the time his skills were bought to unearth secrets—secrets once revealed skyrocketing many a starlet to fame. Johnny's conscience had never been singed before. He managed to find justification for every lucrative proposal.

Until Celeste.

For her, the scrambling world of greed and lust was not an elixir ... rather a deadly poison. She was a butterfly trapped in the spider's web. Not able to kick free, she waited in helpless horror to be devoured.

Johnny understood the never-ending merry-go-round of countless responsibilities, expectations, and schedules. For him, the constant tension energized. He thrived on danger, uncertainty. These were the fodder for another kind of addiction more potent than heroin or wine.

For Celeste, the whirlwind sucked her life away like terminal cancer. Johnny wanted to ease her pain. He had pulled her into his will and captured the whole of her, and she held nothing back from him. Her love had fed his hungering soul. Still, he had crossed a dangerous line. He could not protect her and share her world at the same time.

She'd cried when he told her he'd turned the case over to Jimmy Holloway. Johnny pretended he'd lost interest in her. She must never know the depths of passion he felt for her. Yet, here in the solitude of his making, his eyes moistened.

CHAPTER 15

As good a place as any to stop. Did she really have to make Johnny move out? Conflict. Conflict. Conflict. Readers craved conflict. If she were writing the story for herself, she'd want Celeste and Johnny to be together. They complimented one another. He was darkness, and she was light.

Light ... Light ...

The image of Mrs. Julane popped into Sylvia's remembrance—a Sunday school teacher from years ago. Her hair was always pulled back into a bun, and she stood as straight as her morality. She'd wag a finger as she warned, "What business does light have with darkness, Sylvia Moore?"

Mrs. Julane knew. Lana Longstreet knew too. Johnny and Celeste were Romeo and Juliet, star-crossed lovers caught between their respective worlds, destined for a tragic ending.

Sylvia's stomach growled. Why must she stop creating just to eat? She missed Henry's attentiveness and disliked having to put her creative juices aside just to grab some food. So much easier when she was served.

The day had been as dull as she hoped. Sven, Gunnar, and Thor stayed with Martina's mother allowing the young woman to move about the house as efficiently as a hi-tech robot.

Sylvia's thoughts refused to be corralled and pranced like reindeer. She hadn't slept well the night before and kept rolling over to grab Henry's hand, but he wasn't there. She remembered he had left to take care of important matters, then she tossed with worry, dragging herself to her loft in the early morning hours.

Why did anyone want to sue Fitzgibbons & Associate? There had been threats over the years, and Paul Higgins always managed to find a solution with Berkiwitz's help. She shuddered as she recalled Henry's icy face. Apparently, this problem, whatever it was, wouldn't be so easy to fix.

Guilt replaced worry. She always let Henry bear the brunt of their business, the good and the bad, selfishly enjoying the fruit without the labor, although many argued her books were the greater contribution. But never actual work. Never a chore. Writing was her total world.

How many times did she complain about Henry's disinterest in her career? Then why was she as uninvolved in his?

Paul Higgins was the company's indisputable heartbeat. However, as CEO, albeit a figurehead, Henry shouldered fiscal responsibility. She wanted to help, to listen and stroke Henry's cheek with reassurance, to stand by him regardless of what happened to the company. Though they had enjoyed the pleasures of great wealth, she knew profits were dwindling these past few years with the mounting changes in the industry. Yet she maintained her extravagant lifestyle with little thought to the long-term impact her spending would have on the company.

Remorse curdled her stomach. Whenever Henry talked business, Lana Longstreet had pushed him away with her indifference. "Henry," she'd say, "you bore me to tears. Can't we change the topic?" Then she'd drone on for hours about her characters' plights.

What if the company went bankrupt? The possibility brought no fear for Sylvia, though Lana Longstreet would have palpitations. Sylvia giggled with the irony. If wealth had destroyed her marriage, poverty might save it.

She took the spiral staircase into the kitchen.

What to eat?

She found the leftover meatloaf on the top shelf of the fridge. She threw two slices on a plate and set the microwave timer, then drummed the countertop to the microwave's hum. Her gaze drifted to the back door where she glimpsed her extra laptop propped against the wall, the one she kept handy for those opportune times when she took the train or decided to write at one of the cafés in town. She'd often indulge her spirit by recording surrounding sights and sounds as well as descriptions of interesting people and places, passages she might utilize someday.

The microwave buzzer blared.

"That's it!"

Martina bolted into the kitchen. "Are you all right, Miss Longstreet?"

"Oh. I'm fine. It just dawned on me, is all. I don't have to wait until Wednesday."

"I don't understand."

Of course, she didn't. Rosalie would've nudged Sylvia toward the door.

Excitement fueled the idea. "I need to make a phone call. I'd like privacy, please."

Martina slinked away like a scolded puppy. The poor girl's first few days had been riddled with the unexpected. Sylvia determined to give Martina a substantial tip with her paycheck in spite of Lana Longstreet's indifference.

Taking a step toward her laptop, Sylvia halted when the landline rang. Should she answer? She examined the caller ID—Henry's office. Maybe he called with good news. "Henry!"

"I expected Martina to answer."

"Thought I'd take a lunch break. I was just thinking about you."

His breathing sounded heavy, as if the world had perched on his shoulders. "Look. If it's not too much of a disruption in your schedule, could you come to Manhattan tonight for the weekend instead of waiting until our usual Wednesday get together? You could stay at my apartment if you'd like."

If she'd like? Wouldn't he expect her to? "What's wrong?"

"Nothing."

"Something's wrong. I can tell by your pubescent squeak you're trying to hide something from me."

"I'd rather wait ... discuss it when you get here."

"No need to be so secretive, Henry. I do care, you know."

"I'm only beginning to realize how much."

"Very well, I'll have Erik bring me this afternoon."

"We could have dinner at Chez Philippe."

"I'd like that

"I expect to be here the rest of the day. Call me when you get to Manhattan. I'll meet you at the apartment."

"Sure. I'll be there soon. Henry ... we'll get through this, whatever this is. This time, I want to be there for you."

His silence thudded like a dropped brick. Mere words could never convey the depths of her regret, nor could Henry see her pool of tears.

"Sylvia, how are things there? Any more strange noises?"

"Not a peep since you left yesterday. In fact, the odor's gone. The ballroom feels toasty warm. We should give Martina a raise for all the extra work she's done."

"I ... I don't know what's going on. Martina told me she didn't have time to clean the ballroom. I told her not to worry ... the room could wait for a couple of days."

"Well, the smell could've been a mouse in the last stages of decomposition."

"There's also the possibility whatever interrupted us the other night knows I'm gone."

Why must Henry cling to these idiotic notions? Her house was no more haunted than a church. Lana Longstreet was set to blast obscenities at Henry, except Sylvia longed for Henry's embrace. She must tell him, though the saying of the words seemed as awkward as a first kiss. "Henry, I love you. You do know that, don't you?"

"I love you too, Sylvia. Hurry."

Sylvia set her suitcase down by the door. She'd wait until Henry came to unpack. She called Henry's cell, but it went straight to voice mail. Rather than leave a message, she called his office landline.

"Henry Fitzgibbons's office."

Someone should permanently silence that raspy English tongue. "Monique? This is Lana ... Mrs. Fitzgibbons. Is my husband there?"

Wolves marked their territory. She shouldn't fling her jealousy like canine urine.

"Hello, Miss Longstreet. Henry said you might call. I'll let him know you're on the line." Sylvia's pulse quickened as Monique spoke ... the girl—phony right down to her plastic shoes.

The tart put Sylvia on hold like an annoying customer.

"I'm sorry, Miss Longstreet. He can't come to the phone right now. He'll leave the office in about an hour. In the meantime, he wants you to make yourself comfortable."

Too busy to speak to his wife?

"Tell Mr. Fitzgibbons I'm holding him to that hour."

Monique hung up without so much as a laugh or another word.

Sylvia sat on the couch and thumbed through Henry's golf magazine.

Maybe she should consider taking lessons since Henry enjoyed the sport so much. With David's added responsibilities as a new father, he wouldn't have much time to play. Why couldn't she and Henry spend time together golfing? She analyzed Zach Johnson's stance. Putting the magazine to the floor, she mimicked his posture and took an imaginary swing. "Ouch." The pull on her back muscles might be a huge clue she wasn't built to swing like Zach Johnson. She tossed the magazine back into the wooden rack by the couch.

Maybe taking golf lessons wasn't such a good idea.

What should she do to pass the time? She despised television. She could whip out her laptop and plot sequels, but she'd vowed not to think about writing while she had this time with Henry. Her mind rattled like a half-empty cereal box.

She looked at the clock. The stores were still open. She could go to Nanette's and pick up a dress for Julie. Then she'd go to the maternity shop next to Starbucks to buy an outfit for Bonnie. On the way back, she'd pick up a bouquet of flowers for Henry's empty vase.

Inspired with a mission, she scribbled a note in case he came before she returned.

Gone shopping. Be back soon.

She giggled with the realization she hadn't left Henry a handwritten note in years. She added. *Love, Sylvia.*

Nanette Dubois's boutique was one of Sylvia's favorite places to browse. She sniffed the jasmine-laden air and brisked her way through the aisles of youthful fashions in search of an ensemble for a budding young artist, maybe something Julie could wear for her next gallery exhibit or a less exotic outfit to wear on a date.

The thought boiled over with a subsequent one. Why had Julie been so secretive about this new young man in her life? Some disembodied man with no name ... not even a mention of what he looked like. When Sylvia had told Mother about meeting Henry, she could have filled three pages of description. Mother had winked. "This is the one, Sylvia."

Was this the one for Julie? She hardly dated. That she mentioned the boy at all meant he was special. Patience would have to reign until she was ready to share, or until Sylvia could pry details out like one of her detectives. Maybe Julie was reluctant to say very much knowing her father would have their private investigator check him out.

Sylvia's gaze fell on a slick, tell-all, form-fitting tunic. Stunning, but did she really want her daughter to stand out like a model on display? Lana Longstreet might be interested in it for herself since she gravitated toward the slinky and bejeweled, something glamorous and fitting a romance writer.

Sylvia lifted her head toward the jewelry display and mentally matched stone-studded earrings and necklace. No. She rejected the idea, not wanting Lana Longstreet's selfishness to intrude on her original purpose for coming into the shop. She returned the dress to the display rack.

She peered at the two women by the counter. She recognized Nanette's flaming hair, her slight form, swallowed by an angry, obese customer who waved a blue-sequined blouse in front of the shop owner's nose. She darted to one side and narrowly escaped the woman's flailing arms. "Excuse me, Mrs. Florentine. I'll be right back. I'm certain we can work something out to your satisfaction."

Nanette rushed toward Sylvia, engulfing her with a gigantic hug.

Normally repulsed by public displays of affection, not even Lana Longstreet held any ill will toward the gregarious Nanette. After all, her exuberant interactions with her customers inspired the shopkeeper Louise in *Avenging Mandy.* "If you're busy, Nanette, I can wait. Or I can come back tomorrow."

Nanette released her death-defying squeeze. "I'll not hear of it. Mrs. Florentine's tantrum can wait. She's the most exasperating customer I've ever had. The blouse wasn't torn when she bought it, and I warned her the size was not right. She insisted on purchasing the blouse anyway."

Sylvia stored the image for a possible sequel. "We all like to think of ourselves in lesser terms when it comes to our figures."

Nanette muffled her laugh as she tossed her head in Mrs. Florentine's direction. "Some more than others. But you, Miss Longstreet, haven't changed sizes since the day you first came to my shop. How many years?"

"Do you want me to remind you?"

"No. My guess is more than twenty."

"It doesn't seem possible."

"So. What can I do for you today? Although, I'm surprised to see you out in public what with this scandal so new and all." Nanette sandwiched Sylvia's right hand in a sympathetic grip. "I want you to know, I don't believe a word the news is saying."

"I'm sorry. I'm afraid I don't follow."

Nanette offered an exaggerated wink. "I expected you to say that. Feel free to browse. Signal me if you need assistance." She scooted off to a more subdued but still irate Mrs. Florentine.

Sylvia's gaze caught a display of evening dresses on the other side of the counter. Maybe she could find something appropriate for Julie there.

As she examined options, a loud string of obscenities cracked the atmosphere. Apparently, Mrs. Florentine had found her second wind. She swept the counter with the blue-sequined blouse, sending a newspaper across the room and landing at Sylvia's feet.

She picked it up, her anger rising as she read the headline: *Lana Longstreet Implicated in Publishing Scandal.*

Henry had practiced all afternoon, and he recited his apologies again as he put the wildflowers he'd bought into the crystal vase, then dried his sweaty palms. He'd imagined every possible scenario how Sylvia might react, from the mildly upset to the most violently disturbed. Not one of his rehearsals entertained a pleasant ending.

This much he knew. Sylvia was innocent, and he must stand by his wife.

After he and Sylvia talked, he should call Higgy, tell him about the reconciliation, even if this made the company CEO look suspicious too. He vowed to put his wife's picture on his desk and crowd his office with reminders of his pledge ... push thoughts of Monique out of his head.

He tapped Sylvia's short note, rereading her signature. Would she still love him after he dumped all this madness on her? Would Lana Longstreet's personality rear and trample his manhood yet again?

He had hoped to be here when Sylvia arrived from Connecticut, but Berky had kept him on the phone too long with all his mournful predictions. Why didn't she wait? Oh well, might as well go over his pitch a few more times. He stood in front of his wall mirror, pinning his shoulders authoritatively while he mumbled a few canned phrases.

He sipped his café coffee for a few seconds, then resumed his rehearsal. "Sylvia, I've got some bad news."

No. No good. Ease into the negative. Be casual. Or wait until they had dinner at Chez Phillipe. Maybe she wouldn't be so angry if he showed a little attention before ripping her world apart.

The knob turned. Sylvia pushed the door wide open and stood in the doorway, a rumbled newspaper in her hand.

"Sylvia ... I'm glad—"

"What's the meaning of this?" A ball of newsprint flew across the room and landed like a cannonball on the floor.

Her volcanic rages usually followed a predictable pattern—sputter, spew, then calm. If he waited out the storm, then they could talk. Instead of her characteristic pre-explosive shakes, she paled and thinned like the misty caricatures in her ballroom. Barren of the hope he'd seen just yesterday, her eyes were lifeless, like sunken sockets on a dead soldier.

"Will you at least let me explain?"

She closed the door, then sat in his armchair—not the couch as he had envisioned—where he'd hold her hand before giving her a copy of North's *Fowl Weather*—Henry's segue into, "And he's suing us."

No recourse but to plow ahead. Henry paced as he confessed everything, how Fitzgibbons & Associate might become a footnote in history: *A publishing empire whose brief but notable existence featured the works of Lana Longstreet, perhaps the greatest romantic suspense writer of all time.*

Henry waited for the aforementioned legend to spring into action, hurl something, anything. Instead, Sylvia rose to her feet, far too composed. "How could you let this happen?"

But of course, she'd blame him. Then again, perhaps she should. Wasn't a CEO's responsibility to avert these kinds of disasters? "Sylvia, please be reasonable—"

"Reasonable? I trusted you, Henry. I thought you were intelligent enough to manage my work. My mistake."

True, he argued from a weak position, but Sylvia's stinging words knocked common sense aside. "There's never been a problem until now that I'm aware of."

"That you're aware of? Now why doesn't that reassure me?"

"I can't oversee every published book. We put out too many. I don't believe in micromanagement. I hire competent people to do their jobs."

"Competent? This is the worst case of incompetence I've ever seen." She held up Henry's copy of *The Gathering Flock*. "This isn't even my book. I've never written a story by this title."

Henry studied her eyes. Dry. Cold. Unforgiving.

"I stopped at the bookstore. I couldn't find a copy of *The Gathering Flock,* and no one at the store ever heard of it. Now, don't you find that a little odd? Evan and I always compete for the most prominent display shelf."

Henry pointed to Sylvia's name on the cover, and she scanned the first few pages.

"This isn't my book, Henry. I've never written in first person point of view. Someone in that conglomerate of yours should have picked up on that."

"I don't know how this book was published without more careful scrutiny." If only she'd screech, spew her anger, so they could move beyond this pointless ping-pong of blame.

She crossed her arms as she backed toward the door. Instead of shrieks, her tones were near whispers. "How many times do I have to tell you? I did not write this book. Someone else did and used my name. How could this happen, Henry? Tell me, how?"

He stopped pacing and sat at the far end of the couch, burying his head into his palms. "I don't know."

"I adore Evan North. Why would I jeopardize my friendship with him or copy *anyone's* work? Cheating is not on the list of Lana Longstreet's multitude of sins."

He knew the apology he offered was as shallow as a dry fjord. "I'm sorry, Sylvia."

"This never would have happened if you bothered to read any of my books."

"I read your first one."

"Really? One book out of sixty. How thoughtful. You've never liked my writing. Sometimes I wonder why you ever married me."

Every argument came down to Sylvia's disbelief that he loved her and his inability to offer a satisfactory response to her doubt. Can any man single out a reason why he loves a woman? Most men, Henry observed, never analyzed why a woman attracted them. A bee doesn't know why he picks a certain flower. They just buzz about and land. Women think love has a basis, a smile or a quality of character. The fact he didn't like to read fiction factored nowhere in his decision to marry Sylvia Moore. Henry Fitzgibbons loved her and didn't want to live without her.

"Look, go ahead. Blame me if it makes you feel better."

Henry planned to wait out Sylvia's ill mood, as he had done a hundred times before. Once her ire abated, she might let him comfort her. Her calm frightened him more than the most virulent episode he'd ever witnessed. His ready-made excuses were totally inadequate for the moment. He could give honesty a try. "What do you want me to say? I blew it? Okay, I blew it. I'm sorry, Sylvia. I'm sorry I let you down. I'm sorry I got you into this mess."

He expected her to toss a figurine, or even North's book, or throw the flowers into the trash. Instead of the dramatic, she offered a muffled sigh as she picked up her suitcase. "It's over, Henry. I'm spent with grief because of you. You've let me down for the last time. Please, don't call me. Refer any business matters to my attorney."

As she opened the door, she whimpered like a child wakes from a terrible nightmare, then turned, her tear-filled eyes meeting his confusion. "I don't know if this matters to you or not. Even after all we've been through, I still love you. I expect I always will."

In times past, Sylvia closed a door with resolute finality, leaving no doubt as to the extent of her disapproval. Instead, his marriage ended with a soft click.

FROM JOHNNY GALLANT

C20

"Hello, Johnny." Celeste appeared to him as if in a dream. Dressed in a white-sequined gown, a hallowed aura shone around her. "I'm so glad you came to the gala. It's good to see you again."

"I had to come."

Her eyes filled with tears. No matter if he had stayed or left, he caused her pain.

"I've missed you, Johnny."

Her face wore a question mark: *Why did you leave me?*

Nor could he give her an answer to the unasked with any amount of truth. He could cite company policy, safety precautions, and lofty principles. Celeste knew, as well as he did, these were excuses. If he removed himself from her professionally, then why did he take back his heart?

A woman like Celeste needed more than an occasional romp. She deserved commitment, fidelity. Johnny had faced deserts, floods, and fire, but feared this challenge more than any other.

A part of him wanted to marry her. These weeks without her revealed his barren condition. Before he met Celeste, men envied Johnny's self-confidence—his total satisfaction with a life lived alone. What now? He could not have her and be the man he was, nor could he lose himself so completely and not eventually despise her for turning him into a man he would surely become.

She'd asked for him to accompany her tonight. At least, during this gala, he could walk beside her, journey through the Academy Awards like a dutiful significant other. Come morning, he must distance himself once again. What business did gold have with slate?

Johnny's heart raced as she took his arm. He prayed to an entity he hoped existed, driven to the heavens, not sure of what any god could do for him, or even how to formulate his petition.

For Johnny, the concept of an all-powerful being prompted challenge, not worship. He'd shaken a defiant fist since the day of his birth. Forces connived to take Celeste away from him, and Johnny Gallant could not change himself enough to prevent losing her.

She exposed his empty soul, and he longed for her to fill it. He knew himself all too well. This selfish need for her was sure to twist their love into something unrecognizable, a sinister shadow of what should be. Johnny Gallant had destroyed the heart of everyone who loved him. What chance did Celeste have against his inner demons?

Again, he lifted a vague petition to an unknown God, begging him to shield her. Not from the man who threatened her life, but from the monster within Johnny's heart.

CHAPTER 16

Where did this inspirational bend come from? Totally unlike anything she'd ever written. Could Johnny's desperate plea to a higher power be a manifestation of his creator's own feelings of helplessness?

Lana Longstreet believed in God, a fashionable one to be manipulated in her stories. And as a child, Sylvia Moore attended Sunday school where she sang "Jesus Loves Me." Somewhere along the way, she stopped singing, and spiritual mysteries no longer held her in awe.

At what point did her faith crumble? Perhaps belief left her slowly and silently, from the days of her youth until the revelation of its loss, and left her soul depleted.

She should feel content with all the blessings life brought her—success, wealth, her children, and soon, a grandchild. She could learn to find fulfillment without Henry, for she'd lived half their marriage without him. The truth was her heart had been drawn and quartered. The threatened loss of livelihood paled in comparison to losing Henry.

The only hope she knew rested in a forgotten God. Though not in words, her heart threw out a desperate prayer. Suddenly, from somewhere in the loft, a bang ended her heavenly treatise. Over the years, she learned to tune out the occasional moans and groans, the heaving breaths of an old house. She turned back toward her computer.

The table shook. Pens launched from the holder and flung themselves across the room like thin, featherless arrows. Paper scattered in all directions as if tossed to the wind. A warm liquid bubbled on her arm ... she gasped at the quarter-inch paper cut. She rose to get a Band-Aid, but a gust from nowhere whirled through the room throwing pictures and decorations in every direction before they crashed to the floor.

A voice from deep within propelled her, a warning like Henry's agitated scream. "Sylvia, get out!"

In breathless retreat, she sped down the spiral staircase into the kitchen. The rattles grew painfully louder, and Sylvia covered her ears to drown the shrilling laughter, derision, insults driving her out of this sanctuary, chasing her through the whole house, mists pointing toward the ballroom.

Certain of her insanity, she gasped at the scene before her—shutters ripped from the windows and scattered through the sitting room. Common sense told her to leave the house immediately, but something inexplicably pulled her toward the front portico. When her hand touched the knob, the tumult ceased.

"Well, now." She'd have to stop watching *The Twilight Zone*. Another scare like this one might send her reeling right into the hospital. She peered out the side window at the graying clouds skittering across the sky and the torrential rain. "That's all it was. The wind knocked off the shutters, and a microburst funneled into the house."

She stared at the grand staircase. Did she dare go back to the loft? She took a step forward, stopping mid-step. Soft plunking chords, resembling those from a harpsichord, came from the ballroom. The music beckoned her with a power far more compelling than curiosity. She followed the harmonic summons like a trail of breadcrumbs until a sulfurous gas coated her nostrils. In her mind, she fled the scene. Why then, did she edge closer, sucked against her will toward the flickering, colored lights floating from the fireplace and bouncing off the walls?

Misty geometric forms burst through the flooring seams and zoomed upward, merging with the lights, taking on distorted human likeness. When the music stopped, their thick, bloodied bodies pointed derisive, bony fingers in her direction. They rushed at her, pushing, kicking, biting. Dozens of hands pulled her hair and scratched her face. Something pressed against her whole body, crushing her, robbing her of breath. In vain she flailed against the horde, finally surrendering to their abuse—her last conscious thought floated on the only word she could utter, "Henry."

Henry stopped reading the text and raised his head. Someone whispered his name as if carried on the breeze.

Sylvia.

Not possible. When she returned to Connecticut, she made her position quite clear—she wanted nothing more to do with him. Wooed by a restless spirit, he paced across the carpet, first back and forth, then up and down. He tried to sit, then rose and paced again.

Instinct has no rationale ... he simply knew. Sylvia needed help. He reached for the phone, then hesitated. She warned him not to call. What was the worst she could do if he did? Put a contract on him? Not likely. Her temper usually fell short of homicide. He punched in her landline first.

The answering machine picked up.

He tried her cell.

It went to voice mail.

He tapped an impatient foot while he waited for the prompt. "Sylvia. It's Henry. I know you don't want me to call. But, please let me know you're all right."

What if she thought Henry concocted his worry? She'd never return his call. If she were injured, could she get to a phone? He resumed his pacing. A familiar sense of foreboding accompanied this restlessness—the day Julie fell from the old conifer tree in the backyard, as he recalled. He had stayed in Connecticut over the Fourth of July for a launch party. While Sylvia hustled with last-minute preparations, he paced as he did now. He heard Julie's scream and ran outside to find her unconscious on the ground next to a broken limb. He sickened at the sight, thinking she was dead. He had swept her into his arms and wept, relieved when a raspy breath passed through her blue lips.

The memory jarred him to action, and he called Higgy.

"Look, old friend, I don't have time to explain, I've got to go to Connecticut. Now."

Henry gripped the door handle to keep his balance while Higgy broke every speed limit. Normally, the ride took an hour or a little more depending on the time of day. Higgy zipped in and out of Manhattan traffic and onto the highway in record time. His GPS had them arriving in an unheard of forty-five minutes. Perhaps he was as worried as his partner.

Neither spoke for what seemed like an eternity. Henry broke the silence just as they neared the exit to State Route 40. "Thanks for bringing me, Higgy. I know a good religious man like you doesn't believe in ghosts. But something's in the house—something evil. I shouldn't have left her."

Higgy bit his upper lip and stared straight ahead.

"I should have fought harder to keep us together. I let her go yesterday just like I did fifteen years ago. I should have begged her to stay. Do you know what she said when she left?"

Higgy shrugged his shoulders. "She's a writer. I'm sure she made a dramatic exit."

"But she didn't. She gave me this weird look and said she'd always loved me. What if those are the last words she ever says to me?"

"Don't get me wrong, Fitz. I adore Sylvia, and I'd like nothing more than to see you two put your marriage back together. Do you want me to pray with you?"

God might not hear the desperate plea from one Henry Fitzgibbons, but Higgy's prayer was sure to shake the foundations of heaven. "Yes. Thanks."

Henry expected Higgy to pull off the road. Instead, he blurted out his words with eyes wide open. "Lord, I come before you now on behalf of my friend, Henry Fitzgibbons. He's worried about his wife. I ask for your protection against whatever forces are at play in his house. You are a God who is unrestricted by time. You answer before we ask. So, we thank you for what you have already done. Amen."

"That's it? That's what you call a prayer? That's going to give me peace—a haphazard, off-the-wall petition like that?"

"Fitz, God's already working on a solution before we even know we have a problem. Trust Him."

Henry pounded his fist into the seat. He trusted no one, except maybe Higgy. "Simple enough for you to say. I can't, Higgy. More than anyone else, you know the depth of my sins. I do regret them, but how can a holy God forgive such horrible acts? I feel like all this is part of his judgment. I haven't deserved any of the good in my life, and I don't blame God if he takes everything away."

Higgy shot Henry a sympathetic glance. "Friend, how long will you despise God's love for you?"

Henry opened his mouth in rebuttal, but they had just pulled into the circular driveway. Henry jumped out and ran up the front steps into the house. He darted into the kitchen, then up the spiral staircase, breathlessly calling out her name. "Sylvia? Sylvia? It's Henry. Please, answer me. Sylvia?"

The loft was littered with chewed paper. Pens, pencils, and broken glass spotted the hardwood floors, and the computer had slid half off the desk.

With renewed urgency, he ran through the maze of the upstairs rooms, down the main staircase, gasping when he saw the shutters had fallen. He stopped by the ballroom. Sylvia lay in a motionless heap, covered in soot. He rammed against an invisible barricade and screamed like a helpless child. "Higgy, they've killed her!"

Higgy rushed in, penetrating whatever barrier held Henry back. With Higgy's lead, Henry was freed to follow and fell to his knees by Sylvia's side. He pressed two fingers against her throat. "She's alive, but her pulse's erratic. Better call an ambulance."

CHAPTER 17

Henry paced the hospital corridors for at least two hours. Nurses sped back and forth from rooms to stations. A few visitors approached the staff with questions.

"How's Mother today?"

"Any word on the tests the doctor ordered?"

Buzzers chimed and lights flashed on patients' doors.

Yet, no one acknowledged Henry's presence except Higgy, who maintained a steadfast vigil, walking beside Henry and keeping him supplied with coffee. The hours ticked by with still no word. Finally, a youngish man, wearing blue scrubs, seemingly not much older than David, poked his head into the waiting room. This lad must be a resident or an intern. Doctors should have gray hair and serene looks, not curly locks and engaging smiles.

"Mr. Fitzgibbons?"

News at last? "Yes?"

"I'm Dr. Rodriquez." He offered a handshake. Doctors, unless they were surgeons, shouldn't have such firm handshakes either. Made them seem too self-assured.

"How's my wife?"

"Resting comfortably at the moment. So far, her symptoms have me stymied. Although I don't think she's had a stroke, I won't know for sure until I run a few more tests. Her blood pressure was dangerously high when she came in, but she's stable for the moment. Also, the swelling in her arms and legs is beginning to ease. I am puzzled, however, about the raised red marks she has all over her body ... like flea bites. It looks as if she literally pulled her hair out in places, and there are a lot of bruises on her neck too. She denies anyone attacked her, but is it possible she tussled with an intruder?"

Good bet, Doc. "There's no evidence anyone broke into the house. We had an invasion of wolf spiders in the gardens. I suppose a few could have ventured into the house."

Dr. Rodriquez speared Henry with looks of doubt.

"I'm sorry, doctor. I can't explain her injuries either." *That is, I refuse to get into a paranormal discussion with a man almost half my age.* "What's wrong with my wife? Medically, I mean."

"To be honest, I'm not sure. I'd like to keep her overnight for observation—just as a precaution. She seems to be manifesting minor cognitive impairment. She flails at the air and tells the staff to make *them* go away. Has your wife ever hallucinated before?"

Best to leave the causal factors up to the doctor's imagination. "No. My wife is quite rational. She's a writer, Dr. Rodriquez. Please tell me her confusion's temporary. You have heard of Lana Longstreet?"

Dr. Rodriquez glanced at Sylvia's chart then scratched his head as if unable to make the leap. Henry explained. "I signed her in under her married name, but she prefers to go by her pen name."

If not for the seriousness of what had happened to Sylvia, the doctor's blush would be comical. "Your wife's Lana Longstreet? I didn't know. Well, yes. Of course, I can't say with any certainty until all the tests are in. I anticipate these symptoms are temporary." With an about face, he left at breakneck speed, probably to brag about his famous patient. Henry abhorred name droppers. Then again, if tossing around Lana Longstreet's name provided Sylvia with extra attention, what was the harm? Fame brought privilege.

Higgy returned with more coffee, and Henry recapped the doctor's report. "I'm glad you're here, Higgy. You're a good friend."

"Didn't I always promise I'd watch out for you? Besides, you're the one who saved my life during the war. Remember?"

Henry did remember ... all too well.

"I already called Julie and David. Don't know if I should call anyone else."

Higgy stroked his chin. "What about her mother?"

"Given her advanced Alzheimer's, I don't think I should call her. The last time we visited, she didn't even know Sylvia, let alone the rest of us. I suppose I could advise someone at the nursing home, and they can decide how much to tell Adele."

Henry combed his hair with his fingers. "I might as well go to the house for a bit. Do you mind dropping me off? Erik will bring me back if I'm needed. I'll call you as soon as I know anything."

"Of course."

"Higgy, I can't leave her alone in the house. It's too dangerous. I don't know what to do, and I don't want to dump this North business on your shoulders. My stupidity caused the mess. I don't like the commute, but I don't see any other choice."

Higgy took out his car keys. "As long as I'm the Associate in Fitzgibbons & Associate, I bear equal blame. We'll get through this crisis as we get through all of life—one day at a time."

Henry stopped at the nurses' station to make certain all the contact information was correct. A nurse came to the counter, and Henry handed her a list of phone numbers for

Syvlia's record. "I'm going home for a few hours, to make some calls and take care of a few things."

"Don't worry. Miss Longstreet's in good hands. Dr. Rodriquez is the best neurologist on the East coast."

"I'm certain he's well qualified." Henry turned to Higgy. "I'm ready."

They headed toward the elevator.

"Rosalie. I should call Rosalie too."

"I agree. Rosalie's family."

"I should have called her before this to see how she's doing."

Higgy offered a smile of reassurance. "Don't worry. No news is good news. Besides, she'll understand."

That much was true. As for Henry, recent events were a mystery, pressing against his mind like a hot iron to a garment. Could there be some design, some purpose to all that had happened? One truth remained at the core ... neither he nor Sylvia could go back to indifference. They both must move forward ... to what?

Henry squelched his worry ... Julie carried enough for the whole family.

"I'll book the first available flight I can find."

"Try not to worry, honey. Your mother's a strong-willed person, too stubborn to get sick."

"True."

"David's on his way to the hospital as we speak. Call me when you know your flight plans. And Julie?"

"Yeah?"

He hesitated. "I love you." The words stuck in his throat, but he forced them out with a hard breath.

"You okay? I've always known you loved us. Just seems strange to hear you say so."

"Get used to it."

"I love you too. Listen. I've got news to share. I want to wait until Mother's home."

"Julie—"

She hung up before he could manipulate her into telling him her secret. He hoped for some knee-slapping good news for a change of pace.

Henry checked off Julie's name on his call list. *Now for Rosalie.* He punched in her number, expecting Delbert to answer.

"Howdy-do?"

"Rosalie, what are you doing out of bed?"

"Good grief, Henry. I'm as fit as a fiddle. Can't wait to get this here cast off. Slows me down too much. Somethin' tells me you weren't calling to check up on me."

He wished he had. "I'm sorry Rosalie. I should have called before this."

"I heard of your troubles, Henry. It's all over the news. Can't keep a thing that big a secret. I'll have you know, Delbert and me have been prayin' for both of you."

Until he heard her voice, he hadn't realized how much he missed her sauciness.

"Miss Longstreet's the reason I'm calling. The doctor thinks she might have had a slight stroke." He explained the concerns, leaving out the invisible wall and chewed paper. Rosalie already pegged him as teetering on the edge of insanity. "I thought you'd want to know."

"Anything I can do, Henry?"

"Not really. Thanks for the offer."

"I can keep prayin'."

Was the whole world piling up petitions on his behalf? Strange how the thought brought him comfort now when he had sworn off God for more years than he could count. "All prayers are appreciated."

He clicked end call and scrolled down to Stingray, scanning for something other than rock, and saw the category, Classical Christian. Why not? The first song up was *The Old Rugged Cross*. Yesterday, he'd have passed over anything religious. He recalled a time long ago when Pop stood by a lectern, telling a spiritually hungry congregation how much God loved them while the organ softly played his father's favorite hymn.

Many who had crossed Henry's path professed faith— Pop, Higgy, Charlie, Erik, and Rosalie. He wished he could believe in a *good* God, that the Universe balanced good and evil. A God who cared for him personally, like Pop preached, seemed beyond the realm of credibility. If that was God's true nature, why did he permit so much evil?

His cell vibrated with an incoming call. He worked hard to keep his voice calm, afraid to reveal his unsettled self. "Fitzgibbons, here."

"Mr. Fitzgibbons? This is Alva Gonzalez from St. Raphael's. I promised I'd call. Your wife's awake."

Henry waited for Erik to park the car. When he returned, they rode the elevator to Sylvia's floor. "I vait in lounge room for you. Ja?"

"Thanks Erik. You're a good man."

Sylvia sat upright in a bedside chair when Henry entered. He had steeled himself against the probable hostility. "Henry, you shouldn't have brought me here. All I need is a little rest, something I can do at home."

"Now don't get mad, Sylvia." He drew up a chair. "You were barely breathing when we found you, and the house looked ransacked—like someone had a huge temper tantrum. How do you explain your rash and those bite marks?"

"I don't know what happened, Henry. I'm sure you're making too much of things. I tell you, I'm fine. Dr. Rodriquez just left, and he says I can go home tomorrow if all the tests come back okay. No need for you to play the hero. Besides, I'm far too busy to have a stroke. Simply not doable."

She shook as she attempted to pull a blanket around her shoulders. No matter how much she might deny the truth—she was visibly upset by her ordeal, whatever it was. When Henry reached to assist, she pushed his arm away. "I don't need your help, Henry."

Must you be so blasted independent, woman! He sat back down in defeat. "The nurses said Dr. Rodriquez's the best in his field, so if he thinks you're okay, who am I to argue?"

"He did say I should have someone stay with me. That's silly. I'm not a child, and I don't need babysitting."

"I'll stay, Sylvia."

"No need to put yourself out on my account."

"It's not a bother. You're my wife."

Her eyes closed, and her body stilled. "I can't talk right now, Henry. I want to go back to sleep. I'm tired."

Dismissed again and discussion terminated, Henry stood and put his chair back against the wall. "I'm going to the house. Julie's plane is due in at eight."

"You shouldn't have alarmed the children. Although, I'll be glad to see Julie. David stopped by earlier. I sent him home. I don't want coddling."

Henry shrugged his shoulders and left the room. If he said anything more, he'd ignite another domestic battle he'd be sure to lose. He should verify Sylvia's report. Not one to tell a deliberate lie, she often bent the truth for her convenience. He stopped at the nurses' station. "Is Dr. Rodriquez available?"

An older woman scrolled on a computer, then finally raised her head enough to see who asked the question. "He's nearly done with rounds. If you'll have a seat in the waiting room, I'll let him know you'd like to speak with him."

"Thanks."

Henry found the last available seat in the lounge where Erik the Good leaned against the wall. Not surprising. He wasn't the sort to take a seat away from a patient's relative. "Do you mind picking up my daughter at the airport, then coming back to the hospital to pick me up?"

"I vill, Mr. Henry." Erik donned his hat and left.

Henry flipped through a stack of magazines on the table next to his seat. His eyes fell on the Gideon Bible to the right of the magazines. On an impulse, he picked it up while trying to remember the last time he bothered to read from any Bible.

Pop's funeral.

Mother had insisted Henry read his father's favorite passage. The words burned anew: *Let not your heart be troubled.*

The years failed to answer the question young Henry put to God that day. Why did he permit such senseless acts? A man goes to buy a carton of milk at the corner store and ends up being killed in a robbery. Wrong place at the wrong time.

Henry stood at grief's door once again, mourning his marriage. Not that he blamed Sylvia for wanting a divorce. He'd never been a good husband, and he'd earned every morsel of her animosity.

"Mr. Fitzgibbons?"

"Oh, Dr. Rodriguez. I didn't see you come in."

"Let's go somewhere to chat, shall we?" Henry followed the doctor across the hall into a consultation room.

"Your wife seems to be in good physical condition. As I said earlier, I can't find any rational reason for her spell. Could be she simply fainted as she claims, and perhaps hit the fireplace when she fell. That could explain some of her bruises and marks. As for the bite marks, your wife promised to call an exterminator when she gets home, which she's adamant should be tomorrow. I have no reason to keep her in the hospital. She can leave in the morning."

"Thanks, Doctor."

"I'm curious, though, Mr. Fitzgibbons. Has your wife been under any stress lately, besides this recent scandal?"

Yeah. She's been terrorized by eighteenth-century fiends. "Possibly. We don't actually live together. I don't know everything about my wife's personal business. Why do you ask?"

"I served in Afghanistan, and I saw husky men develop heart trouble from sheer fright. Extreme stress can cause all manner of physical symptoms from shortness of breath to ulcers. I recommend your wife get some counseling."

"I will be staying at the house for a while, at least ... until I'm sure she can manage by herself. I can't promise she'll see a shrink, though. My wife's an indomitable woman."

"So I noticed."

"Thanks, Dr. Rodriquez."

Henry left the floor, took the steps to the main lobby, then stepped outside to wait for Erik. He wondered about the doctor's recommendations for Sylvia to see a psychiatrist. Could counseling for either of them unravel the knotted mess their lives were in? Not likely.

He punched in Higgy's number.

"Higgy? It's Henry. I've decided to stay in Connecticut. I'll have Erik drive me into the city as needed."

"Your call. Although, a commute for a claustrophobic like you won't be easy."

"I'll pay Martina extra to stay with Sylvia when I'm away. And I'll rent a car for her because Erik won't be available to bring her back and forth. It's the right thing to do."

"I suppose."

"Do you mind bringing me to pick Sylvia up tomorrow? Sunday's Erik's day off, and I hate to ask him to miss church. Besides, I think she'll take the news about me staying at the house better if you're there."

"Henry, you're absolutely right."

CHAPTER 18

Sylvia glanced at the wall clock. Erik should arrive any minute now. She shouldn't have agreed to stay overnight in the hospital. How could she possibly make up the lost word count? The petite volunteer smiled while she helped her charge into a wheelchair, then covered Sylvia's lap with a hospital blanket. "It's a little cold outside, and I see you didn't bring a coat. This will keep you warm. Who's coming for you?"

"I expect my chauffeur soon. My daughter's staying with me for a few days."

"That's good. Dr. Rodriquez prefers you don't stay alone—in case you have another spell."

Lana Longstreet reared, bragged, and lied. "My dear girl, I'm rarely alone. I have servants, you know." The volunteer straightened like a bristled porcupine, feet readied for a quick getaway. Sylvia softened. She hadn't needed to be so snooty. "Thank you for your concern, though."

"I'll tell the nurse you're ready for your discharge papers." The aide put the wheelchair on lock, exited the room, and left her patient's back to the door. Sylvia grunted. Lana Longstreet preferred to meet the world head on.

Might as well put the unpleasant experience to good use. How would Johnny Gallant react to a hospitalization? Seeds of a sequel formed ... *Stroke of Genius*. A good title.

"Hello, Sylvia."

With her back to him, Henry couldn't see her tears. "What are you doing here? Why isn't Erik driving me home?"

"It's Sunday. Erik hoped to go to church. I told him we'd pick you up."

"We? Is Paul here too?"

Paul leaned over the back of her wheelchair and kissed her on the cheek. "Hello, Sylvia. I see you're more yourself today. I hope you don't mind riding in my Lexus. Not quite as sporty as your Porsche, but it has a back seat. I threw a pillow in for your comfort."

"It's a ten-minute ride, Paul. You needn't worry about my comfort."

A nurse wedged her way into the room. Turning the wheelchair around to face the hall, she reviewed Dr. Rodriguez's instructions, including a follow up appointment in two weeks.

Feign agreement and cancel in the morning.

"Do you have any questions, Miss Longstreet?"

"No. I don't think so."

Offering a sweet smile, the nurse gave Sylvia the written instructions. "Goodbye, Miss Longstreet. I'm a huge fan, you know. I look forward to your next book." Then she hurried out the door, and the volunteer helper reappeared. "I'll give you a ride down."

The two men trotted behind her like an entourage. The volunteer helped Sylvia into the backseat of Paul's Lexus, then spun off, probably relieved to be free of the tension. After the men got into the front seats, Henry turned toward her, his face firm with unfamiliar insistence. "Get mad if you want to. I'm still your husband, and I'm putting my foot down. I will not have you staying alone in that house—especially after the last two incidents. You have one of two choices. Either I stay with you, or you're coming back to the apartment with me."

"Henry, I'm in no mood for your jokes—"

"There's no room for debate, here. Now, tell Higgy where to take you."

Too tired to argue, she'd have to put up with Henry until he got it out of his head she might be in danger. Sir Lancelot would never leave his queen. "Home."

As Paul eased the car into traffic, she leaned back against the seat, still not wanting to give up the fight. "Henry, you are out of your mind. How can you stay at the house and still take care of business? Have you forgotten we're being sued?"

Henry's jaw clenched. "Erik can drive me into the city as needed. I've arranged to rent a car for Martina so she can stay with you when I'm gone. David has agreed to serve as backup for Sundays, if needed, so Martina can go to church."

"You commute? What about your claustrophobia? You'll be in the hospital next with acute anxiety."

"I'll take a sedative if I have to. You'll not talk me out of this."

So, Henry wanted to play Johnny Gallant after all. Pure lunacy. Lana Longstreet's laugh sounded sinister even to Sylvia. "You're going to protect me? Henry, you can't even aim a flyswatter?"

He growled. "Your sarcasm won't change my mind either."

And Henry accused her of being dramatic. "How am I supposed to get any writing done with all this traffic in and out?"

"We'll see to your privacy. If you still want a divorce, I won't stand in your way. Until this lawsuit is settled, and we know what'll happen to the house, I refuse to leave you alone."

The house? Of course, the house was an asset. If they lost the lawsuit, the court could attach the home for payment of the claim.

She put the pillow behind her head and leaned back. "I see this argument's unwinnable right now. Very well, Henry. I won't oppose you as long as you stay out of my way."

Henry snorted.

Paul blushed.

Henry continued his case. "Sylvia. It's a big house. I promise to stay out of your way as much as possible. Besides, I'd like to see the landscaping project through. And the improved gardens will increase the value of your house."

My house?

Why wouldn't Henry take any ownership? Sylvia's head ached, and the refueled anger pulsated through her veins. Did he assume she bought it for herself? Well, he might as well know now. "It's your house too, Henry."

He clenched his teeth. "I hardly think so. You used your own accounts."

"But you've never seen the deed, have you?"

"What are you saying?"

"I put both our names on it. Surprise! You're the proud owner of a two hundred and sixty-year-old colonial mansion."

Henry turned away. "No, I didn't know."

If she must sacrifice her home, Henry should feel the loss as much as she would. Once she had been so full of hope. The memory brought tears to her eyes, and she turned her head away before Paul could see her in the rearview mirror. She had rushed home after she signed the deed, full of excitement, a hoped-for-moment as sweet as when she announced her first pregnancy. Instead, Henry stormed through the apartment, accusing her of unfaithfulness. "I know you never wanted a part of Connecticut. I just thought you should know the house has always been yours, even though you refused to cherish it as I have."

No one spoke again until Paul parked the car in the circular drive. "Now, if you two can manage to stop bickering for a few seconds, maybe Henry could help you into the house."

"I don't need any help, thank you." She got out, slammed the door, then marched into the house where she could release her pent-up tears in privacy.

"Mother? Are you okay?" Julie rushed up to meet her. "Where's Dad?"

Tears would have to wait. "He's right behind me. I'm so glad you're here. I've missed you so."

"Dad didn't tell you? I have to fly back tomorrow morning. I will be back in August though for the big anniversary bash. I'm so excited. David and I have been planning this for months."

Sylvia hoped her disappointment over Julie's short visit didn't show. She'd try not to argue with Henry, for Julie's sake. "Well, let's have a cup of tea. Tell me all about this art show, and, of course, this young man you wrote me about. Really, the scant details you've provided wouldn't even fill back cover copy."

Julie smiled. "And did you tell Dad?"

"He knows there's a boy you like. Nothing more than that."

Sylvia led Julie into the kitchen.

She patted the counter and pulled up a stool. "You sit here, Mother. I'll make the tea." She set the water on to boil, then continued. "I've got some news."

"Oh! You sold your painting, the one with the farm. I hope you got a good price for it."

Julie smiled. "No, I wish I had, though. At least since I'm here, I don't have to make the announcement in an email or text. Sort of happened suddenly, about a week ago."

"So, tell me, already!"

Julie's cheeks glowed like Johnny Gallant's waitress, excitement pinking her cheeks. She was in love.

"I've been anxious to tell you but was waiting for the right time. Seems like, where you and Dad are concerned, there's never a right time."

"Well, tell me now, and we'll let your father know later."

"This boy I wrote to you about ... he came out to see me last week." Julie flashed a small diamond ring on her left hand. "I'm engaged!" Instead of empathy for her daughter's joy, Lana Longstreet fumed as she gazed at the puny ring. Julie's fiancé apparently did not come from money. Hopefully, he at least had a job with some prospects.

Sylvia managed a smile. "I guess this is wonderful news. But are you sure he's the one? You've only known each other since February."

"Nonsense. You and Dad only knew each other a few months before you got engaged, and didn't wait very long before you got married."

"True."

"I know you and Dad will like him. I've invited him to the party in August, so you can meet him then. We're getting married in October."

Sylvia forced a smile, pushing Lana Longstreet's snobbery aside for the moment. How could she not wish her daughter happiness? One thing was certain. With an October wedding, no way could she divorce Henry before late fall. Julie didn't deserve the tension and uncertainty a divorce would bring to ruin her special day.

Motherhood demanded Sylvia share in her daughter's exuberance. "So what is my future son-in-law's name? Where's he from? I only know you met this charming fellow on a cruise. Tell me everything. You know how I adore a good love story."

As Julie talked, Sylvia marveled at her daughter's radiant face. Julie hadn't rattled on about a boy since her high school prom. Then the boy was Anton Galloway, a fashion model Henry knew from New York City. Sylvia had never told Julie her father arranged for them to meet. So uncharacteristic of Henry ... a very unpredictable thing for him to do. Anton and Julie did hit it off splendidly but wisely broke up when they headed for different colleges.

This aura hovering over Julie held familiar hues. Sylvia recalled how she bubbled all night when she told her parents how Henry proposed.

"His name's Jonathan Delaney," Julie purred. "He has the most delicious blue eyes I've ever seen on a man."

"I like him already. Tell me more."

"I told you I met someone on the cruise ... how incredible is that? We took the same rock-climbing class." Julie answered the call of the teakettle without missing a beat. "We have so many things in common, it's creepy." She placed three tea bags into the teapot, filled it with boiling water, then placed the teapot on the counter. "There. We'll let it steep for a few minutes."

Sylvia watched Julie's movements with awe, her confidence surprising since she'd grown up with everything handed to her. Perhaps living on her own had domesticated her. Maybe her fiancé's lack of money would be no problem ... at least not for Julie.

"Tell me more about your Jonathan. Where does he live?"

"Right here in New Haven. Can you believe it?"

"No!"

"Yeah. I go on a cruise and meet a man from my hometown. How incredible is that?"

"Pretty incredible."

Too incredible, Julie. Sylvia shivered with sudden worry.

A million miles into dreamland, Julie plunked an unopened package of Lorna Doones unto a plate, then slid it across the counter. Perhaps making tea was the limit of Julie's newfound homemaking skills. "You do still like Lorna Doones, don't you?"

Sylvia acknowledged with an enthusiastic nod. "So, what kind of work does Jonathan do?" Judging from the size of Julie's ring, he probably wasn't in a lucrative occupation.

"In a way, he's an artist like me."

Sylvia opened the package of Lorna Doones. They tasted better when shared over tea and a love story. "What does he paint? Landscapes—like you?"

Julie laughed. "I meant it figuratively. Actually, he's a writer—like you."

Sylvia grasped Julie's hand in feigned approval. "Well, then, I shall have to adore him, won't I?"

"He's been working on a novel and published two short stories in *Atlantic Monthly*."

"I *am* impressed. What does he write?"

"Action and mystery interwoven with romance. He's a great fan of yours. His stories border more on suspense than romance. Like his boss's."

Intuition sparked a new fear. "His boss?"

"Evan North. Jonathan's his assistant. I'm surprised you don't know him."

CHAPTER 19

Henry had gone around the back into his room to avoid the ballroom and to give the women their space. Why hadn't the architect designed a way to the west wing without having to go through the ballroom? He'd entertained an idea of having a contractor construct a hallway to the old servants quarters from the foyer. Why hadn't he asked Sylvia about the concept?

Oh, well. Moot point now. They shouldn't invest anything more in the house until they knew which way the lawsuit would go.

He had wanted to ask Julie about her life, her hopes, her dreams, matters he should have talked to her about before she left for college. Five years too late was better than never, though there was no opportunity last night. She'd sealed herself in her room by the time he'd come home from the hospital.

Excuses still managed to erode his vow to live life differently. She rarely came to Manhattan since leaving for college and then moving to California. Julie's last visit had been during her spring vacation of her senior year of high school, and she spent most of her time in New York visiting art galleries. While in the apartment, she did nothing but sulk because she didn't have a date for the prom.

What's a father to do? He'd met Anton the week before during a book cover photo shoot. Since he was the right age and liked art, why not introduce the two of them? Of course, slipping Anton a hundred dollars to take Julie to the prom didn't hurt. Turned out pretty well.

Unfortunately, the role of heart mender fell way beyond Henry's purview most of Julie's life. He'd ask Sylvia about what Julie had to share ... if his wife ever decided to talk to him again.

Let Julie and Sylvia have their mother-daughter moment. How he wished he could connect with Julie as easily as Sylvia could. Perhaps their connection was deeper than parent-child. Each was an artist in their own right— something foreign to Henry's psyche.

Perhaps his love of sports was the driving force behind his better relationship with David. At least with him, there were many fond memories of his visits to New York, taking in a baseball, football, or hockey game. Henry would hurriedly slot David's visits into his calendar the moment he was told. Some things were worth suffering the maddening crowd.

Tap – tap.

Henry froze until he realized the sound came from Sylvia's raps on his outside door and not the ballroom.

Surprised she had taken the back path, he let her in. She stormed to the opposite end of his room, plopping into a side chair, then crossed her arms and legs, her eyes twice their size—frazzled to near despair.

"Henry, we have to talk!"

"I'm not sure we should. Every time we do, we end up arguing."

"It's Julie. Did you know she's getting married?"

At Sylvia's news, Henry sat on the bed, dumbfounded.

"I didn't know she was seriously seeing anyone, just a mention of a boy she met on her cruise. She didn't say much about him. Is he the one? When did you find out?"

"Just now. I didn't know she was serious about anyone either. I sent her upstairs to pack. She has an early flight tomorrow morning and wants to bring some clothes back with her. I told her I couldn't wait to tell you the good news."

"Is it good news, Sylvia? You don't act like its good news."

She scowled. "Have you mentioned the lawsuit to her?"

"No. David heard about it on Channel Six News. Julie doesn't read a paper or watch television. I suppose she should hear it from us. But who is this mystery man who dares propose without coming to me first? Is there no sense of propriety left in the world?"

"Get over it, Henry. You never asked my father."

"Oh, but I did. He just never told you. He liked me, you know. Sports man too."

"And that's the measuring stick Daddy used to deem you worthy of his daughter's hand? I hope you don't use the same protocol to size up Julie's fiancé."

"How I assess the man wanting to marry my daughter remains to be seen. Suppose you tell me what you know. Then I'll decide ... after I have a sit down with the young man, of course."

Sylvia rose and paced, her face red ... anger ... worry? Normally about this stage, she picked up the nearest object and smashed it into a wall. Thankfully, she'd come for help, not confrontation, and skipped over the part where she told him she'd married the most clueless man on the face of the planet.

"Have you ever heard of Jonathan Delaney?"

"I don't think so. Why? Is this who Julie wants to marry?"

"Henry, must you be so dense? Yes. And he works for Evan North."

"And you've never met this Jonathan Delaney? I thought you and Evan were tight."

"No. I wasn't aware Evan had an assistant. The way he brags on himself, I assumed he did all his own work. Of course, I adore Evan, though he's large on ego and short on acknowledgements. He doesn't even include them in his books."

Henry sighed. Things kept getting more and more complicated. If this Jonathan was somehow involved with Ethan's scheme, how would this complicate life for Julie?

Sylvia's smile was more of a sneer. "I figured you'd eventually see the dilemma we're in. What are we going to do? I wish his working for Evan were a simple coincidence … why can't I?"

"Maybe because you're finally seeing what a snake Evan North really is."

Her eyes moistened, her hard exterior tenderized by her little cub's possible danger. Now perhaps Evan North would taste the torrent of a Lana Longstreet tirade.

"Henry. I can't bear to see Julie hurt over this. I'd do anything to shield her from pain, but I'm afraid my daughter will be caught in the middle no matter what we do."

Henry bristled. "She's my daughter, too, Sylvia."

"Let me talk to Julie. She has your courage, Sylvia. She might surprise us both. I'll ask Higgy to get our private detective to investigate Jonathan right away. Julie's too smart to get mixed up with a crook, even innocently. And she's a good judge of character."

Sylvia turned away. Why couldln't she even face him? "What if your private detective finds out Jonathan's tight with his boss? What then?"

"We tell Julie the truth. She's a grown woman, able to draw her own conclusions."

"I hate to admit when you're right. I'm going up to talk to her now."

"She should hear this from both of us."

Sylvia nodded.

Henry dared take a step closer. "How much do we tell her about us?"

"I haven't changed my mind about the divorce, Henry. Though we'll have to put up a front for a while longer."

For Sylvia, the die had been cast. Why did he, a man who didn't believe in them, still hold out for a miracle? "Do you want to go up now?"

She led the way outside, along the cobbled paths, through the kitchen, up the spiral staircase, through the catacombs of her chambers, to the children's old rooms. Henry smiled to himself that she again avoided the ballroom. For his benefit or hers?

As they walked, he silently rehearsed what he'd say to Julie. How does a father tell his daughter the man she loves might be a fraud? He couldn't spurt out, "Julie, I hear you're getting married. Oh, by the way, your fiancé's a liar."

Julie's door was already opened. Henry gulped. She was throwing clothes into a suitcase with enough force to shake her bed. When he and Sylvia approached, Julie looked at them with tear-swollen eyes as the radio blared, "Coming up next, the latest on the dueling authors, Evan North and Lana Longstreet."

Too late. Now what? "Julie, I didn't want you to find out like this."

"Well, I did. And it hurts."

He wished her back to infancy when he bounced her on his knee and played the Friendly Giant who solved all her problems.

"Dad, I stayed in all night, and we hardly talked. Why didn't you tell me Evan North was suing you and Mother? I hate it when you treat me like a kid. I feel like such a fool. Jonathan never told me either."

Best to let Sylvia take the lead since the two women operated on the same wavelength.

Sylvia sat on the bed and motioned for Julie to sit too. "Sweetheart, things have been rather hectic around here."

"I know, Mother. I should have told you about Jonathan before this, but I was afraid you might not approve. He doesn't have much money."

Henry plunged in. "I'm going to have our private detective do some digging."

Julie shook with anger ... so much like her mother. "You can't be serious, Dad. You're going to investigate my fiancé? How could you? Jonathan's too sweet and kind to do anything nefarious."

Henry had known a few women who he might characterize as sweet and kind. Not exactly adjectives he'd use to describe a man, especially one who could stomach working for a snake like Evan North.

"Think about the facts, Julie. You took the cruise in February, and you haven't known Jonathan for very long. You have to admit ... this is an awfully big coincidence."

Julie pitched a pair of shoes into the wall. "This rots."

"Honey, we only want to protect you."

"From the most wonderful man in the world? I finally find someone who loves me, and you two ruin my life by getting into a fight with his boss."

"Calm down, Julie. We didn't get into this mess on purpose."

Julie fell into her mother's arms. "What should I do, Mother? I love him."

"Do whatever your heart tells you."

Probably best to retreat since Julie obviously wanted only her mother. Henry stepped into the hall, feeling as useless as ever. He pulled out his cell phone. "I'll call Higgy right now. And Julie? Your mother's right. We don't expect you to make a choice between us and Jonathan. I just hope you can at least try to understand our point of view. We have to know his complicity in all this."

Henry managed to find the way back through the maze, down the spiral staircase, and into the kitchen as he punched in Higgy's number. "Higgy? Henry. You're not going to believe this."

CHAPTER 20

Henry rebuked the rain, but the deluge continued, buffeting against the diner windows, rattling the wet panes. The bustle of busy waitresses darting in and out of the kitchen added to the din.

David looked at Henry across the table as he raised his voice. "Looks like the rain's gonna keep up all day." He scanned the menu. "I think I'll have the lumberjack special. What do you want, Dad? My treat for once."

A short, but full-figured coed approached and stood in front of David as she tapped an order pad. "Hello, Coach Fitzgibbons. What'll ya have?"

"Could you give us a sec more, Bernie?"

"Sure thing." The perky brunette dodged several round serving trays as she headed to another table.

Henry, startled at the girl's familiarity with David, studied her as she zoomed back to the kitchen and quickly returned with a pot of coffee, practically hopping from table to table to refill. He leaned over the table and whispered to David, "Is that Bernadette Brown?"

"Sure is. She graduates in June."

"What lucky college is getting her?"

"Yale offered her a full scholarship, so she's decided to stay right here in town. Word is, she plans to turn pro next season. Would you believe she did her practice round yesterday with only fourteen putts? The girl's amazing."

"You've done a great job, Coach."

"Thanks."

Henry took a sip of coffee, then put his cup down. "I still think it's a shame you didn't turn pro yourself. You had the talent, son."

David leaned against the back of the booth. "Not too late. Maybe after Patrick's born ..."

"Patrick?"

"Didn't I tell you? Well, we're hoping for a boy. We decided to name him after his two grandfathers—Patrick Henry Fitzgibbons."

"Hope he doesn't grow up to give long-winded speeches. Are you priming him to be a politician?"

Bernadette returned as David let out a loud laugh.

"What's so funny?"

"My father, here, Bernadette, thinks he's a comedian."

"Your father? Thought he was your brother?"

Henry blushed.

"Ready to order now?"

Henry glanced over the menu. "I'll have the two-by-two-by-two deal with bacon."

"How do ya want your eggs?"

"Over easy," and David joined him for the rest, "Homemade toast and a small orange juice. Coffee now." He handed Bernadette his menu, then leaned in with a laugh. "Have you ever done *anything* differently in your whole life, Dad?"

Probably not very much. "I happen to like bacon and eggs. Rosalie used to make them for me every time I visited. Sure do miss her."

David closed his menu. "I'll have the lumberjack special. And be sure I get the check"

Bernadette scribbled the orders. "Sure thing, Coach. Enjoy your breakfast." She tucked her pencil behind her ear and sped off to a nearby table.

David snickered. "I get tired just watching her."

Henry peered at David's scruffy cheeks and chin. "In a hurry this morning, son?"

"Didn't get much sleep last night. Bonnie's having a lot of gas and can't sleep. Her tossing and turning keeps me awake." He yawned as if to prove a point. "Won't complain, though. We're pretty excited about the baby."

When had this scraggly boy grown up to become a molder of people—a math teacher, golf coach, and now soon-to-be father? Henry burst with pride for David's accomplishments; though, in truth, he'd become all these things apart from his father's guidance.

David poured two creamers into his coffee, stirred it four times, tapped his spoon on the rim twice, put his spoon down, then took a sip. Just the way Sylvia used to prepare her coffee. Henry should have been around during David's teen years, then maybe he'd drink coffee black like his father.

He leaned back against the booth and yawned again as he spoke. "What time do you need me to stay with Mom?"

"Martina, Erik, and the kids are there now with Thor, of course. Erik's taking me into the city later this morning. I won't be back until early evening, so why don't you come around when Martina leaves, about three-thirty."

"I guess I could leave school a little early. By the way, nice of you to get Martina her own car."

"No big deal. This way she's more flexible with her hours." Henry's stomach growled, and they both laughed. "Hope our breakfast gets here pretty soon. I'm starved. Really, I was happy to get the car for Martina. With Erik driving me into the city so much, your mother needs her to run errands. So, everyone benefits."

"Whatever your motives, getting her the car was still a nice thing to do."

Bernadette arrived with their order. When she slapped their plates onto the table, the juice spilled over. "Sorry, Coach. I'll wipe it up."

"No need, Bernie."

David sopped up the spill with a paper napkin as Bernadette flitted toward the kitchen, a "Thank you, Coach," trailing behind her.

David snickered. "Good thing she takes more time to line up her putts."

Henry worried he was asking too much of an expectant father to babysit his mother. David had a lot of responsibility on his young shoulders. "You know, your mother insists she doesn't need looking after. If I asked anyone else to stay with her, she'd refuse all together. She only agreed because she enjoys your company."

David put one thumb up while he gulped the rest of his coffee. "I enjoy hers, too, except when she starts in on one of her books. I've read them all ... I just don't get most of them. I know she's talented. I suppose I'm more of a *Sports Illustrated* guy. No plot twists to get hung up on."

Henry raised his coffee cup for a toast—David followed his lead. "Here! Here!"

A husband should come to his wife's defense. "Don't forget those books you don't enjoy have afforded you and your sister a comfortable lifestyle. Neither one of you *has* to work. Your mother never asks much in return for your allowances either."

"You're right, of course, and I am grateful, even if I don't show how I feel. I don't want you or Mom worried about us kids either. If this lawsuit goes bad, we'll adjust. Don't forget we have our trust fund, and Bonnie has a trust fund too."

Henry dispelled the distasteful image of having his children support him in his old age. "We won't lose, David. Berkowitz's a genius, and I'm confident we'll find a compromise. Fitzgibbons & Associate will be around for the next generation of writers." Now, if he could only convince himself.

Walking this emotional gangplank made Henry's face taut. Time to steer their conversation in a different direction. "So, what did you do yesterday since our golf game got kiboshed?"

"We went to church."

Caught halfway through a swallow, Henry coughed up his last bite into a napkin. *Et tu,* David? "When did you become a church goer?"

"We decided to start when we found out about the baby. We usually go to the Saturday night service at First Fellowship."

God squeezed him. Higgy. Charlie. Now David. What did the Almighty want with Henry Fitzgibbons ... why corral him like a wild horse?

"Bonnie said she'd go to whatever church I wanted. Problem was I didn't know squat about religion of any kind. Not to be disrespectful, but I don't recall much teaching on the subject growing up."

"We wanted you kids to decide for yourselves."

"I understand. You meant well. Bonnie used to go to church before we got married. She wanted our baby to be brought up in a home of faith. I resisted at first. Then I had a long talk with her former pastor."

"Let me guess. You found Jesus."

"I guess you could say that. We prefer to use the word *saved*. I'm new at this Christian stuff, but I've got to tell you, Dad, it's been great. I feel like a new person. I've started reading the Bible too."

"I've noticed you're pretty chipper these days. I figured the pregnancy lightened your steps. I know I danced when your mother told me about you."

Bernadette returned. "Can I get anything else, Coach? More coffee for your young-looking dad?" She winked. "Musta had you while he was still in high school."

Nice to know a young girl didn't think him as old as Methuselah.

She placed her hand on Henry's shoulder. "He's cute, Coach." She left. When she returned, she handed the bill to David while she sang, "You asked for it ... you got it ..."

David handed her thirty dollars. "Keep the change, Bernie."

"Thanks, Coach." She skipped off like a kid with a lollipop.

David chuckled. "I always leave her a bigger tip. She's a better golfer than a waitress, but she needs the money for some new clubs." He put on his jacket. "I need to get to work. I'll see you when you get back from the city. I'll be thinking of you today, and I'll say a prayer for Julie too. I think you're wrong about that Jonathan guy. Julie's got a sixth sense about people. No way she'd get mixed up with a scammer. I gotta believe his connection with North is just a coincidence."

As they stood to leave, Henry pulled his son into a manly hug.

When they walked out of the diner, Erik pulled up almost immediately, jumped out, and came to Henry's side, covering him with an umbrella. He smiled. "You spoil me, Erik."

"Iz pleasure to serve you, Mr. Henry."

"Give the umbrella to David, please. His car's probably a block or two away."

"Four, actually. This is a popular diner."

As David turned the corner out of sight, Henry slipped into the passenger side. While Erik fastened his seat belt, Henry thought how ironic he'd come to depend so much upon a man he'd originally purposed not to like. Except for his height, Nordic handsomeness, and Swedish accent, Erik and David resembled each other in many ways. Both loved their wives with a renaissance gallantry, and both rejoiced in a simple sunset. Erik romped with his sons, encouraging their imaginations, while David would be a better father than Henry had been.

Maybe faith made people better parents. Not surprising, his son eventually turned toward religion. Henry recalled a six-year-old David who, out of the blue, asked to say grace at the dinner table. Henry had laughed the matter away, refusing to pray. "We'll have no praying in this house, young man. Waste of time."

Pop always prayed, a towering mystery, more unapproachable than the God he served. At sixteen, Henry gathered the courage to defy them both. "I don't believe like you do, Pop. I'm never stepping foot in a church again."

His father's words echoed now in Henry's soul. "My boy, do you think you're stronger than the Almighty? You wait. Someday, God will bring you to your knees and rid you of your arrogance. Mark my words. He'll bring you down because he loves you, just like I disciplined you out of my love for you."

Two months later, Pop uttered his dying words to the officer who cradled him. "Tell my son God loves him, and so do I."

Sylvia threw down her notepad with disgust. Two hours and still an empty page. To cope, she switched gears and shifted between writers' loops and emails.

Still, hopelessly blocked.

Not one word added to her count since she came home from the hospital.

This was Henry's fault.

A cup of tea might free her creative juices. How she missed Rosalie's perfect attention. Henry tried, but only Rosalie understood Lana Longstreet's peculiarities. She'd have to make her own tea or bother Martina.

Lana Longstreet thought making her own tea beneath her, cooking too. Sylvia used to be a fair cook before fame and fortune turned her into a writing zombie.

A memory floated through the loft. She could almost smell macaroni and cheese baking in the oven. Lana Longstreet believed the concoction ruined the pallet, and Sylvia sensed her alterego's condemnation. "Pick up the phone and order caviar, Sylvia. You don't want macaroni and cheese."

"No! Not this time. I'm going to make macaroni and cheese whether you like it or not."

Sylvia got as far as the grand staircase, stopped, and retreated through her chambers to take the spiral steps. "Silly woman. Now, you've become as much a victim to your paranoia as Henry."

Before the fainting spell, she laughed at his sprints across the cobblestone path. "You chose the room, Henry, because you wanted to be as far away from me as possible." Sighing, she scolded herself for arguing with an absent spouse. Once in the kitchen, she found an old ceramic mug, filled it with water, then placed it in the microwave. While she waited for the timer, she searched every nook and cranny for elbows and a brick of cheese. Rosalie had stored enough food to open her own grocery store, but no cheese and no elbows could be found. Sylvia brightened with the idea. She could ask Martina to go to the store and purchase the ingredients she needed.

Sylvia found a container of tea bags on the counter. "Now, all I need is a package or two of Lorna Doones." She shook her head at this recent need to talk to herself almost constantly. Was she now afraid to be alone? She grabbed a couple of packages from the cookie jar next to the coffee pot. "See, Henry. I can manage fine without you."

She glanced at the wall clock.

Two-thirty.

Spurred with a mission, she scribbled the ingredients for macaroni and cheese on a slip of paper and then went in search of Martina. Because of the rain, she'd kept the boys indoors. Training her ears for the pitter-patter of little feet, she strolled through the downstairs rooms, still avoiding the ballroom at all costs. Not hearing any playful noises, she figured the boys were watching television in the secluded den.

Martina might feel uncomfortable leaving the boys. But bringing them with her could cause her day's work to get behind. Sylvia smiled with the thought. What if she offered to read to the boys while Martina was gone? Lana Longstreet reared. "You don't have time for low-class food or entertaining children. You have a deadline."

Sylvia managed to subdue her inner voice for the moment with memories of reading to Julie and David all afternoon when they were little. Sometimes, Henry would come home to find them all asleep.

She peeked into the den where the boys watched *Dumbo* on their portable DVD, the volume so low she could barely hear. Thor lay between them, ready to pounce if duty called. How could she disturb so sweet a scene? She basked in remembrance as she observed them, resisting the urge to tell Dumbo he didn't need the magic feather to fly.

When the credits rolled, Sylvia made her pitch. "Say, do you boys want Miss Longstreet to read you a story?"

The twins jumped with a resounding, "Yay!" Sven hugged Sylvia's knee. "Could you read us *Cat in the Hat*?"

"I'd be delighted. You know, my children loved that story. I expect they still do. Where's the book?"

"Mama put our books in a toy chest on the veranda."

Before Sylvia could stop him, Sven made a mad dash into the ballroom with Gunnar in hot pursuit. "Mama said I'm in charge of the books, Sven. Let me get it."

Both boys rushed off to claim victory over the book before Sylvia could warn them to use the cobblestone path. She gasped when she heard Sven's shrill cry. "Stop it! Mama, help us!" Thor clawed the air, snarling at some invisible threat, then paced the length of the foyer, running towards the children only to retreat with a defeated whine. Scraps of hardwood flew in all directions as Thor scratched at both sides of the archway. She rushed to enter but was pushed back against the wall while the boys' curdled screams mingled with frantic barks. She beat against an invisible wall while a thin mist rose from the floor and hovered over the terrified children. "No! You can't have them, I tell you! Go away!"

Martina rushed in from the old servants' hallway and shouted an unintelligible command. Sylvia could only watch in wonder as the mist evaporated, and Thor charged toward the boys who lay in a heap on the ballroom floor. Sylvia trailed behind Thor, helping Martina carry the children from the room.

She turned, her eyes wild with worry. "Miss Longstreet. We have to get out of here now."

"I don't—"

"Come with me."

In unquestioned obedience to a subordinate, Sylvia followed Martina to her car. The boys' little bodies were covered with bite marks, and a wet stream trickled down their cheeks. She could no longer deny an evil presence lurked in her home—a presence that would devour anyone who dared to infringe on its domain—even innocent children.

Henry pulled Higgy to the side before he entered the conference room. "Did our private investigator find out anything yet?"

Higgy nodded. "He did, and you're not going to like what he discovered."

"Hit me, then."

"He found out Jonathan Delaney brought the book in question to North's attention. Evan might never have realized the similarities, or we might have caught the problem before the book was released. Seems, regardless of Julie's belief the boy is innocent, he had something to do with this mess, all right. To what extent is still a mystery."

"There's more, isn't there, Higgy."

"When I talked with Julie, she said Jonathan had a copy of *The Gathering Flock* when he came to visit her a few weeks ago."

Henry squirmed. "That's strange. I did check our release schedule. For some reason, distribution got delayed. The only copies that were sent out were to Sylvia's review team. Jonathan would not have been on the list. Of course, North always receives an advance reader copy at Sylvia's request. If Julie's fiancé is in cohoots, Evan might have given Jonathan the ARC."

"Or Jonathan might be working with someone on our staff to get inside information. That would explain how he knew about the forgery and brought it to North's attention. We can't ignore the possibility."

Treachery from without was something Henry could accept. To think one of his own could betray him in some way seemed beyond the realm of plausibility. "I refuse to believe we have a mole."

The meeting went as Henry expected. Berkowitz had successfully delayed the initial court date to September, giving him additional time to launch a defense. Berkowitz's account parroted Higgy's earlier version—someone within the Fitzgibbons & Associate family might have fed information to Jonathan who then piped the intel to North. Who among his staff could be so devious?

Berkowitz calculated the next steps. "First, let's make a list of all past employees who might have a grudge and include anyone you fired recently. I think we need to take a long hard look at all correspondence over the past year. Start with your editorial staff."

Henry flashed a roster of recent hirings … no one fired in the last two years. Henry outsourced much of the editorial work, except for Sylvia's. She insisted only the most experienced editors handle her books. "I'll have Monique get right on the paperwork trail. There isn't much she doesn't know about the staff …"

Higgy coughed an objection. "I don't think we should bring *any* employees into this, Fitz. Not even Monique. Did you know she has ties in New Haven?"

"No, I didn't. I thought all her family lived in England."

"Either she lied to you, or you just assumed this. She lives with her parents here in the city. And interestingly enough, her father has recently bought up huge portions of real estate in New Haven. If she lied or kept the information from us, there may be a good reason. However, given the peculiarities of this lawsuit, until we're certain of our little English princess's motives, even Monique is under suspicion."

"Not Monique."

"I'm sorry, Henry. Berky suggests we hire an outsider, an undercover agent to do the investigation."

"You're kidding, right? Do we have to be so paranoid?"

Higgy clasped his chair until his knuckles turned white. "I insist, Fitz. Remember, you might be CEO, but I have controlling interest. You and Sylvia both agreed to give me the extra percent because you two couldn't agree on anything."

Not since the Persian Gulf did Paul Higgens pull rank. "Then I guess the matter's settled." With burning cheeks, Henry stormed into his office.

He sat, forcing all this latest information into some kind of cohesive pattern, so deep in his thoughts he hadn't heard Monique come in. She clicked her tongue. "I know you can't tell me what's going on, but I don't need to be a mind reader to tell this awful business is draining on you. Is there anything I can do to help?"

"No. Thanks for the offer. Hold my calls, will you? I need my space for a bit."

"Of course, Henry." She closed his door, but her scent remained. Sylvia wore the same perfume lately. Wanting to give his wife a nice gift for her birthday, he'd asked Monique what scent she wore, then picked up a small bottle to give to Sylvia. She seemed pleased with his selection, though he hadn't told her why he'd chosen that particular brand. At the time, the whole matter seemed innocent enough. What did he know about perfumes?

Maybe Sylvia's rages against Monique came from insight Henry lacked. Though he denied Sylvia's allegations, he did, on occasion, entertain thoughts of taking on a mistress ... someone like Monique. Fleeting thoughts, to be sure. For at the end of the day, Henry Fitzgibbons realized he could love only one woman, failing marriage and all.

Henry put his head on his desk and drew in four deep breaths. No help. His anxiety persisted, and his throat constricted. He turned on the radio, hoping soothing music would help him process his conflicting thoughts ... wanting to know if someone had betrayed the company. If so, who? He couldn't believe Monique would do such a thing. He banged on his desk a few times, but the tantrum did nothing but refuel his anger. He stretched on the floor and counted his pushups. As a soldier, he could do a hundred with one hand on his back. Now, he took pride in managing twenty-five with both hands firmly planted.

He retrieved a putter and three golf balls from his closet, draining each one into a makeshift cup on the first putt. Yet, his rage continued to swell.

"Pray."

He must be hearing things. Then he realized the command rolled off his own tongue.

For the second time today, his father's words echoed in his memory. "Someday, God will strip you of your arrogance."

Pop, today's the day.

Henry had waged war against himself far too long. He hungered for peace. The putter plunked to the floor as Henry fell to his knees, not certain of how to pray. As if time funneled around him, he sensed his mother's presence. In his memory, she knelt with him beside his childhood bed. "Just talk to God like He's right here, Henry. He'll listen."

He sobbed between broken phrases uttered from a little boy lost. He confessed his arrogance and begged forgiveness. He confessed his pride, anguished over his ruined marriage, and asked God's protection for Julie. He expressed thanks for those sent as beacons to bring him home—Higgy, Erik, Charlie, Rosalie, and David.

Monique's sultry voice over the intercom shattered his concentration. He glanced at his desk clock. He had spent the better part of an hour in contrition, slumped by his chair, spilling a lifetime of sins.

"Sorry to disturb you, Henry. Your son's on the line. I told him you didn't want to be disturbed, but he said it was urgent."

Henry pulled out his cell. He'd silenced it during the meeting and hadn't put the sound back on as yet. One text from David ... call me immediately. No wonder he'd used the office phone."

"I'll take the call in here."

David's frantic words pinged Henry's ear. "Did Mom call you? I'm here at the house, and there's no one home, and Martina's car is gone."

Henry fell to his chair, spent of all strength. "It's possible your mother needed something and didn't want to wait for Erik."

"I don't like the looks of things here, Dad. The tire marks where Martina parks her car look as if someone sped out in an awful hurry. I found the door unlocked, and a DVD player still running."

"Your mother never locks her door. I'm sure there's a logical—"

"Dad, the floor's dug up in front of the ballroom, and there're claw marks on both sides of the entryway."

Oh, God. Please protect them.

"David, get out of the house. I'll be there as quickly as I can."

CHAPTER 21

Sylvia's heart still raced three times faster than normal. How could Martina be so calm?

She released her tight grip on the squirming children and eased them from her lap to the floor. "Thank you for seeing us, Pastor Mark."

Mrs. Estes placed a serving tray laden with tea and cookies on the coffee table. "Why don't you let me take the children into the playroom? I'll put medicine on their bites, then slip a movie into the DVD player." She pulled two lollipops out from a multi-pocketed apron decorated with bees, butterflies, and giraffes. "I have more treats in the other room."

Martina nodded permission, and the boys followed Mrs. Estes out the door while Thor trotted along side. Children and pets bounced back so quickly from terror, but Sylvia's heart pounded as if fear had found a permanent home.

With the boys out of earshot, Martina turned toward Reverend Estes and explained the events prompting the hasty flight. "The house is possessed. I'm sure of it."

The conversation between Martina and Reverend Estes existed on an ecclesiastical plane, far too high and wide for Sylvia to grasp. The words they used were familiar, like a language she'd been exposed to once upon a time, yet unable to truly grasp. Reverend Estes and Martina, however, understood one another perfectly.

Reverend Estes leaned forward as he spoke. "Did you exhort the demons?"

Martina nodded. "I've never seen this kind of oppression before."

How did a simple housekeeper understand the intricacies of theological puzzles? Did Satan live in Lana Longstreet's home? Preposterous. A twisted plot from a B horror film.

Memory burst from a sealed room in her mind. She was seven, and her parents had taken her to Myrtle Beach for a family vacation. She wandered off and got lost for hours. Giving up hope, she leaned against a boulder and cried as the waves broke around her ankles. There, in front of her, stood an elderly couple. They looked a lot like Grandma and Grandpa Moore, though this couldn't be them since they lived on the other side of the country.

"What's the matter, dear?" The woman's voice sounded kind.

"My parents are lost. I don't know where to find them."

"Come with us. We'll see if we can figure out where they might be."

When Sylvia reunited with her parents, they didn't scold her. Instead, they smothered her with hugs. "We were so worried. We thought we lost you."

"I wasn't lost, Mama. I knew where *I* was. I didn't know where *you* were." A logical statement for a child. Her parents had laughed, then took Sylvia for ice cream.

As she scanned Reverend Estes's office, she felt lost again. Not from her earthly father but another Father from whom she had wandered away. And once again, a kind person offered help.

Lana Longstreet scoffed at the minister, his wife, and the cluttered study. The shelves contained a mishmash of theological and secular books arranged in no logical sequence. Sylvia sunk into the leathery softness of the overstuffed recliner. The faint scent of Old Spice reminded her of Daddy's chair. She could almost see him as he read the newspaper while Mama baked cookies. Sylvia mourned the lost memories, wishing she had never allowed Lana Longstreet to subdue them and change timid Sylvia into the woman she always wanted to be—strong, independent, no longer frightened of solitude.

At what price, though? To emerge herself into Lana Longstreet's soul, Sylvia had sacrificed the love of a husband and suffocated happy childhood memories. If only she could exorcise her alter ego along with the evil possessing her home. Perhaps Sylvia and Lana were far too integrated to be separated. Lana Longstreet ordered Sylvia's otherwise chaotic creativity ... yet, without her domination, Sylvia's life could bloom again, maybe even become as beautiful as the lavender roses in her garden— full and glistening after the rains.

From the depths of her psyche, she willed Lana Longstreet from her soul. The tyrant, however, was too entrenched, pulling at Sylvia's resolve like taffy. The writer within was winning. Perspiration beaded on Sylvia's forehead— scalding acid burned her throat. She heard herself scream, "Leave me!" The room turned upside down, numbness taking over until there was complete blackness.

Ammonia assaulted her nostrils. Mama must be washing the floor. No. It wasn't Mama. It was Martina, and she waved a stick under Sylvia's nose.

Reverend Estes handed her a glass of water. "Drink this, Miss Longstreet."

"What happened? Did I faint?"

"I'm afraid you did. Only a few seconds, though. Martina managed to keep you upright. I keep smelling salts in my drawer as a matter of course. Counseling sometimes triggers severe reactions in people."

Compassionate eyes scanned her soul. Reverend Estes pulled his chair from behind the desk to the other side of the coffee table, poured two cups of tea, then handed one to Sylvia. "Martina has filled me in on what happened. I'd like to hear your thoughts, Miss Longstreet."

"Please, call me Sylvia. Sylvia Moore Fitzgibbons. That's my real name." Something rattled. Her body convulsed. Reverend Estes took her cup and saucer, setting them down on the table. Martina held her hand while Reverend Estes held the other. They prayed. Sylvia's sobs drowned their words, but their intent burned within her.

Soon, peace filled the room. And her soul emptied for a few seconds. Then she felt a filling, an identity too long exiled. Sylvia drew in three deep breaths, and the shaking subsided. "I think I'm okay now."

Reverend Estes leaned forward, concern on his face. "Mrs. Fitzgibbons, I'd like to help you. To do so, I need to determine where you are in your spiritual life. Are you a Christian?"

Lana Longstreet would have responded with colorful expletives. Thankfully, she was gone ... far from reach ... hopefully, never to be found again. "If you're asking if I attend a church, no I don't. I haven't for a long time."

Both Reverend Estes and Martina gazed her way as if expecting an explanation. "As a girl, I attended Sunday school. Sadly, somewhere between protests and my first book contract, I lost interest. I told myself living a good life should be enough ... I didn't need to attend church to worship God. I could do that on a mountain top. I never entered a church again, nor did I ever climb a mountain."

Reverend Estes leaned forward. "How do you feel about God now?"

"Until these disturbances flared up, I didn't think about God at all. Strange. Why now? They've apparently inhabited the house for years before I bought the estate."

Free of Lana Longstreet, Sylvia spewed confession upon confession while Reverend Estes listened. She kept nothing hidden, including her unhappy marriage and the lawsuit.

Reverend Estes handed her a box of tissues. "Mrs. Fitzgibbons, you are not the first person who has tried to live a moral life based on self-interpretation of good and evil. What many fail to understand is the fact God has done the work of conquering evil. He wants to put a spirit inside of us—one that desires good. Do you remember from your Sunday school teachings how Jesus died on the cross and how his sacrifice makes forgiveness for sin possible through faith?"

"Yes. I do."

"God loves you, Mrs. Fitzgibbons. There is a fountain of forgiveness in the power of Christ's name. You only need to ask."

"I'd like forgiveness, Reverend Estes."

The trio slid from their chairs, kneeling while Sylvia prayed aloud. "It's been a long time since I talked to you, Jesus. I've made a mess of my life, and I've hurt the ones I love. I can't solve these problems by myself. I need you. Of all the sins and omissions in my life, I most regret forgetting how much you love me."

She continued to pray through moans and tears, emotions only God could understand. A feeling like quickening during pregnancy filled her. Was this evidence of new life beginning within her soul?

As her senses leveled, she noticed the dull afternoon sun. The rains had ended. She looked for a clock but found none. "Reverend Estes, what time is it?"

He looked at his watch. "My goodness, it's a little past four."

"My son must be frantic. He was coming over to the house at three-thirty. I don't have a phone with me. We ran out of the house taking only the children and Thor."

Reverend Estes handed her his cell phone. She punched David's cell number, relieved when he answered. "David? It's Mom."

"Glad I took the call. I didn't recognize the number. Where have you been? I was just about to call the police. Dad and Erik are on their way home. He told me to leave, but I thought I should stay here in case you came back. Is Martina with you?"

"We're fine, David. I'll explain later. I'm with Martina and her pastor."

"You sure you're okay? You sound different."

"I think maybe I am. Could you pick me up here? I don't want Martina to have to drive me all the way back to the house when she lives only a couple of blocks from the church."

"A church? Sure, what's the address?"

"Here, let me hand the phone to Reverend Estes. He'll give you directions."

While Reverend Estes spoke to David, Martina smiled. "Are you sure you're okay now, Miss Longstreet?"

"Please, call me Sylvia. I think, in a way, we've become sisters." She accepted the gift of Martina's embrace.

Reverend Estes pocketed his cell phone. "Your son is on his way, Mrs. Fitzgibbons. Martina, my wife will help you get the kids into the car."

"Thank you, Pastor Mark." Martina left, no longer Lana Longstreet's housekeeper but Sylvia Fitzgibbons's friend.

Reverend Estes took Sylvia's hands into his. "Are you sure you want to go back to the house?"

"Why shouldn't I? Since I've confessed my sins, the disturbances will stop, won't they?"

He handed her a book from his shelf: *The Power of Darkness/Deliverance by Light.* "Maybe this book will explain what I'm trying to tell you. There is spiritual warfare going on in your home, Mrs. Fitzgibbons. Take heart and remember ... God's more powerful than any of Satan's minions. The believer is protected through God's grace. However, if demons have already rooted in your home, they may not want to leave. Exorcising them may take more than a simple, short prayer. I believe God wants you and Henry to be reconciled. However, healing from the wounds you have described takes time. And Satan does not like losing."

Panic rose. "Are you saying things might get worse before they get better?"

"Possibly. From what you've told me, these apparitions started bothering you soon after Henry moved in for the summer, worsening when he decided to give your marriage another try. If this is true, Satan seems determined to keep you and Henry apart. The closer you come to reconciliation, the harder Satan will fight to prevent your marriage from healing."

"Just before the children ran into the ballroom, I did entertain the possibility that I'd been too hard on Henry about the lawsuit. Could that have prompted the attack on the children?"

"Possibly. "

Though she was drawn to Reverend Estes, his words seemed to bridge on insanity. "Should I leave? Henry might let me stay at his Manhattan apartment."

Reverend Estes paced with eyes half closed. Was he praying? She determined to follow whatever advice he gave regardless of her ability to understand his instructions or however ridiculous they might seem.

"Don't leave yet. If you're willing to ride this out, I sense God's protection. Satan cannot abide where God is praised. I suggest, however, you close off the ballroom to the children—at least for now. In the meantime, I'll arrange for our church members to conduct a continuous vigil until we're certain the house is cleansed."

Lana Longstreet would never have allowed an invasion of church people into the privacy of her home. But with her gone, Sylvia Fitzgibbons could decide for herself. "If you think a vigil would be helpful, then by all means."

"Good. I'll make the arrangements. There'll be a minimum of two believers praying for two-hour intervals around the clock."

What about the noise? How could she meet her deadline? "I do appreciate your kindness, Reverend Estes. Are you certain we need the calvary? Seems a tad metaphysical."

"No mystery about this at all, Mrs. Fitzgibbons. We pray and sing. Like a church service without a boring sermon. If we fill the house with praise, evil will be crowded out. We'll start as soon as I can formalize a list."

"Thank you."

Mrs. Estes stepped in. "Your son's here, Miss Longstreet."

"It's Fitzgibbons."

The war for her soul had been fought and won. Yet, another war lingered—one against a malignant force who had set its heels in her home, determined to wrench the good germinated since Henry first moved in for the summer. Confidence replaced fear. Whatever battles she now faced, she was no longer alone. A force greater than Lana Longstreet now abided within.

CHAPTER 22

Henry bolted through the kitchen door. "David!"

"I'm in the foyer."

He embraced his son, briming with relief. "I thought I told you to leave. I saw your car outside and feared the worse."

"Everyone's fine. Mom's resting upstairs, and Martina took the kids to her house. I'll let Mom explain everything because I'm not sure I understand what she's telling me," he said, dragging a sheet of plywood across the floor, then propping it gainst the wall beside the ballroom entrance.

"What're you doing?"

"Mom'll tell you."

Henry shook his head. "I don't know, David. Your mother's always been angry with me but now worse than ever. I don't blame her. I let her down, and sometimes I think she'd be better off if I weren't in the picture."

David eyed the entrance as if mapping out major construction. "I always thought Mom was unflappable, but I've never seen her so unsettled before."

"I'll send Erik home. We don't need anything more tonight, do we?"

"I don't think so."

"At least the rain's stopped. I'll start a pot of coffee. You could use a break, right?"

David put the hammer down. "I can't stay much longer, but coffee does sound good. I've already called Bonnie. Her feet are swollen, and she's hankering pizza ... so I promised to pick one up on my way home."

Henry left David, sent Erik on his way, prepared the coffee, then grabbed two cups, placing them on the counter. Should David know that his father had joined the club of believers? Henry yelled into the other room. "Coffee's ready."

David came in and sat on a stool. "What's going on here, Dad? Mom wants me to close off the ballroom before the Hagstadt kids come back again, mumbling something about the room being unsafe. Does Mom think the house's haunted? Until now, she laughed about you and Julie's visions. Of course, I've never seen anything in there but dust and spider webs."

Henry filled the cups, then set one in front of David. "Both times your mother passed out we found her in the ballroom."

"Really?"

"The doctor suspects she suffered a shock. Nobody knows for sure what caused her to faint on those two occasions. Nor do I have any idea what happened this time."

"Mom said the boys ran into the ballroom, and something attacked them, like bugs. When she tried to help them, an invisible wall blocked her. Martina ran in and grabbed the boys and told Mom to get out of the house. Then Martina drove over to her minister's. I'll tell you Dad, the whole story sounds kind of creepy. I'm not sure if I believe in ghosts, but there's something unhealthy in that room. That's for sure."

Henry took a sip of coffee, then set his cup back down and met David's gaze. "I'm not sure either. But not everything can be explained through reason and logic. Whatever's in there could be a creation of our imagination ... the mind does play horrible tricks on us. I've read cases where people share hallucinations. There're some who believe a haunted house is simply energy imprints from previous residents— left after a violent death. Others believe ghosts are actually demons at work."

"Seems like an odd thing for you to say, Dad." David cocked his head to one side. "Did something happen to you too?"

"I suppose so. My father predicted God would bring me so low, I'd cry out to him for help. Well, today was that day. I wish you could have known your grandfather. He was a good man, and I think you're like him in a lot of ways."

"You never talked about him much."

Henry took another sip. How could he explain the rift between his father and himself? They loved each other, yet could not understand what made the other tick. "We didn't get along very well, and he died when I was a teenager."

David's eyes filled with sympathy. "I saw a picture of him and Grandmother Fitzgibbons on their wedding day. You'd think Julie and I got dressed up and had our picture taken."

Henry should not have robbed his children of their heritage. They deserved to know their grandfather was once an army chaplain and had been given the medal of honor for risking his life to save a drowning crewman during the Vietnam War. Henry had a medal too but had never told anyone about his award. His father had deserved his medal. Not Henry.

"David, I'm sorry I didn't tell you much about your grandparents. I haven't been a very good father. I want to change, to be more involved in your lives."

"You could have done worse by us, Dad. Don't be so hard on yourself. So, why the turnaround?"

"Let's just say, I've made *my* peace with God."

"Interesting. Mom says she found peace too. I'll have to admit, I'd love to see the two of you stop arguing all the time."

"You could hear us?"

"Yeah. I just tuned out the shouting, but I could hear Julie crying. Sometimes, I couldn't wait for you to go back to Manhattan because the fighting stopped as soon as you left."

"I'm sorry, David. I'm sorry our selfishness grieved you kids. I wish I could undo those years. I can't. I can only do better from now on."

David swallowed the last of his coffee, then stood. "Forget I said anything. As far as I'm concerned, it's ancient history. Everyone has regrets. I know I do. Still, sometimes, I wish things could have been different between you and Mom."

Henry embraced his son with newfound love. "You're a good son, David. I wish I had been half the man you turned out to be."

"Dad, you don't need to be perfect in my book. Fighting aside, you've always been my hero."

When David left, Henry strolled along the garden path toward the retaining walls to see how the budding roses had fared the day's heavy rains. Most of them stood tall, dripping with moisture. Had the wall given them shelter from the storm?

He crouched down, gently lifting the delicate sprouts and examined the beds. Where the mulch had eroded over the years, infant blooms hung from broken stems. The beds Charlie replenished fared better, even the older bushes. He had trellised the growth and pruned the dead shoots, refortifying the mulch with fertilizer. The new growth, laden with moisture, hugged the ground. But their stems remained straight and strong.

A heart, he reasoned, might be like a rose bush. God had bolstered Henry's soul with a trellis of love, even before Henry knew he needed a Savior. Because of God's mercy, these current storms had not broken him entirely. He would bloom again regardless of the dire forecasts.

He went to his room and scavenged for a Bible, finding none. He pulled out his mostly unused laptop from its case, then searched for Scripture online, downloading a version from Amazon. He'd buy a hard cover one in the morning but was grateful today's technology let him find comfort from God's word with just a few clicks. He read from the Gospel of John, remembering Pop's preference for the book. When he finished reading, he stretched out on the bed. Gentle breezes thumped against his window, lulling him into the most restful sleep he had ever known.

CHAPTER 23

Refreshed from the blessing of deep sleep, Sylvia stretched to greet the dawn. She dressed and went to her loft, then clicked her computer screen to manage the hundreds of emails accumulated over the last couple of days.

Preferring to use her computer rather than her cell phone, which she retrained herself to keep nearby, she sorted through the threads generated by writers' loops, topics varying from novices wanting to know how to write a fiction proposal to experts sharing their latest publication news. She deleted most, keeping only those messages pertaining to copyright issues, information that might prove valuable given her current circumstances.

She opened the message from Reverend Estes: *Mrs. Fitzgibbons. I received a call from Charlie Michaels. He has asked his pastor, Dr. Foster, and congregation to participate in the vigil. Our church has readily agreed. Attached you will find a schedule with times and names of prayer warriors. Martina and Erik requested to be among the first. The vigil begins at four o'clock this afternoon.*

How did Charlie know? The Hagstadts? Or maybe Henry blabbed every detail. She smiled at his unlikely friendship with the bean-pole hippy.

She moved the folder to her personal files, then deleted the items in her spam folder.

Now for fan mail.

She looked forward to notes from her readers. Some complained of her predictable plots—justified criticism. Lana Longstreet wrote over sixty novels. Of course, her plots were recycled. Then again, with God in her life now, Sylvia Fitzgibbons's well could now be tapped, a style swallowed by the other's ambition.

Most of the fan mail bordered on complementary, although fewer and fewer since the lawsuit hit the tabloids. One fan commented how her stories influenced the reader's life. *For the better, I hope.*

No longer haunted by Lana Longstreet, what kind of writer would Sylvia Fitzgibbons become? Hopefully, one motivated by substance rather than profit, one whose faith was evident, a different writer than either of her personalities ever dreamed of becoming. The thought moot. If the lawsuit went badly, there might be no more writing career to pray about.

She opened an email signed A New Evan North Fan: *I used to be a devoted fan of yours. Now I see you're nothing but a fraud. I hate you for what you did to a great writer like Evan North.*

This stranger's words stung more than if written by someone she loved. Fans were fickle. Ask any celebrity whose devotees turned tail after a flop. Human nature, Sylvia observed, only wanted to run with winners.

She opened dozens more saying essentially the same thing. Thankfully, a few good wishes intertwined with hateful messages. As recommended, she moved the fan email to a separate folder then forwarded the files to Berkowitz.

With no subject line, Sylvia couldn't be certain if this post was fan mail, spam, or mail with malicious intent. She glanced at the odd address: *n505@millroad.com.* It rang familiar.

She scanned the email for viruses. Finding none, she opened it: *I have information to prove your innocence. Meet me at ten o'clock at the abandoned raincoat factory on Mill Street. Come alone. Do not call the police or tell anyone of our meeting. If you will meet me, send a blank reply.*

The similarities could not be coincidental. Sylvia's words penned in her first suspense novel, *Shadows at Noon*—except the abandoned building had been a T-shirt mill on Factory Street, the time midday, and the message delivered by courier instead of an email. The courier's name was Ned who lived at 505 Mill Road.

She clicked *505millroad.com* into a search engine. The top item linked to a website displaying the book cover for *Shadows at Noon*. Odd. The book went out of print five years ago. She minimized the email while she considered its content. Probably a prank. Then again, perhaps whoever sent it really wanted to help. If Erik brought her, he could wait down the street. Technically, she'd have come alone. She doubted anything sinister, yet discretion still remained the better part of valor.

The invitation intrigued her. Even if the email was a hoax, the plot twist might work well for the Johnny Gallant series. Go or ignore? She felt a sudden chill, and went into her bedroom chambers to get a sweater.

Tap—tap. Tap—tap.

Henry awoke to rhythmic vibrations as the sun's rays burst through the window and bounced off dancing dust particles. The room needed a thorough cleaning. He'd ask Martina to concentrate on his room ... if she came tomorrow. Poor girl couldn't keep up with all the commotion.

Tap—tap. Tap—tap.

He dressed and went around to the garden where a somber Charlie knelt beside a bed of crushed roses while three men hoisted a stone structure into a standing position. In all the confusion, Henry had forgotten about the new shed.

Charlie cupped a broken bloom in his hand as if grieving its death. "The hard rain was awfully brutal to your roses, Henry. I might be able to save the ones where the stems are bent. I'll have to bolster the roots, give 'em extra support, then replenish the fertilizer and mulch. The retaining wall saved a few of the older beds."

Charlie pointed to the unsheltered beds by the veranda. "I'm afraid there's no hope for those. The shoots're completely severed from the roots. I'll have to dig 'em out, put in new bushes."

Henry thanked God, he'd only been bent. "Do what you have to do, Charlie. I trust your judgment. Need a hand with anything?"

Pulling a wheelbarrow behind him, Charlie walked toward the temporary storage bin. "I got everything under control. 'Bout another hour before I wrap up for today."

"In that case, I'll go back inside and check on my wife. They attacked her again yesterday."

"I heard."

"How'd you know?"

"Erik called me wanting to know if my church could help out with the prayer vigil his church was organizing for your house. I called my pastor, Dr. Foster. He's coordinating efforts with Mark Estes."

"Prayer vigil?"

"Maybe you should talk to Miss Longstreet about it."

"I will." *What have you been up to, Sylvia?*

Henry entered through the kitchen as hammering echoes rang in his ears.

Tap—tap. Tap—tap.

The incessant tapping filled the house, traveling from room to room like a yodeler's resound. He trailed the noise, saving the ballroom for last.

Tap—tap. Tap—tap.

Saliva coagulated as he entered the foyer, relieved to see the tapping was from David's handiwork, a stack of plywood at his feet. "Good morning, Dad."

"So, you're the one making so much noise?"

David laughed. "Yeah. Why? Did you think the spooks got loose again?"

"That's not funny. I thought you had to work today."

"I took a few personal days."

"Does your mother know you're here?"

David picked up a sheet and braced it against the ballroom doorframe. "Give me a hand with this, will you?" Henry grabbed the other side, steadying it while David nailed it in place. "I popped in a few minutes ago. Mom's busy at the computer and asked me to hinge this one section. Said she's hosting a prayer vigil starting today. What's that about?"

"Not a clue. I better ask ... maybe later."

David laid his hammer on a carpenter's stool and snickered. "What're you afraid of?" He slid another plywood panel from the stack. "What's the worst she could do to you?"

"I could wear a bicycle helmet, I suppose."

"I know what you mean. She never aims at a person, but I've had to duck a few times myself just to be safe. Look, Dad, I know this is a big house ... but sooner or later, the two of you have to start communicating."

"I suppose you're right. Can you manage this by yourself?"

"I'm almost done, anyway. Just want to nail this board in place, then I was going home. Bonnie wants me to start painting the nursery."

"I'd like to help with the nursery project."

David snickered. "Thanks, but no thanks. I've seen the way you paint."

"I've never been very handy around the house. At least, let me pay for the furniture. Bonnie can pick out what she wants. Okay?"

"Thanks. She'd like that." David twirled the hammer like a gunslinger's pistol, then holstered it in his tool belt.

Henry arched with pleasure at his son's virile abilities. "You're a regular pro, son. Where did you learn all this stuff? Not from me, that's for sure."

"Don't know. I like fixing things. I'm not as good as Charlie's crew, though. The shed went up faster than an Amish barn raising." He yanked on the newly fastened plank and tested the hinged portion. "Should hold. I'm out of here. See you later. Now, quit stalling and go talk to Mom."

Better go with ammunition. She might not throw things if I have a tray full of food.

Henry hadn't made coffee and figured Sylvia probably hadn't had anything to eat yet. He trained his ear toward the spiral staircase. No clicks—the only sound was the faint whir of the saws from outside.

He started the coffee. If memory served him right, Sylvia used to like cinnamon toast. Or was that Monique? He risked the toast and fixed the tray Rosalie style, then took deep breaths as he climbed the spiral staircase.

Sylvia wasn't in her loft. Maybe he should leave the tray and make a quick exit. He set the tray on the computer table, accidentally knocking the mouse.

An email came up, its large font begging him to read it. *Come alone.*

CHAPTER 24

Sylvia rushed into the loft from her bedroom, her sweater thrown over her shoulders. "I thought I heard someone coming up the steps."

Henry made no reply but seemed fixated on her computer.

"Why are you reading my mail? Are you spying on me now?"

Henry looked like a cornered, mischievous waif. "I'm not spying on you. I brought up your breakfast and hit the mouse by accident when I set the tray down. I couldn't help but notice."

His face drooped, most likely disheartened by her gruff reaction. She prayed for grace to stop hurling insults at him, to appreciate his attentiveness. He had taken great pains to put the tray together nearly perfectly imitating Rosalie's precision. Maybe her acidic quips caused Henry's hasty departures from Connecticut even more than the ballroom demons. Introspection hurt—a mirror revealing her haughty disposition. Lana Longstreet couldn't be blamed for all of Sylvia's mistakes.

She stepped between Henry and the computer, then minimized the screen. "Well, thank you for breakfast. Anything else?"

Henry stared at the computer screen. "You're not seriously considering meeting this person, are you?"

"Do you take me for a fool?" The note said to come alone. If Henry knew her intentions, he might follow her or insist on going with her. She couldn't lie. Henry always saw through her fabrications, even half truths. He said the right corner of her mouth veered upward when she fibbed.

She brought the email back up. "Here, I'll forward the email to Berkowitz. Satisfied?"

"Sylvia, don't pay any attention to these crazy emails. Don't even open them. This lawsuit isn't just about money. I believe whoever's behind the plagiarized book has some other ulterior motive, and there's no telling to what lengths they might go."

In spite of Henry's warning, instinct told her she should follow up on this lead. "Thank you for breakfast. There's another reason you came up, though, isn't there?"

Henry crossed his arms, the way he always did when he reached the height of his frustration. "What's going on with the ballroom? David's playing Mr. Fix-it, and Charlie said something about a prayer vigil."

"Well, if you paid more attention to things around here ..."

Henry groaned, turned, and headed toward the stairwell. She had chastened him again. If only she could bridal her vicious temper. "I'm sorry, Henry. You've been a dear, really—and I haven't shown you how much I appreciate all you've done. Let's go out for dinner tonight. My treat. I'll even make the reservations. What do you say? Seven?"

"Don't change the subject, Sylvia." He returned and sat by the window, his face a muscular wall of resolve.

She pulled up a chair to sit next to him. "All right, if you must know, Mark Estes thinks these hallucinations of yours are satanic in some way. He thinks a prayer vigil will rid us of them."

"You've seen something strange in there too, haven't you? Why can't you be honest with me?"

Why *had* she persisted in disbelief? Henry deserved to know what she thought she saw. As the words flowed, she shook uncontrollably. Henry held her, and the trembling stopped. She looked up at him. His eyes were full of compassion while her own were filled with tears. When was the last time they cried together? Ah, yes. Her miscarriage—she'd bought the house soon after."

"This is the first time you've ever leveled with me, Sylvia. At least, since we separated."

Separated.

Yes, their true condition. A state neither would admit to. Instead, they skirted the real issues and blamed one another for their mutual unhappiness. Sudden realization filled her.This vigil would fight for more than a dispersion of evil forces—strangers fought for their home.

Hers and Henry's.

Their marriage.

Oh, God, help us!

She rested her head against his chest, and he held her even tighter. "Henry, how did we end up so far away from each other?"

"I don't know for sure, Sylvia. Somewhere along the line, we stopped living for each other. I'm sorry for the hurt I caused you."

"Where to now, Henry? Can we ever find our way back?"

Henry sighed. "If you still want a divorce, I won't oppose you. We'll weather the lawsuit and Julie's problems together. A divorce doesn't mean we can't find a way to be friends. After all, we've managed to keep a business afloat through the worst of our arguments."

"Do *you* want a divorce?"

"No. I love you, Sylvia. The thought of letting go of what good might still exist in our marriage tears me to pieces."

"Is there hope for us, then?"

He oozed another sigh, seemingly one of contentment. "A few days ago, I thought our marriage couldn't be saved."

"And you feel differently now?"

He nodded. "I don't expect you to understand, but something happened to me yesterday."

"What?"

"Let's just say I believe my days of being mad at God have ended."

"You're right. I don't understand."

"I think I told you my father was a minister."

"Yes, and a drug addict shot him during a convenience store robbery. You could never talk about him without flaring up, and I never knew why."

Henry took out his handkerchief and wiped his eyes, so unlike him to be emotional. "When my father died, I wanted nothing to do with a God who let such things happen. I'm only beginning to realize, though I fought hard against him, God never left me ... not even in the Persian Gulf."

Sylvia prayed while Henry talked. Like those vines strangled the roses, she and Henry had let weeds of discontent destroy their marriage. Only God's grace could untangle the mess their neglect of each other had created.

"Don't you see, Sylvia? I've wasted too many years being mad at God. I'm in my fifties ... who knows how many years I have left."

"Don't say such things, Henry. You're still in good health ... too much cholesterol in your diet maybe, but otherwise you take good care of yourself." She stroked his chin. "You're still a very handsome man."

"I hope to be around for a few more years ... I want to give them to God."

Should she tell him of her own experience? Not yet. "And our marriage?"

"To answer your original question, no. I don't think we'll ever find our way back, nor should we try."

"I'm sorry to hear you say so, Henry."

"Not what I mean. I'm not a writer like you, and it's hard to put words to what I feel."

"Try."

"I think maybe God wants to move us forward—not back—forward toward something better."

Her knight in shining armor found courage again, to say all those things, knowing full well Lana Longstreet might shred his dignity like a lettuce chopper. How was he supposed to know she had left the building ... hopefully for good.

Sylvia rested her head on Henry's still strong shoulder. "You won't believe what I'm about to tell you."

They talked for hours, holding each other. He marveled at her story, yet a part of him felt saddened. Separately, as children, they once believed in a God who loved them. What might their marriage have been if they had held to their faith? He dispelled remorse and clung to hope. This newness, this rain of revelation, might yet cleanse their troubled marriage.

He brought her into a kiss, filled with reassurance. There would be a sequel to Sylvia and Henry, this book written by God's intervention.

Sylvia searched his eyes. What did she hope to find? "I have to tell you something. I promise I'll never lie to you again. I want to meet the person who sent the email you saw. I have to, Henry. What if it isn't a prank? What if someone—someone who has as much to lose as we do—wants to help us?"

Sylvia shared the innuendos and the eerie reference to *Shadows at Noon*. Her logic held true. Regrettably so.

Still, how could he ignore the risk? As if drawn into one of Sylvia's novels, a plan took root. "I'll agree to let you go on one condition. You keep your phone on while I wait outside. If I don't like where the conversation is going, I'll call the police. Agreed?"

"I suppose we should be cautious."

"I'm taking you up on the dinner invitation. We can go to Regina's. The restaurant's about five blocks from the warehouse, and we can walk from there. No need to involve Erik."

Sylvia's wry smile was intoxicating, and they shook hands like two boxers before a bout. Henry glanced at the clock. "Do you realize how late it is? Past noon already, and you never touched your toast. What do you want for lunch?

"Nothing right now. Let's just sit here and talk for a bit longer."

"About?"

"About your move from your room to mine?"

"I'd like that."

They talked for hours more, imagining the future, with hope but yet with trepidation ... so many unknowns. Would they have to sell the house? If so, would Sylvia be willing to move back to Manhattan? Though turbulent times certainly stretched ahead, from now on they'd bridge them together.

He glanced at his watch. "It's three o'clock. Martina and Erik will be here soon."

Sylvia put on her sweater, then glanced in her mirror. "You go on ahead. I need to freshen up a bit."

"Okay. I'll see you in a few minutes." As he started toward the loft, something like a wolf's howl pierced the quiet. He thought his stomach growled until Sylvia ran up behind him.

"What was that? Sounded like an airplane overhead."

"I thought I imagined ..."

A wind funnel rifled through the loft. Pictures dropped to the floor, and the computer began to creep across Sylvia's desk.

Henry grabbed Sylvia's arm. "Let's get out of here!"

Before they could reach the spiral staircase, a force pinned them against the wall. Sylvia called out into the wind, "In the name of Jesus, I command you to leave at once."

The air stilled.

This woman amazed him, as if Lana Longstreet and Sylvia Fitzgibbons merged into one confident being. "How did you know what to do?"

"Something I learned from Reverend Estes. He told me the only power Satan has over the believer is fear, and he must bow to the power of Jesus's name."

"We've so much to learn."

Deciding to take the grand staircase, Henry led Sylvia down the steps, both of them gasping when they reached the foyer. A sheet of plywood lay scattered across the ballroom.

They stood hand in hand—a unified protest against the evil desiring them. Henry gazed into Sylvia's eyes, and they said in unison, "You cannot have this house. It belongs to Christ alone."

FROM JOHNNY GALLANT

C28

Johnny Gallant paced the floor, his thoughts disturbed by memories of Celeste. Though he'd sent her away only two months ago, her absence seemed more like an eternity.

He knew beyond any shadow of doubt that he was destined to break her heart sooner or later. Maybe sooner was better than later. His half truths may have seemed cruel on the surface ... how else could he protect her? He'd taken advantage of her, betrayed her trust in him. He didn't deserve her love.

Gold became tarnished when touched by an inferior metal. If he'd stayed with her, he'd have only caused her ruin. Jimmy Holloway proved himself to be as competent as they came—an eagle's eye and canine hearing, his wits like radar wherever danger lurked.

No matter how Johnny justified rejecting Celeste, his longing could not be squelched. If he could smell her perfumed hair or hold her milk-soft hands once more ...

No!

His self-loathing was a sledge certain to smash her generous heart to pulp. He had reached a crossroad—to die for his want of her or to kill their love with his egotism.

CHAPTER 25

Sylvia stopped typing and stretched her fingers. The words flew like a Texas deluge after the drought.

Her life had turned a hundred eighty degrees in the matter of a few weeks. Once she required absolute silence while she wrote. What miracle helped her to work while strangers took over her home?

Kind people helped her and Henry clear the ballroom, setting up chairs, and singing hymns while they worked. Perhaps the vigil energized, rather than served as a distraction. Once set up, they told them to feel free to go about their necessary lives while they prayed for them.

She made her way down the grand staircase to rejoin the worshipers before she and Henry left for Regina's. Stopping at the ballroom foyer, she allowed the soft candlelight to warm her spirit. Paul was standing next to Henry while a group sang chorus after chorus, some she remembered from Sunday school. She must find a way to thank Erik and Martina who refused extra pay for their services as well as supplying the guests with sandwiches and snacks. Even Sven and Gunnar pitched in and passed out candles. Martina kept one lit at the entrance way, and guests tipped their candles into the taller one.

The schedule promised a minimum of two people every two hours to assure continuous prayer. Surprisingly, the ballroom bulged with warriors. Father Gilbert, Rosalie's priest, and Charlie arrived early. Sylvia felt humbled by the generosity of these saintly people who answered her need for no profit of their own.

She brought in a folding chair and set it between Henry and Paul, enjoying his melodic baritone. The songs seemed to spread a sweet aroma ousting the sulfuric odors so often hovering in the room. Whatever evil presence had lurked before could no longer be sensed in this holy presence.

So, this is worship.

She wanted to linger, but God propelled her toward a meeting of a different sort.

Henry took her hand and guided her from the ballroom. Paul followed. "I asked Higgy to join us in our little rendezvous. He has as much at stake as we do."

Sylvia huffed. "Why don't we call in the National Guard while we're at it?"

Paul laughed. "We'll keep the entourage to just us. Henry filled me in on your plan. You two can ride with me to Regina's, then we'll walk to the factory from there. I wanted to call the police, but GI Joe thought otherwise."

Sylvia squeezed Paul's cheek. "You are the dearest man I know."

Regina's had long been one of Henry's favorite New Haven eateries. Decorated in colonial style, the aura reeked of early eighteenth-century charm. Yet, the spicy offerings contradicted perceived revolutionary favorites like Yankee Pot Roast. The waitstaff, well-trained in expeditious hospitality, proved to be both efficient and amiable.

Higgy helped Sylvia into the booth, then sat on the opposite side of the table. "I always enjoy eating here when I'm in New Haven."

Henry nestled next to Sylvia, pushing the booth curtain to one side to gain full view of the restaurant. "Place has quite a history. If one believes the hype, Regina's has been in business since the early seventeen hundreds. First as an inn. Then about 1945, Lorenzo's father bought it and turned it into a first-class restaurant."

The rotund Lorenzo waddled to the table with a rose-filled vase and greeted his favorite patron with a kiss on the cheek. "For *a you*, Miss Longstreet." He clicked his chubby heels together, bowed, and left.

Higgy covered his mouth as he whispered to Sylvia. "Lorenzo's affectations never cease to amuse."

"*Ssh*. He's coming back."

This time Lorenzo handed Sylvia a complimentary bottle of champagne. "I do not believe a word of *a dis* gossip, Miss Longstreet. A woman as *a pretty* as you? She could *a never* do such a thing."

Sylvia rescued the mission. "Thank you, Lorenzo. But we need clear heads for a meeting after dinner. May I save this for a later time?"

"By all means. *Pleez*, enjoy your meal. If not to your liking, you *a tell* Lorenzo." This time he winked then returned to the kitchen without further ceremony. In good order, the three feasted on stuffed manicotti with marinara sauce, Lorenzo's specialty.

The small talk about weather and the current stock market brought a welcomed respite from the recent heaviness. Higgy savored his last bite, sipping his water before settling back against the booth. "While I finally have the two of you together, I wanted to share something with you I think you'll find interesting."

Sylvia smiled. "Do tell, my dear Mr. Higgins."

"Berky conducted a title search ..."

Sylvia's face whitened. "Paul, I don't want to lose the house."

"Just to be sure, Sylvia. I don't believe it will come down to that."

Resilient as always, she propped her elbows on the table and cradled her head as if in jest. "So, what wonderful bits of information did you discover? I did the same thing when I bought the place. I'm not completely devoid of business sense, you know."

Henry's cheeks heated. He should have been more curious about their little piece of history. No time like the present. "You've got my attention, Higgy."

"I didn't stop with the government abstract. Our private investigator hired a research expert who dug up some interesting history. As Sylvia already knows, Theodore Trumbull, a distant relative of then Governor Jonathan Trumbull, built the main house."

Henry's sparse knowledge of Connecticut history couldn't fill the proverbial thimble. But he did recognize the name Trumball, jarring a piece of stored trivia in the recesses of his mind. "Wasn't he one of the few governors allowed to remain in office during the American War of Independence?"

Higgy's face gleamed. He always smirked when he spun a good yarn. In their Army days, Higgy stole the limelight with his renditions of ancient mideastern history. Henry glanced toward Sylvia, her eyes bulging as Higgy continued.

"Right you are, Henry. Connecticut managed to escape the worst of the fighting although the colony supplied much of the goods for the Continental Army, and Theodore's political connections allowed him to conduct meetings relatively unencumbered. Many suspected his famous balls were a mere militaristic opportunity, a place where generals gathered to discuss war plans."

Sylvia leaned back. "Tell me something I don't already know. It's possible George Washington attended at least one of Trumball's affairs."

Higgy winked. "But did you know about the Massacre of 1779?"

Henry and Sylvia joined in chorus, "What massacre?"

"A lot of rumor and conjecture mixed in with a few facts, of course. The official account reports renegade loyalists butchered more than fifty guests along with Theodore, his wife, and their two grown children."

Henry pulled at his stomach, and his chest constricted as memories flickered under the black light of remembrance. Not of colonials but of screaming Muslim women and children:

Sarge flung a cigarette to the ground and crushed it. "Stevens, I want you and your squad to go house to house inside the village. See if there're any friendlies who'll help interpret. Watch your back. The rest of you secure a perimeter. No one goes in or out until it's sanitized. I'd like to avoid bombing if possible. The major thinks there are dissidents hiding out in some of the houses. Typical of these extremists … to use women and children to shield them."

Stevens tipped his helmet, his wide grin nearly as ridiculous as Bozo the Clown's. "Sure, Sarge. Bones and Isaacs—start at the south end. Farrell, Johnson, and Frosty—take center. Bartholomew and Higgy will follow me to the North. Fitz, you're with us so we can keep an eye on you." Stevens tipped Fitz's helmet with a bayonnette. "Can't have anything happening to you when you're due back home shortly. Or didn't you know Sarge got your orders straightened out."

Fitz gulped. No he didn't know Sarge had gone to bat for him. He'd be glad to leave Iraq.

Stevens laughed. "I see you're as clueless as always, Fitz."

Sarge turned to the others and barked orders. "Mark each clean house, so we don't do a double search. Any questions?"

Voices roared over his head like dubbed subtitles in a foreign flick, lips moving out of sync. Henry forced himself back into the present.

"... Trumbull's brother," Higgy continued, "inherited the property but gave the estate to Josephine Bonet, the beloved governess, in exchange for her care of Theodore's younger children, not present at the time of the massacre since Miss Josephine, according to the records, had taken the younger children on a rare holiday the day before. Sadly, the two younger children drowned while visiting the Trumball's ocean bungalow some months later. After their deaths, Josephine married Alvin Donner, an ancestor of the previous owner, Alfred Donner. Some rumored Josephine was a loyalist spy and the lover of Captain Briggs, the leader of the renegade squad who conducted the raid. He and his troops had been swiftly captured, tried, and hung."

Talk of wars and massacres once more brought up memories Henry so desperately wanted to forget.

"Fitz, watch out! Enemy at eleven!" Fitz dropped at the warning. Everyone fired without hesitancy, not realizing their targets were barricaded by women and children dressed as dissidents. The cries of the wounded mingled with rat-tat-tats and soldiers' shouts. Dust rose from the bevy of bullets as the extremists came out from behind their human shields and fired back. Spits and gags blended with a descant of frenzied moans from the bereaved.

His face buried in the crusty sand, Fitz reached for more ammo while a warm, sticky substance drizzled down his pant leg. Higgy was face down in the dirt, barely conscious, blood seeping from a shattered knee, while a second stream flowed from his skull.

From some leftover boy-scout instinct, Fitz pulled a towel from his backpack and wrapped Higgy's head and tied a piece of torn pant leg around his thigh—a makeshift tourniquet. "Don't you die on me, Higgy. You owe me ten bucks. Remember?"

Fitz raised his eyes. Dead women and children dotted the horizon. The site nauseated him, and boiling acid churned his stomach.

Stevens's commands rose above the sudden silence. "Look guys. Do your best to secure the place. This was just a horrible accident."

The company medic crawled up beside him. "Go, Fitz. I'll take care of Higgy."

Fitz pulled himself up, puking every few steps as he approached the remains of battle. Squashing his repulsion, he rolled the riddled, blood-bathed body of a small boy. A stick jutted from underneath. As Fitz turned from this slaughter, his eye caught a flutter of white. He turned and saw the prone body of a teenaged girl. Around her stiffening fingers, something silver glistened in the afternoon sun.

Stevens approached. "What's this?" He slipped the tip of his bayonet between the dead girl's palms, retrieving the treasure. "Well, what do ya know? Ain't that pretty?" He pocketed the silver cross with no sign of remorse. "My girl will like this."

Fitz fell to his knees. His vomit mingled with the blood of innocents.

Henry thought he heard Sylvia cry out from among the dead. "Do you think Josephine planned the massacre and turned in her lover? Oh my, but that's a good plot ... Henry? Are you all right?"

Henry stepped forward to receive his medal while others stood in line to await a similar honor. When he returned to formation, he leaned toward Higgy. "How's this possible? We should be court-martialed, not honored."

"You saved my life, Fitz. Don't look at the negative."

There could be nothing heroic in the murder of women and children. Did the government buy his silence with a medal and a ceremony? Did no one care that a band of frightened soldiers massacred a village over a little boy's stick?

The army called the fiasco a tragic accident while Henry wore the lie in the form of a medal, an earlier than anticipated discharge, and an eternal reminder of his cowardice.

Sylvia's jab to his side broke his stupor. "Henry? Are you still with us?"

"I'm sorry, Sylvia. I went away for a few seconds."

Higgy threw him a knowing glance. "It came back to you, didn't it, Fitz?"

Sylvia's eyes quizzed Higgy first, then Henry. "What came back? What're you talking about, Paul?"

"It's time for the truth, old friend. Are you going to tell her why you're claustrophobic or should I?"

Sylvia poised herself like a detective preparing for a confession. "Henry? I thought we cleared the air this afternoon. What're you hiding from me?"

Henry drained his water glass, then oozed a long sigh. "War does horrible things to a person, Sylvia. I enlisted for three years when I got out of college to help pay for my loans, still pretty innocent about life. I spent the last few months of service during the first ground invasion of Iraq. I was supposed to be mustered out, not deployed. Higgy here was bound and determined to keep me safe from harm."

Henry spewed the horror, every scream and bloody image. Sylvia didn't pull away from him as he expected. Instead, her eyes filled with sympathetic tears. She took his hand into hers. "Why haven't you told me before now? I knew you had recently been discharged from the Army when we met, but I never knew what you had gone through.

All these years, I thought your phobia was an excuse, a cover-up for not wanting to be with me. I might not have understood, but I would have loved you through your pain."

Silence reigned for a few moments as if no one knew quite what to say ... no other words of comfort could be offered. Henry waved the waiter to refill their water glasses as Higgy broke the silence. "Your husband left out the fact he saved my life during that fiasco. You're too hard on yourself, Fitz. The rest of us accepted the incident for what it was—an extraordinary disaster during extraordinary times, fighting unconventional warfare. But you—you've chained yourself to an unshakable memory."

Henry leaned back and stared at his friend. "You mean you never thought about what happened?"

"Of course, I remember. The horror brought me to my knees where I found forgiveness. You took a little longer."

Sweat teemed from Henry's face, and his clothes were soaked from perspiration. He took out his handkerchief and wiped his face, then Sylvia kissed his clammy hand. "War, Henry, makes criminals of us all. Sometimes we are helpless to undo the harm. We can only hope the rest of our lives will atone for the past."

Her words soothed him. Maybe God would ease his self-recrimination as he'd done for Higgy.

"If you'll excuse me, I think I'd like to throw a wet towel on my face before we leave."

As he pushed against the men's-room door, a sultry, British accent caught his attention. Why was Monique in Connecticut—and so late? He must be hearing voices. A brawny, male laugh joined the woman's English lilt. Perhaps he should say hello. He stepped forward but stopped at her words. "Oh, Evan. How I adore you."

CHAPTER 26

Sylvia's heart jumped with every creak.

Something scurried over her shoe. She lowered her flashlight and caught a glimpse of a gray mouse as it scampered under a set of boxes. Shivering half from the eeriness and half from the cold, she turned the flashlight on each corner of the room. What if this was nothing more than a cruel hoax? She should turn around right now and go home.

She whispered into the phone, "I've had a lot of bad ideas in my day. I think this takes the cake. I'll stick to writing about private investigators instead of becoming one."

She held the phone up to her ear, keeping the volume as low as possible. Henry's voice reassured her. "We'll give you five more minutes. Then you're coming out, or we're coming in. No debate."

"You'll get no argument from me. This place gives me the creeps."

"We're right outside the door. Whistle if you need us."

Snap.

The sound came from behind. She reeled, and her flashlight flew from her hands across the room.

Henry's panic rang in her ear. "I don't like the sounds of that. We're coming in."

"Good!"

Enough intrigue for one night.

Sylvia picked up the flashlight, giving it three whacks. Yes. The flashlight could be used as a weapon if needed. Against what? She practiced a couple of karate moves she learned researching *Hero's Last Stand.*

A woman's shadow came into view. "Miss Longstreet, it's me, Monique. I'm sorry if I gave you a fright."

Sylvia tightened her grip on the flashlight. "What're you up to, Monique? You're lucky I didn't smack you with this."

Henry and Paul rushed in like the SWAT team on a movie set, each armed with boards.

Monique's laughter combined with Sylvia's. "Easy, Henry. I counted on one or both of you trailing Miss Longstreet." Monique turned toward a stack of boxes. "You can come out now, Jonathan. Everybody's here."

A young man, late twenties, dressed in sweats and a Yale University baseball cap, peered around a stack of boxes. Then he shuffled to where Monique stood. "Are you okay, Monique? I warned you this mystery theater might get someone hurt."

The shadowy figure turned to face Sylvia and her musketeers. "Miss Longstreet, I'm Jonathan Delaney."

Sylvia chomped on her amusement, saving her ridicule for another time. After all, Henry and Paul had thought themselves her rescuers, and she should allow them their momentary delusion of heroism. "Gentlemen, put your boards down. I don't think these two are a threat."

Henry dropped his board, his grunt proof of his distrust. "I'm glad you find all this amusing, Sylvia. So happens, I overheard Monique at Regina's while she dined with Evan North."

"Is this true, Monique?"

Monique's flashlight quivered. She was probably as frightened as her invited guest. "Yes, Miss Longstreet, but I can explain. I didn't know you were there. Honest."

Henry stepped forward. "I'll bet. Higgy was right about you all along."

Monique sobbed her rebuttal. "Mr. Higgins? You told Henry not to trust me? How could you? Of all people, I thought you were a good judge of character."

A silhouetted Paul coughed. "I simply told Henry not to trust anyone, including you. I'm sorry, Monique. I meant to keep the employees out of this mess as much as possible. Still, I'd like to know why you dined with Evan North and at a place you know we frequent. What am I supposed to think?"

Monique upended five wooden crates. "These will have to do for chairs." As if she owned the place, she scooted to the other side of the room, flipped on the overhead lights, and returned. "Don't worry. Daddy owns the factory. He hasn't decided what to do with the property yet. I just thought you'd be intrigued if we met in the dark at first."

Sylvia smiled. Might as well give Monique a bit of credit where credit was due. She could have been a script writer. Her parallels to *Shadows at Noon* offered an entertaining mystery. Shame Henry couldn't appreciate the mastery.

Monique sat first. "Things are not always as they seem, Henry. Words I've heard you use many times. Look, I'm on your side. You've got to believe me. I told you, I can explain. Sit down ... please. I promise you, everything will make sense by the time we're done. I didn't mean to scare anyone. Jonathan wanted so desperately to explain everything to you, for Julie's sake. I told him this was a capital way to make certain Miss Longstreet met with us. He thought the idea crackers, but we couldn't be sure you'd meet with us in a conventional way."

Henry grunted. "Probably not. I tried to talk Sylvia out of this absurdity, but she wouldn't listen." He approached Monique as if skirting a rattler. "You expect us to believe you've lured us here for benign purposes?" He took two steps toward the door. "Sylvia ... Higgy ... let's go. I'm not in the mood for games. If this boy can't be man enough to face us on his own, I'm not sure I want to listen to anything he has to say."

Sylvia took a deep breath. Writer's intuition told her Jonathan Delaney was the key to this whole litigation riddle. She pulled Henry back into the scene. "Monique and Jonathan have gone to extraordinary lengths to get our attention. Don't you think we should give them the benefit of the doubt, for Julie's sake, at least?" Sylvia plopped down on a crate. "Now sit, both of you."

She studied Jonathan's slender, muscular build, focusing on his acclaimed delicious blue eyes, his cherub face belying an otherwise masculine aura. When he spoke, his voice lilted across the room with melodic vibrations. "Monique's right. We only wanted to get your attention. We never meant to frighten you, Miss Longstreet."

"You may call me Mrs. Fitzgibbons."

Henry smiled.

"Mrs. Fitzgibbons, I love your daughter. I would never hurt her or her family."

A calmer Henry and Paul reluctantly sat on either side of Sylvia. "Why all the secrecy? There must have been a dozen places we could have met." Henry glared at Monique. "Regina's seems to be a favorite hangout these days."

She wailed like a stepped-on cat. "I'm sorry you overheard us, Henry. I only pretended to be interested in Evan so I could help Jonathan."

Sylvia bristled. "Jonathan's engaged to my daughter, Monique. I hardly think that's a defense."

Jonathan stiffened, his eyes large with infantile fear. "Maybe I should do the talking, Monique. You're getting us into serious hot water here." He turned to face his accusers. "Mr. Fitzgibbons ... Mrs. Fitzgibbons ... Mr. Higgens ...

The Gathering Flock isn't plagiarized ... well not by Lana Longstreet."

Paul took out his cell phone, snapped a picture, then hit video. "What are you saying, young man? North's *Fowl Weather* appeared on the market before *The Gathering Flock*'s review copies were sent out."

Jonathan's eyes bulged at Paul's threat, but Sylvia smiled. Something about the lad's bungled attempt to prove his innocence endeared him to her. "Please. Hear him out, Paul. Might prove interesting if nothing else."

Paul saluted with one hand and held his cell phone in the other.

Jonathan breathed like a diver about to plunge. "*The Gathering Flock* is *my* book. I wrote it."

Monique gushed. "You have to admit, Henry, it's a marvelous book."

Sylvia groaned. "Ten to one, he hasn't read it."

Henry scowled. "My reading history is not the issue here, ladies. Jonathan, are you admitting to copying North's book?"

"No, I'm not admitting anything, Mr. Fitzgibbons. *Fowl Weather* was the plagiarism. Mr. North stole my book."

Creaks from a decaying building and a howling wind filled the silence. Jonathan's accusation ate at Sylvia's stomach like a third cup of coffee. Either Evan North was a crook or Jonathan was a liar—neither alternative appealed to her. Evan wasn't merely a neighbor—he was a dear friend—they attended each other's signings and launch parties. How could he have stooped to stealing someone else's work? If he did such a horrible thing, why did he frame her?

"Jonathan, none of what you're saying makes much sense."

"Mr. and Mrs. Fitzgibbons, please believe me. I love Julie with all my heart. I'd gladly die for her."

Henry rose, visibly shaken, then took a step toward Jonathan, his hands fisted, readied for combat. Jonathan recoiled, perhaps more out of respect than fear. Henry hardly posed a threat to a younger man like Jonathan.

"Henry, nobody wants to talk to you when you're menacing. Relax. Let the boy say his piece."

He exuded a long snort, then sat. "Fine."

Sylvia motioned for Jonathan to continue. "We're listening, aren't we, Henry? Although, my husband has every right to distrust you, and what you're proposing seems ludicrous. I've known Evan North for years."

The bulge in Jonathan's throat traversed the entire length of his neck as he gulped. "With all due respect, Miss Longstreet—"

"Mrs. Fitzgibbons."

"My apologies ... Mrs. Fitzgibbons."

"Apology accepted. Continue."

"Even the wealthy and powerful reach a point of utter desperation. I've been Mr. North's assistant for two years, and in all that time I never saw him write a thing. He claimed he was too busy lecturing at Yale. When he asked to read my book, I assumed he meant to help, especially since he kept it for a few weeks. When he gave my manuscript back to me, he threw it on the table and said my writing was the worst tripe he'd ever read. In the meantime, Fitzgibbons & Associate had offered me a contract for *The Gathering Flock*."

Henry riled. "I sign those contracts, boy, and I don't recall your name at all."

Monique coughed. "Henry, in case you forgot, you let me sign your paperwork. The senior acquisitions editor sent me the contract. Since you and Mr. Higgins were out of the office, I signed off on your behalf."

Sylvia glared at Henry. Should she be angrier he gave his Voguish secretary so much authority or that he didn't even know what authors the company contracted? "Go on, Jonathan."

His gaze flitted from one perspective in-law to the other. Poor boy, caught in the web of a family torn asunder. "When I told Mr. North I'd received a contract, he threatened to fire me. We argued, and I said he had no right to run my life. I'd quit first before he could fire me. He cooled, and I thought the matter dropped until his book, *Fowl Weather*, showed up in bookstores across the country nine months later just before my book was due to be released. He offered me a bribe to keep silent. 'Compensation for artistic contribution,' he said."

Sylvia inched closer to Jonathan, clasping his hands in hers. "What a terrible thing to do, stealing an artist's work."

"I thought you'd understand, Mrs. Fitzgibbons."

Henry snarled. "Another mystery. You and Julie. How convenient the two of you happened to take the same cruise before North's book came out."

Jonathan reddened. "I can explain."

Henry folded his arms against his chest. "Go ahead. Try."

"Julie doesn't know this, but I've been in love with her for years before the cruise. I never told her we went to the same high school because she wouldn't have remembered me. We hung out in different crowds, and I was a few grades ahead of her. I was incredibly shy and too afraid to ask her out. After college, I returned to New Haven, hoping to break into a career in writing. Meanwhile, I followed Julie's art career, signing up for her blog and newsletter. When I read about her upcoming cruise, I got a ticket and pretended our meeting was coincidental. I didn't want her to think I was stalking her ..."

Henry smirked. "Weren't you?"

"Maybe. I suppose I should tell her the truth, even if she calls off our engagement."

Henry's posture seemed to relax some ... perhaps amused by Jonathan's predicament. "She deserves nothing less than the truth." Crossing his legs, Henry continued his interrogation. "Let's assume what you've told us is true. How did copies of your book get printed with my wife's name on the cover? If you didn't plagiarize Evan's book, you've stolen my wife's identity. Still a crime. Right, Higgy?"

Contemplating, Paul didn't answer immediately. "I don't know what to think. I'm no lawyer, and there're a lot of unexplained things in this whole mess. One bit of info helps confirm Jonathan's story, though. I investigated the distribution order for *The Gathering Flock*—twenty thousand copies were planned—a small number for one of Sylvia's books. Even more curious ... only four thousand were actually printed and sent to her list of reviewers and designated authors, Evan North among them."

Monique chimed in. "I can explain, Mr. Higgins. You see, I told Asaim, our exchange worker, Mr. Delaney was going to be the next Lana Longstreet. Asaim's English isn't very good. He thought I meant Miss Longstreet wrote the book and changed the template. Then Jonathan told me what Mr. North had done. Fortunately, I was able to cancel the distribution until we could figure out what to do about Jonathan's book. Unfortunately, not soon enough to stop the advance reader copies from going out. I sent a memo to all the reviewers, including Mr. North, explaining the error, and requesting they disregard and destroy the book."

Paul scowled. "You should have told us, Monique. Maybe this whole thing could have been avoided."

"You're right, Mr. Higgins. I didn't mean to be deceitful. I wanted to help Jonathan, and I didn't want Asaim to get into trouble. I overstepped my authority. By trying to make the mistake disappear, the situation got out of control. I was afraid you'd fire me."

Sylvia met Monique's worried glance. "That could still happen. So, then, if what you're saying is true, Evan's using our company's incompetence to cover up his crime."

Jonathan took Monique's hand in his. "I'm afraid so. Monique felt responsible, so she agreed to go out with Mr. North to see if she could put a stop to all this. I begged her not to. Mr. North can't be trusted. I'm afraid he's used her good intentions to further his self interests. She's got a good heart. Not wanting to be accused of using her influence to get Fitzgibbons & Associate to publish my book, she kept our relationship a secret."

"Relationship?" Anger surged through Sylvia's veins as she viewed their interlocked hands. "What about Julie?"

Jonathan squeaked his explanation. "I'm afraid we've given you the wrong impression, Mrs. Fitzgibbons. You see, Monique's my cousin ... our mothers are sisters."

Sylvia sighed relief.

"I'm afraid I have no way to prove my innocence. Even Julie doubts me. Please believe me when I say I'm just a simple boy who wants to be a writer. I've always been a huge fan of Lana Longstreet. Both Monique and I have tried to reason with Evan North. But our pleas haven't done any good. He's bribed at least a dozen people at his publishing company to vouch for the timeline on his stolen book. They doctored all communications, shredding any incriminating documentation, including my letters of protest. Since, technically, Mr. North's contract precedes mine with Fitzgibbons & Associate, and he has an earlier release date, granted only by a week or so, I'm afraid there's no proof other than my testimony."

Sylvia smirked. "I'm not so sure Evan would go the nth degree on this lawsuit, now that I know the story. But given what I'm just heard, I expect he'd be willing to milk this fiasco to our ruin. His book is flying off the shelves, I'm told. The publicity alone is making him very rich."

Henry stood, his body more relaxed and his cheeks less red. "I don't know why I should believe you ... yet, strangely, I do. You took a big risk tonight. I can verify any correspondence between our company and you. That should, at least, clear up authorship and exonerate my wife. You'll dig those out for me, Monique?"

"Yes, of course."

Henry scratched his chin. "As you say, I'm afraid we have little proof of your version of the story. Sorry, but you appear as guilty as we do. Any ideas, Higgy?"

"I'll talk to our private investigators. If Monique and Jonathan are telling the truth, North must be desperate. Desperate men are often careless, and we might uncover a flaw in his scheme—put an end to this mess."

Sylvia listened intently as all was explained and considered Paul's suggestions going forward. She glanced at Monique, panged with guilt over the jealousy Lana Longstreet had nurtured toward the girl. Monique was as loyal as she was beautiful. This much was certain ... somehow, someway, the truth would come out.

CHAPTER 27

They walked in silence from the warehouse back to Regina's and on the ride back to the house. .

"Why don't you stay the night, Paul?" Sylvia asked.

"You two go on in. I'll see you in the morning. There's a matter I need to attend to. Let this thing rest overnight and then we'll examine the facts again in daylight."

Sylvia cocked her head to one side. "What business could possibly be so important at one o'clock in the morning?"

Higgy laughed. The man might deceive Sylvia but not Henry. Something rattled in his brilliant brain. "All this intrigue has left me with a humdinger of a headache, and I didn't want to worry you. I just need to sleep on all this."

"But why drive all the way back into the city if you're coming to Connecticut again tomorrow? We have plenty of room, and I'm sure Henry could lend you a set of his pajamas."

Higgy smiled as he fidgeted with the wheel. "I appreciate the offer, but I'll sleep better in my own bed. It's only an hour's drive."

As he left, Henry didn't make a move toward the house where so many were still gathered, stealing a private moment with Sylvia. "It's a nice night, tonight."

"Yes, it is."

Cupping her chin, he drew her into a kiss.

"What was that about?"

He embraced her. "I've come to a realization, Sylvia. I've been so busy hating Connecticut, I forgot to count the good things, like the cooler summer nights, and the serenade of the birds in the early morning."

Sylvia returned his kiss.

Henry tried not to yawn. Deep into the wee morning hours, thirty or more people still remained in the ballroom. He and Sylvia slipped in, adding their voices to the praise choruses. By three o'clock, Sylvia excused herself, though Henry stayed wanting to pray for a few minutes more. The worshipers dwindled down to four—four committed to pray through until dawn.

Pop once organized an all-night prayer vigil on behalf of a critically ill parishioner. Fifteen-year-old Henry ridiculed Pop's efforts, refusing to participate. "Pop, if you want my opinion, this all-night prayer stuff's nothing more than a pompous, religious farce." Young Henry stormed out the door. When he returned, he found his father grieving the man's death. Prideful, arrogant Henry had felt no sympathy. "I told you so, Pop."

How he wished he could have the moment back. Why can't life give a man a mulligan or two?

A slight twinge shot up his arm as he realized remorse was futile. Pop believed God threw confessed sin into the sea of his forgetfulness to be remembered no more. Henry prayed for grace to forgive himself. He thanked God for the peace within this house, his house together with Sylvia. He asked for discernment in their dealings with Jonathan and God's protection for the business.

Henry's thoughts returned toward Monique and Jonathan. Every piece of evidence pointed to their guilt, and no reasonable person should trust either one of them. "I don't know what to think, Lord. I'll let you figure it out."

He prayed for Sylvia. Could he make up for all the years he failed her? In many ways, she still resembled the forlorn, rain-soaked waif who captured his heart all those years ago. The memory warmed him.

Discharged only a few months, he'd managed to get an editorial job with a sport's magazine. Wondering what his future might be, he had just closed his umbrella to enter his magazine's building when his eye caught a woman hugging her soaked garments, laughing in the rain, her near-black hair stringing over her shoulders like wet spaghetti. When she twisted her soggy curls as if to wring them dry, their eyes met. She seemed to him like a drowned, unsheltered rose. He offered his umbrella.

"I don't need one, thank you. I have my own." She took one from her purse to prove her independence. "I wanted to feel the rain against me to describe a scene I'm writing in my novel."

"You're a writer?"

"Actually, until today I worked as a senior editor at *Fashion Daze Magazine*." She pointed to the large building behind them where Henry had moments before readied to enter. Strange they hadn't met before today. "I just landed my first book contract."

"Congratulations. What's it called?"

"*A Life Gladly Sacrificed.*"

"Do you always celebrate by getting soaked in the rain? Aren't you going back inside where it's dry?"

"No. I'm headed home. I quit my job so I can write full time."

Her bus pulled up beside them. If he got on it, he'd be late for work, not to mention his hatred of closed places included cars, trains, buses. He threw all his fears to the wind, obeying a whisper.

The bus ride became Henry's greatest adventure yet to be told. Even with the bumpy roads, he never once regretted taking the bus to win Sylvia's heart.

His eyes drooped, sleep loudly calling to him. He climbed the spiral staircase into Sylvia's chambers, pulled the sheets down, and slipped into bed next to her.

The lawsuit seemed trivial compared to the peace he felt at this moment. Knowing their history, could this feeling last?

FROM JOHNNY GALLANT

C30

Johnny spotted her from across the room, always in white and always feeling as if heaven called to him. When Celeste looked his way, the world stopped, and there were only the two of them. As good a bodyguard as they came, Jimmy's eyes swept the room while Johnny held Celeste, the party having slowed its pulse as if permitting him this moment with her.

He should have noticed the man in the misfitting tuxedo before he pushed Jimmy aside and charged toward Celeste as if on a suicide run. By the time Johnny saw the small pistol in the man's palm, he could do little else but pull Celeste behind him, away from the line of fire. His flesh ripped open as the bullet felled him, and the room folded like a book with him inside, her hallowed beauty shimmering against the growing blackness.

"Johnny, don't leave me now," she cried as tears cleansed his grief for his plan to abandon her.

He prayed whatever sins he committed in this life might be erased by this one selfless act, surrendering his fate to a greater power than Johnny Gallant as the last flicker of light vanished.

CHAPTER 28

The story couldn't end there, not if she were to write a sequel. Should she allow Johnny to live and find faith? Lana Longstreet never hesitated to leave her readers screaming at her hero's unfair treatment, whereas Sylvia wanted to provide her characters with hope. For Celeste to never know the depth of Johnny's love seemed an outrage.

Soft singing wafted through the stairwell. Mark Estes was right. Evil couldn't coexist with praise.

Sylvia glanced at the clock. Nearing time for Charlie to leave. She had never thanked him for his kindness ... no time like the present. She took the spiral staircase into the kitchen, appreciative of the aroma from a freshly brewed pot of coffee. Why not surprise the men and bring the serving tray out to them? She hedged toward the pantry for a china cup, turned, and reached for a third mug instead—a *rose by any other name*. She grabbed several packages of Lorna Doones and took the kitchen path to the veranda.

Henry stood by the shed and glanced her way, appreciation radiating from his eyes. "Coffee!" He pointed toward the shed. "Nice job, don't you think? Just like the one we tore down only this one doesn't have spiders."

Henry put his arm around Charlie's shoulder. "Come join us."

"Don't mind if I do." Everyone pulled up a wicker chair, and Sylvia put the tray on the patio table. "Thanks for the coffee, Miss Longstreet."

"Please, call me Sylvia."

"Sylvia it is."

She scanned the backyard. "Looks like you've accomplished a lot in a short time. I wish you'd let us repay you in some way."

Charlie stroked his bread, then took a big gulp of coffee. "Well, there's something you might consider. Mind you, it's only a suggestion. Don't want ya to feel obligated."

Henry took a long sip before meeting Charlie's gaze. "Sorry, needed that! Go on, we're listening."

"My church helps poorer folks fix up their yards ... a ministry of sorts. We supply them with tools, shrubs, basic flowers—I give lessons on lawn care. We believe in the self-help approach. As they learn, we ask they teach others. This way, we've beautified entire blocks in the slums of New Haven. If you'd care to make a donation, I'll let my pastor know."

Henry beamed. "What do you think, Sylvia?"

She nodded. Until now, she resented Henry's generosity. His easy giving had unmasked Lana Longstreet's miserliness. Could she change? She hoped so. "By all means, Henry."

"Sounds good. Count us in—financially, of course. I don't think I'd make a fit teacher."

Charlie snickered. "Don't be so hard on yourself, Henry. You did quite a bit on your own today." He turned to Sylvia, offering an exaggerated wink. "He's right handy with a shovel there. If he gets any better, he'll put me out of a job."

"Fat chance of that happening. Takes me twice as long as Charlie just to prune a shoot."

Sylvia looked toward the fortified bushes. "I should spend more time out here. The early blooms are beautiful, and the mid-season buds are starting to pop."

Charlie nodded. "Mr. Donner preferred mid-bloomers. Henry said he wanted blooms all summer, so some of the new beds I planted are summer sprouts. Before I finish up this fall, I'll plant more early blooms. Gardens fare better when you have variety."

Sylvia squinted from the unusually bright morning sun. "What's the plan for the hole between the shed and the roses ... where the vines used to be?"

Charlie put his cup down. "Why don't you tell her, Henry?"

"Well, actually I wanted to surprise you."

"Your typical response when you haven't made up your mind."

Henry smiled. "Not fair. Charlie and I really do have a plan."

"I guess I'll have to wait and see, then."

Charlie sat up straight in his chair. "Not meaning to push you people, but have you given any thought 'bout where you might want to go to church? There're a lot of good ones not too far from your house. I can give you a list if you'd like."

The worship group would temporarily fill a void, but neither she nor Henry mentioned what to do when the vigil ended. Of course, they should find a church home. She liked Reverend Estes but felt equally drawn to Dr. Foster. David said how much he enjoyed the church he attended. Since she and Henry came from different religious backgrounds, how could they ever decide? "A list might be helpful, Charlie. Thanks."

"Well, time for me to get a move on. Glad you're happy with your roses. I think you'll be pleased with what Henry's cooked up for that hole yonder." Charlie shook hands and left.

Henry squeezed her hand. "We should join the others in the ballroom, don't you think? Reverend Estes will conclude the vigil tomorrow since he feels whatever lived in the ballroom has disappeared. He can't guarantee for how long, though. I wonder, Sylvia, do you think we will bring the evil back?"

"What do you mean?"

"Whatever roosted in there seemed to feed on our anger. Then the closer we drew to each other, the more agitated the spirits became. Maybe I'm crazy, but I think if we stay here together, this ... this thing ... will keep trying to drive us apart."

Sylvia gulped. "What're you saying? Do you think we should abandon the house now when you've finally decided to stay?"

"No. Sylvia. I'm not suggesting we leave Connecticut. One thing I know for sure, I'm never separating myself from you again. I'll manage the commute, somehow. I don't know what part the house plays in our future ... I just know we'll face challenges we never imagined."

"You're right, of course. There'll be slippery roads in store. This time, however, we're not fighting each other. And, we have God's help."

Henry's cell buzzed, and he drew it from his pocket and looked at the caller ID. "I should take this." He stepped toward the farside of the veranda, gasped, then turned toward her, his face ashen.

Sylvia assumed the call was from Paul. What could he want? He promised to come by today. In fact, he should've been here by now. Maybe his headache turned into the flu ... why Henry looked so worried.

Henry's face contorted as if in sudden pain. "I'll be there by nine tomorrow."

"Henry?"

His eyes blanked as he stared into nothingness. "That was Monique."

"Monique? Calling this cell? How did she ... Henry, you didn't give her your private number too, did you?"

"With explicit instructions to call only in dire circumstances."

"What's the emergency this time?"

"Higgy's gone."

"Paul? Gone? Gone where?"

"Higgy's dead, Sylvia—a cerebral hemorrhage. The housekeeper found him in bed this morning. She said he looked so peaceful, at first, she thought he'd just overslept."

Sylvia let her tears flow, then dropped to her knees as one with Henry's grief. Paul Higgins had been as true a friend as one could ever ask for. Sadly, she'd never told him how much he meant to her. "It can't be. How will we ever manage without our dear Paul?"

CHAPTER 29

"Wait for me outside, Erik." Henry let himself out of the Porsche and took the steps to Higgy's fourth floor office, pausing at the entrance, not wanting to intrude on the man's sanctuary. He'd left clear instructions, requesting to be buried with his prize possession—a golf ball autographed by Jack Nicklaus.

The legend had interviewed a dozen or more publishers for a potential autobiography ... Higgy, representing Fitzgibbons & Associate, had been on Jack's shortlist. Higgy never got a call back but gleamed with pride at every opportunity to recount his moment with Jack Nicklaus, the story enlarging with each telling like a fisherman's tale of the one that got away.

As he lifted Higgy's pride and joy, a white envelope addressed *HENRY* fell from the desk. When he picked it up, he noticed a yellow post note attached from Higgy's housekeeper:

I found this on Mr. Higgins night stand the morning he died. I thought you should have it but didn't know when you were coming back to work. I figured you'd be coming in for Mr. Higgins's golf ball. He'd told me once he wanted to be buried with it. Ingrid.

Henry stuffed the envelope in his pocket to read later—much later—after the pain went away.

The Reverend Isaiah McAllister read from John's gospel—the same passage Henry had been forced to read at Pop's funeral ... *Let not your heart be troubled.*

Henry felt troubled—just as troubled now as he did when Pop died. Where had his new faith fled to? What more could God take from him? He'd lost his pride and probably his business. Why did God take his best friend too?

A widower with no children, Higgy made Henry his executor for his final wishes. There was an elderly half brother and a few cousins, but no one was as close to Higgy as Henry. Nothing much to arrange, though. Higgy had catalogued his last wishes to the letter with a funeral director, requiring Henry to make only a few calls to confirm arrangements.

He put a defiant hand into his pocket and fumbled the envelope. When did Higgy write this? He died only a few hours after they last saw one another. What could have compelled him to write this before he went to bed? Did he have some kind of premonition? Aunt Claudia wrote her last will and testament before she went to bed one night and put it on her nightstand. They found her dead in the morning, just like Higgy had died in his sleep.

"... Peace I leave with you, my peace I give unto you: not as the world giveth, give I unto you, let not your heart be troubled, neither let it be afraid." Reverend McAllister raised a dark-skinned hand. He proved to be more than a gifted orator, his austere presence every bit as formidable as Pop's.

From the platform, Henry studied the crowd consisting of employees, distributors, agents, authors, community leaders, journalists, a myriad of representatives from every corner of Higgy's influence, including a few of Higgy's extended family. The little South Bronx church was full to overflowing. Henry had never been here before, although Higgy invited him more than once. His generosity toward the church came as no surprise—he gave away most of his wealth as fast as he acquired it. Apart from his Lexus, condo, personal affects, and controlling interest in Fitzgibbons & Associate, Higgy left few worldly possessions.

"My dear friends, I have been Paul Higgins's pastor for nearly twenty years. I tell you, without a doubt, he lived his faith ..." Reverend McAllister continued his recap of a life well lived, every word as gospel as the Book in front of him. The world was now a poorer place without Paul Higgins.

An African American girl, about seventeen, came to the platform. "My name's Tesha Johnson. I want to share what Paul Higgins did for me." She told the congregation how Higgy's generous scholarship brought her out of a life of drugs and homelessness. "Thanks to Mr. Higgins, I don't sing for meth anymore ... I sing the love of Jesus." Then she sang "Shall We Gather at the River."

Henry gazed around and wondered why his were the only dry eyes in the church. Perhaps resentment kept the floodgates dammed—the scene was too reminiscent of Pop's funeral, and the same anger had returned.

He could not abandon his fledgling faith, but Higgy's death made no sense. Henry was even angrier at himself for feeling angry at God. How could he say he now believed and still doubt?

When the hymn ended, Reverend McAllister concluded with a congregational reading of the Twenty-Third Psalm. Henry knew the words ... he'd heard Pop quote the passage often enough. To echo them now seemed hypocritical. How could he say *I fear no evil*? Confusion reigned as he witnessed the good Higgy had accomplished during his time on earth. Why did God take him now?

Selfish thoughts reigned, and Henry chided himself for harboring them. How could he and Sylvia weather this storm Evan North had brought without Higgy's guidance?

The crowd left the church in silence, and Sylvia came to his side. "Reverend McAllister invited me to ride with him to the cemetery since you'll be riding in the hearse with the pall bearers."

Good. He didn't want to hear Sylvia go on and on how Higgy was in a better place. Henry's chest heaved with grief. He didn't want to be comforted—he wanted his friend back.

While he rode in silence with the pall bearers—six tall, burly African Americans from Higgy's church—Henry kept his grief imprisoned. As the men eased Higgy's casket from the hearse, full of respect for a man they seemed to admire, every pall bearer marched with a tear-stained face.

Retired soldiers from the American Legion formed an honor guard lining the way from the hearse to the gravesite as lightning ripped the sky, releasing a deluge. As quickly as the rain descended, the squall left and then heaven's temper ended. Did God mourn for Higgy too?

Reverend McAllister held up both hands to signal the start of the graveside service. "My friends, we who are left wonder why death must be the stepping-stone between our earthly existence and eternity with the Father. No matter how old our loved one, it always seems too soon to say goodbye. Know this. God weeps with us this day, and he cares about our last breath as much as the first. Paul Higgins may have been alone in his home when called to the arms of Jesus, but he did not die alone. Although no human saw his passing, I am certain he entered eternity accompanied by thousands of angels."

Henry stood next to Higgy's half brother while each celebrant passed by the casket, placing a single yellow rose in tribute. As Reverend McAllister closed with prayer, Sylvia squeezed Henry's hand. "I loved him too, Henry."

She stayed at his side while the others dispersed, and a private-duty nurse helped Higgy's brother into a wheelchair. The older Higgins feebly shook Henry's hand. "Thanks for making all the arrangements. There's no way I could have done this."

"I understand, Mike."

His voice trembled. "You were more like a brother to him than I was. We loved each other, sure enough. But we weren't close, me being so much older. I'm glad he had a friend like you." He wiped a tear from his eye as his nurse wheeled him away.

Sylvia clasped Henry's hand. "We should go."

Henry couldn't move, needing, wanting to stay.

"Let him go, Henry," she said. "You're not honoring Paul by wasting away for him."

He nodded and let the yellow rose fall upon the others, then squeezed Sylvia's hand. "I'll be along shortly. You go on ahead with Erik. Charlie's going to drive the Lexus to Connecticut for me, so I'll ride with him."

Charlie, among the last to leave, embraced Henry unashamedly. "I'll wait for you in the car."

Finally alone with his grief, free to shed his pent-up tears, he caught the movement of a shadowy figure emerging from the last row of gravestones. As the man approached, rage replaced sorrow. How dare Evan North show his face—today of all days?

Sylvia stopped short. No. Henry was not going to send her away like a protected child. Her place was with her husband. "You go on ahead, Erik. I'll ride with Henry and Charlie."

"If dat is your vish, Miss Sylvia."

As she walked back, Evan North stood tall and arrogant next to Henry. "Evan?"

Henry tapped his clenched fists against his thighs. "I'll handle this, Sylvia. Mr. North was just leaving."

In a faulty Indiana Jones imitation, Evan tipped his leather hat. Such pomposity might charm his students and at one time might have even impressed Lana Longstreet. Not today. Evan North could no longer charm his way into the graces of Sylvia Fitzgibbons. Lana Longstreet no longer existed, and Sylvia had been reborn. Why hadn't she grasped the man's true character before now? She'd been as duped in their friendship as the horde of lovers he left brokenhearted. Wearing three-hundred-dollar cowboy boots and designer jeans to a funeral only enhanced her newer, low opinion of him—a pretentious lout devoid of conscience.

"Hello, Lana."

"I go by Sylvia now." If her words sounded more like a growl, too bad. Evan North didn't deserve the slightest hint of civility.

"I wanted to pay my respects and thought I should do so privately. As I guessed, my presence isn't welcomed. Believe it or not, I admired Paul Higgins. The industry has suffered a tremendous loss."

She should pummel Evan to the little man she now knew him to be. Instead, she grabbed Henry's arm to maintain composure. "So, you've paid your respects. Now leave. You're right. You're not wanted here."

The scoundrel didn't even pretend to leave.

"You heard my wife, North."

He tugged his hat. She wished she dared yank that hat off his head and throw it to the wind. "I don't blame either of you for your hostility. I never meant for things to get out of hand like this. Look, can we go somewhere to talk?"

If Evan North confessed, Hell had indeed frozen over. "You can talk to our attorneys. My husband has just buried his best friend, and I'm sure your lawyers know we are at your mercy. Now leave us alone."

Evan took off his hat, running his knotted thumb along the edge. "I still can't believe Higgins is gone. I talked to him only a few hours before he died."

Sylvia shot a glance toward Henry. "A bold-faced lie. We were with Paul before he died."

"It's true. Higgins came to my place around one or one-thirty in the morning. I'd just gone to bed, but I knew he hadn't come for a social call so late at night. We chatted. I just assumed he told you. Maybe he never got the chance."

Henry fumbled in his pocket as if clutching something precious. "What're you saying? Did Higgy offer a deal?"

"Look, meet me at Regina's tonight. I'll explain everything. Please."

Sylvia studied Evan's face ... his smirk belied his phony contrition. Evan wanted something. "If Henry agrees, we'll be there."

Henry's knuckles whitened. "Fine. This doesn't mean I trust you."

"I don't blame you. I'll see you at seven?"

"For the record, Sylvia," Evan said as he placed his hat back on his head. "Jonathan Delaney's a good kid. Your Julie could not have picked a better husband." He gestured a half bow then faded into the descending mist.

This time, they ordered the lamb chop special. Sylvia looked at the clock. Evan never showed up on time for anything. No reason to expect tonight to be different.

Always pensive, Henry's withdrawal seemed far deeper than normal. Nor did Lorenzo's waddle, almost always prompting a witty remark, cure Henry's pensiveness. Sylvia tapped his water glass. "I know you don't feel like talking, but we do have business to discuss. The sooner, the better."

"Sylvia—"

"Berkowitz pulled me aside before the funeral started. Did you know Paul split his controlling shares between us? We're now equal partners." At least Henry stopped spearing his peas.

"Yes, I knew. I hadn't told you yet."

Patience, Sylvia. Henry grieved with an intensity lacking in all other areas of life. He'd marooned himself for seven days after her miscarriage.

"How're we going to handle this? I don't care anything about business matters. I left everything up to you and Paul."

"And you think I know anything more about business than you? I played at being CEO ... Higgy did all the real work. You married a fraud, Sylvia."

"Henry. Get over yourself ... you're not a fraud. Look, we need a unified front if we are to face Evan's league of lawyers. If not, they'll take full advantage of any division between us."

Henry's lip lifted in a hateful grin. "What do you suggest, then?"

"Maybe I should give you enough shares for controlling interest? But can you still be CEO and have controlling interest?"

"I don't know. Guess we'll ask Berky where we should go from here. I suppose one of us should have the final say. Whatever you want."

"I think I'd rather you make the decisions. Although, I promise, I won't distance myself like I have in the past. I was wrong to blame you for the mistakes when I offered no help. My talent's writing, not contracts."

Henry grunted. "Apparently, I don't have the talent for contracts either, or we wouldn't be in this mess."

Lorenzo must have sensed the tension and waited on them with silent efficiency, removing Henry's half-eaten dinner, then setting down the coffee service. He poured two cups and left his customers to continue their conversation.

Henry took a sip of coffee before he spoke again. "Higgy gave me far too much responsibility. He made a career of straightening out my messes. Apparently, he spent his last hours on earth fixing yet another Fitzgibbons's fiasco. He made a big deal about me saving his life in the Persian Gulf—truth was, though, his getting shot in the first place was my fault. He flung his body on top of mine to protect me from the bevy of bullets. I can't help but wonder if Higgy would still be alive if I hadn't screwed up again."

"Henry, you can't blame yourself for Paul's death." She thought herself in control until fresh tears came. "I need your handkerchief. I left my purse at home."

As Henry reached into his pocket for his handkerchief, an envelope fell from his pocket.

"What's that?"

"A letter," Henry said as he bent to pick up the envelope. "From Higgy. Or at least I think it's from him. Ingrid, our custodian, is also his housekeeper. She left the envelope in his office with a note she'd found it on his nightstand. I saw it when I picked up the autographed golf ball. I don't have the heart to read it yet."

Sylvia rubbed Henry's hand. "Do you want me to read it?"

He tossed the envelope across the table. "Here."

Sylvia scanned the letter's content: *In the interest of reconciliation, I, Evan North, write this ...*

"Henry! This is Evan's confession. How did Paul get this?"

Henry yanked the letter away, his eyes widening as he scanned the paper, slamming his fist against the table when he finished. "I don't believe this. Higgy must've had quite a conversation with North. It's all here, like Jonathan said."

"Well, then, we're home free. Aren't we?"

Henry pushed against the table. "No. At least, I don't think so. I'll ask Berky to be sure. Sylvia, I'm afraid this is just a piece of paper. Without a witness to collaborate its authenticity, North can deny he ever wrote a confession or say he was coerced into writing this. It's a computer printout with no signature."

"Then, why *did* he write this?"

"Because I wanted to make amends—starting with the wrong I did to Jonathan." Evan squeezed in next to Sylvia. "Compromise can make a has-been like me drown in his own well."

Her face heated. "Hello, Evan. I didn't think you'd actually show up."

Henry held up the letter. "Pardon me for being a skeptic. I don't think you've had a sudden change of heart, and you know this so-called confession isn't worth anything. Are you here to gloat?" Henry threw the letter into Evan's face. "You can have this back. Be my guest."

Sylvia gasped. "Henry!"

Evan folded the letter and glanced at Sylvia. "It's all right. I deserve Henry's hatred. I just wish *you* didn't despise me so."

She glared at Evan, his face unreadable. "What do you want from us? Is Henry right? Did you come here to make a deal to ease your conscience?"

Evan picked up Sylvia's unused cup, filled it with coffee from her carafe, and put it in front of himself. "I can explain if you give me half a chance."

"Well, then get your own coffee." Sylvia yanked the cup away, tossed in two creamers, stirred, tapped her spoon, and took a long sip, glaring at Evan through her ritual.

"Fair enough." He motioned for Lorenzo, then pointed to the urn. In a matter of few seconds, Evan had his own urn and cup.

"Like I told you, Higgins came to see me. He told me how Monique and Jonathan conjured up your secret meeting— even showed me a video of your conversation. Very clever, I might add. Anyway, Higgins offered me a way out if I'd write a confession ... sort of a gentlemen's agreement."

Henry slammed a fist on the table. "What kind of agreement since you're obviously no gentleman."

"Higgins put the whole matter right out in the open. He told me he knew how I stole Jonathan's book, *The Gathering Flock,* and asked what I intended to do to rectify the wrong. Higgins's frankness threw me off guard. To tell the truth, I've regretted the whole messy business from the start, especially after my publisher canceled any future contracts."

Sylvia leaned in. "Why did they do that?"

"The official reason ... they have realigned their imprints, and my stories no longer fit. The real reason—I speculate— they didn't want to be associated with the negative press. They did offer me a substantial kill fee on the sequel, and I accepted. I needed the money more than I needed my honor. Anyway, Higgins offered to buy the rights to *Fowl Weather* if my publisher agreed. I didn't anticipate any problem since they were anxious to sever all ties with me. Higgins said he'd repackage both books under one new title and buy back any unsold copies in distribution."

Reptilian seemed too kind a description for North. She shuddered to think she ever befriended him. Wait. Lana Longstreet had been Evan North's friend ... Sylvia had disliked him from the moment they first met. "You're a weasel. That's what you are. What do you get out of all this?"

Evan leaned back, stretching his feet under the table, too cocky, too self assured. "Don't you see? Paul Higgins provided a way for me to save face as well as my career. All he asked in return was this confession—more of a moral statement of contrition than a legal document."

How she wanted to douse Evan with hot coffee. Instead, she checked her anger with a deep breath. "So, now what? Paul's dead, and we know nothing except what you've told us. Why should we believe you? Even if we did, your agreement with Paul is moot."

Henry's posture relaxed as he leaned across the table. "Not necessarily, Sylvia. Am I right, North?"

"Kindly enlighten me?"

Henry smirked, and Evan sprawled against the back of the booth while Sylvia worked her glances from one to the other. "Why should we honor Paul's deal," she asked, looking at Evan, "and you get off scot-free?"

Henry scowled. "And if we don't, you think we'll lose the lawsuit. You win no matter what."

Evan smirked. "I'd rather put an end to this, Henry. What do you say? This way, everyone wins."

"I still don't understand why you stole Jonathan's work in the first place. You of all people."

"A fair question, Sylvia. I've written twenty-five books in my career. Not as many as you but all best sellers. Then the well of inspiration dried up."

She understood the fear of an empty page more than Henry could. "Every author experiences writer's block. You do something else for a while, then the ideas come eventually."

Evan's head drooped. "That's what I've always believed and why I took the teaching job at Yale, even hiring an assistant as a front—to make people think I was still writing, but I came up with nothing. After my first runaway success, I lived in constant fear I'd never publish another book. The feeling never left me in spite of successive hits. I liked the fame, Sylvia."

Her loathing turned to pity. "You're a coward—the worst kind. You sacrificed an innocent."

"Your version. If I didn't produce something soon, I was doomed to fade into oblivion like a Norma Desmond. Don't forget, I gave Jonathan a lot of money for his book."

"After he threatened to expose you. I do understand your fear, Evan. Although I still think you're the most despicable person on the planet right now, we'll think about honoring Paul's offer. Not because we're coerced. I'd fight to the death if winning could change things. We've Julie's happiness to consider in all this."

Evan leaned on his elbows, full of himself. "I knew you'd see things my way. Are we in agreement, then?"

Henry stabbed a response. "Sylvia said we'd give your proposal some thought. I'll have Berky contact your lawyer in the morning with our answer."

"Tomorrow." Evan tipped his hat and sauntered out.

Henry stroked Sylvia's palm, and his eyes met hers as she stretched a grin. "What?"

"Maybe the idea's God-inspired, Henry. Who knows? Maybe I do have some business sense after all. Let's go home. I'll explain later."

EPILOGUE

Late August

Henry gazed at his beautiful wife as she giggled with playful disdain. "When are you ever going to learn how to wear a tuxedo?" Another barb. After all these years, he should be picked clean by now. Then again, her barbs were simply part of her charm. She snuggled into him, kissed his cheek, and adjusted his cummerbund.

One hundred guests waited for them downstairs. "Are you done making me presentable?"

She giggled again. "You'll pass inspection, soldier."

"Happy anniversary, Sylvia. Now, close your eyes. I have a surprise for you."

"Oh?"

He snatched the small square gift box from his dresser and closed her hand around it.

"Can I open my eyes now."

"Yes."

She scrunched her face into a half frown. "Henry, what did you do?"

"Just open it."

Her hands trembled as she gazed at the matching ring set. "Henry! They're beautiful."

He dropped to one knee as he had rehearsed. "Sylvia, I love you with all my heart. Will you do the honor of marrying me again?"

She squealed with girlish delight. "Of course, I'll marry you again."

He stood and swiped his brow with feigned worry. "I'm glad you said yes, because all those guests down there are expecting a wedding ... not just a party."

"Really?"

"Really."

"And you planned this by yourself?"

He shrugged, shifting his weight from one foot to the other. "As much as I'd like to take the credit, I have to admit only to the idea. Julie and David did the rest since they'd already planned for a bash."

Henry started to slip off her old wedding band.

"Wait. Let me put this in a drawer. Maybe I could put it on a gold chain someday. A keepsake for Julie."

"Whatever your heart desires."

She slipped across the room, put the ring in her armoire, then rejoined him. "Okay ... I'm ready."

"So am I." He took her hand in his. "Let's get this Henry and Sylvia show started, shall we?"

She nodded.

While they made their way down the grand staircase, confident the once ghostly inhabitants of the ballroom would no longer threaten them, the small orchestra played, "I Saw Her Standing There."

David and Dr. Foster greeted them as they entered the foyer.

"Do you have the rings, Dad?" David asked.

Henry laughed as he handed the box to David. "Of course, here. Can't think of anyone else I'd rather have as a best man."

Julie approached, holding a cross-shaped bouquet of white and pink roses crafted by Charlie from the rose garden's best blooms, and handed Sylvia a similar but larger arrangement.

They mingled with the guests for a few moments before the ceremony, stopping to chat with Martina, who anchored Sven and Gunnar by the shoulders. Gunnar held his white, heart-shaped cushion with pride, and Sven tugged at Henry's tuxedo jacket. "See, Mr. Henry? We are taking good care of these pllows."

"Thank you," Henry said as he tossled the boys' hair, then offered Erik a handshake. "You have a wonderful family."

"Tank you, Mr. Henry."

"Don't you think it's time you dropped the Mister?"

"Vee look forward so much to dis new job of ours. Vee cannot tank you enough."

"Well, I'm sure the house will be bustling by next year."

Sylvia hugged Martina, and the women giggled like teenaged girlfriends, forever bound through shared faith. Finally free, Sven and Gunnar made the rounds to show off their pillows.

Martina turned to face Henry. "Reverend Estes seems as excited about the new ministry as we are—a boarding home for homeless immigrants. What a wonderful idea."

With perspective found only in his new faith, the concept seemed logical. Trumbull built the house during a time of uncertainty—a symbol of hope—until another's selfish ambition sundered his dream. For centuries after, the Donner legacy sought atonement for their stain of guilt, fighting the same demons that had pursued Henry and Sylvia. Only fitting that Trumball's mansion, finally cleansed through God's mercy, should return to its original purpose—a testament to new beginnings.

The ghosts had not just been figures in the ballroom. Satan did not want the home's owners to reconcile and used every arrow in his arsenal, including the lawsuit and Higgy's untimely passing. Herny wondered if the ghosts in his and Sylvia's pasts gave the devil even more fodder to drive them apart. Just as God cleansed their home, he turned a marriage doomed to fail into a stronger bond than they could have ever imagined.

Sylvia left Henry's side to speak with Bonnie, no doubt to rub her tummy and feel the baby jump. So much to look forward to—Julie's wedding in October and a grandchild in December, then a delayed second honeymoon—far different from their first.

He rejoined Sylvia as Jonathan approached and shook Henry's hand. "Thanks for including me in your plans, Mr. Fitzgibbons. By the way, Evan North sends his regards."

"Jonathan, if you're not going to call me Dad, then please call me Henry and drop the Mister stuff. By the way, how did North react to the news you're taking my place as CEO?"

Jonathan laughed ... a hardy guffaw Henry found endearing. "Not well at first, but he quieted down after he punched a few holes in his office wall. How did you manage to get him to withdraw the lawsuit?"

Visions of a riled Evan North did provide some modicum of revenge, though Henry tried hard to pray for his rival as Reverend Estes recommended. "I gave him a five-book contract with a hefty advance on the condition he released any ownership of your book. Your new title will be *Birds of a Feather*. Keep your eye on him, Jonathan. Make him earn those contracts. As the new associate in Fitzgibbons & Associate, *you* have the upper hand now."

"Yes, I guess so, but according to our agreement, not until Julie and I are married. I have to admit, though, following in Mr. Higgins's footsteps will be a challenge."

Henry encircled Jonathan in a manly hug. Shame Higgy hadn't lived to see this day, all his prayers answered. Maybe he watched from a heavenly perch, for he seemed somehow as near as the first day they met during the Gulf War.

A then frazzled Henry had welcomed the friendship of the older soldier with an honest face.

Sarge read Henry's orders, then circled him as if suspicious of the new recruit. "I see the brass blundered again. This boy's due to be discharged in six months, not to go into combat." He paced with exaggerated steps, stopped, and put his nose a breath from Henry's face. "So, who'll make sure this kid gets home in one piece."

Higgy squeezed Henry's fear out with a bear hug. "Don't worry, Fitz. I'll always look out for you."

"When will you and your wife leave for the mission field?" Monique's question brought Henry back to the present, not even aware she'd sidled up next to them.

Jonathan glanced toward Julie and cocked an eyebrow. "Mission field?"

"My parents will be helping Reverend Estes with the missionary school he's building in Brazil. They're leaving in December ... right after Christmas, unless Bonnie goes past her due date. Sort of a second honeymoon, they never really had a first one."

Sylvia oozed a half sigh with her smile. "It'll be difficult to leave a new grandchild ... thankfully, we'll only be gone six months."

"Time for the bride to get ready for her entrance," Julie said as she tugged on Syvlia's gown and pointed toward the curtained alcove next to the ballroom.

"Come with me, Dad." David ushered Henry toward the front of the ballroom while guests took their seats, each row designated with a lavender rose. Dr. Foster joined them, then Charlie's crew unfurled the white runner while the organist played, "There is Love."

When the music stopped, a tenor took front and center, singing "You Are the Sunshine of My Life." Julie began the procession with Sylvia a few paces behind.

Henry could not imagine his life any fuller than at this moment, his joy never more complete as he took his bride's arm, pledging himself to her anew—this time before the Lord.

The ceremony completed, guests retreated to the refreshment table, giving Henry an opportunity to steal Sylvia away to the veranda for a few moments of solitude. Underneath an orange moon, they gazed at Charlie's redemptive work, truly a landscape masterpiece. Sylvia oozed a sigh of pleasure. "I love what Charlie did with the old wooden garden cart. How clever to encircle it with wild flowers."

Henry brought Sylvia into a passionate embrace. Lana Longstreet had bought a house ... one filled with evil, nearly bringing their marriage to an end. Though evil thought it could send the final blow, God intervened. How like the Lord to reimagine near disaster into something profoundly beautiful.

THE END

BOOKS BY LINDA WOOD RONDEAU

Published by Elk Lake Publishing, Inc

A Christmas Prayer

Fiddlers Fling

Hosea's Heart

It Really IS a Wonderful Life

Miracle on Maple Street

I Prayed for Patience: God Gave Me Children

Second Helpings

Snow on Bald Mountain

The Fifteenth Article

Who Put the Vinegar in the Salt

Wolf Mountain Legacy

See also:https://www.amazon.com/Linda-Wood-Rondeau/e/B006FNG1BI

ABOUT THE AUTHOR

Award-winning author, Linda Wood Rondeau writes stories that grip the heart, inspired by her nearly thirty years of social work. When not writing or speaking, she enjoys the occasional round of golf, visiting museums, and taking walks with her best friend in life, her husband of forty-five years. The couple resides in Hagerstown, Maryland, where both are active in their local church. Readers may learn more about the author, read her blog, or sign up for her newsletter by visiting www.lindarondeau.com.

SOCIAL MEDIA

Facebook author page: https://www.facebook.com/lindawoodrondeau

Instagram: https://www.instagram.com/authorlindawoodrondeau/

Twitter: https://twitter.com/lwrondeau

www.ingramcontent.com/pod-product-compliance
Lightning Source LLC
Chambersburg PA
CBHW052001020726

47501CB00004B/959